Praise for Moira Rogers's
Cipher

"[W]ritten exceptionally well...readers are sucked in from the beginning."

~ *Library Journal*

"*Cipher* was another great installment to the Southern Arcana series. The plot was awesome, the characters had depth and strength, the romance broke my heart and I can't wait for the next book."

~ *Pearl's World of Romance*

"[A]n absolutely fantastic addition to the Southern Arcana series. Moira Rogers has really outdone herself with Andrew and Kat's story."

~ *The Romance Studio*

"*Cipher* gave me the satisfying story I wanted for these two and anted up with a killer plot that never failed to shock and awe. The Southern Arcana series is sublime and I can't wait for the next installment!"

~ *Joyfully Reviewed*

"The Southern Arcana series by Moira Rogers just keeps getting better. I have been waiting for Kat and Andrew's book and it certainly was worth the wait."

~ *Long and Short Reviews*

Look for these titles by
Moira Rogers

Now Available:

Cipher

Moira Rogers

SAMHAIN
PUBLISHING

Samhain Publishing, Ltd.
11821 Mason Montgomery Road, 4B
Cincinnati, OH 45249
www.samhainpublishing.com

Editing by Anne Scott
Cover by Kendra Egert

First Samhain Publishing, Ltd. electronic publication: September 2011
First Samhain Publishing, Ltd. print publication: August 2012

Dedication

This is dedicated to Mari Fee, who not only helped us with titles for this series, but is the reason we wrote any of it to begin with. Merci beaucoup, lady.

Prologue

Fourteen months earlier

Kat tried to open the office door three times before she realized she was using the wrong key.

Her cheeks heated as she lifted the ring until the silver keys caught the faint glint from the streetlight. "Don't say a damn word."

Next to her, Andrew chuckled. "Hey, my lips are zipped."

"Better be." God, she loved his laugh. And his smile. And his eyes. She was supposed to be mad at him, but her lips tugged up in a smile of her own as she found the right key. "This'll just take a few minutes, and then we can head back."

"I'm in no hurry." He rested his hand on the door and waited for her to unlock it. "With Derek MIA right now, work's a little weird."

The reminder brought a stab of worry. Derek was hip-deep in the latest shapeshifter mess, one that came with danger and execution orders and an instinctive need to bundle his baby cousin off into protective custody.

It was annoying. It was condescending. And it was hard to stay mad when protective custody meant spending time with Andrew—even if he *had* gone over to the dark side by joining the ranks of the overprotective assholes.

She could fume at Derek. She'd never been good at staying angry at Andrew.

Kat unlocked the door, and it swung open without a squeak. Inside the office was dark, so dark that her mind jumped straight to all the things she and Andrew could do in the dark. Theoretical knowledge only, more was the pity, but sometimes she caught Andrew watching her in a way that made her think he'd make it worth the wait.

Someday.

"What were you looking for, again?"

"My binder with the research notes for this stupid OS class." The door clicked shut behind her, and she pivoted only to find herself staring up at Andrew, his handsome face turned darkly mysterious in the uncertain light.

For one perfect moment, the world went soft-focus. Awareness and potential filled the air—not the magical kind fueled by her empathic gifts, but plain, old-fashioned excitement.

Their friendship had danced along this line for months, no longer just friends but not yet something else. The enormity of what they could be trembled inside her, whispering of epic love, humbling and intimidating. She still felt young and untried, too inexperienced for grown-up relationships with high stakes and ever afters.

She wasn't ready. Not yet...but soon, and it would be worth it.

He would be worth it.

Andrew's thumb brushed her cheek. "You're making big eyes at me."

She wrinkled her nose and considered sticking out her tongue. "I wouldn't be if you'd let me come to the office by myself. This is revenge."

"Nowhere by yourself, those are my orders."

The soft *click* to their left was out of place, and it took Kat a moment too long to figure out why.

Triumph spiked through the room in a painful lash of

emotion so strong she staggered. Andrew reached out, but rough hands had already closed on her shoulders, dragging her back so fast her heels skittered across the carpet as she belatedly started to struggle.

"Kat!" Andrew's voice shook with terror—and anger. "*Kat!*"

A dark figure loomed behind him, and Kat's lips parted on a warning that came too late. "Andrew—"

Brutal fingers slammed over her mouth, muffling her enraged scream as a huge body crashed into Andrew. Her brain flitted in too many directions, and instinct took over. She crashed her heel down, aiming for her attacker's toes, but pain splintered up her leg as her floppy sandal smashed against a steel-toed boot.

The man holding her laughed. "You're feisty for a human. Or are you the little psychic secretary?"

They weren't humans, not if they knew who she was. *What* she was. Dread froze her in place as Andrew struggled.

One of the dark-clad men punched him, a hard right across the jaw, but he continued to fight. He kicked a second intruder in the ribs, and the man stumbled back, gasping for breath.

Hot breath spilled across Kat's ear, and terror cracked her shields, letting in a sick twist of Andrew's pain and the exhilaration of his opponents. Feral, primal—Andrew was an unanticipated but welcome game, a hunt in which they could indulge themselves.

Shapeshifters.

The second the thought formed, her attacker tightened his grip. "We're not here to hurt you, but if your friend doesn't stop fighting, we'll kill him."

With his emotions sliding over her skin like slime, she knew the words for truth. As soon as the hand eased from her mouth, her begging plea tumbled out. "Andrew, stop." God, she sounded scared. She *was* scared. Andrew was strong for a human, but shapeshifters would rip him to pieces. "*Please,* Andrew!"

The shifters stepped back, forming a half-circle as their prey rose and faced them. The man behind her growled. "Tell us where Jacobson's safe houses are. I don't want to torture you into talking, but I will."

For a moment, she thought Andrew might back down. Then one of the men made a low noise of anticipation, and Andrew swung.

He was going to die, trying to protect her.

She was going to watch it happen.

Fear shattered into a thousand pieces and took her self-control with it, the breakdown so complete that she didn't realize she'd lost her grip on her empathic projection until everyone in the office froze.

The hands on her shoulders clenched until she thought they might crush bone. One of the men shuddered, a queer-sounding whimper ripping free from his throat. Low, terrified—barely human, and so afraid.

"You goddamned little *bitch*—" Rough fingers twisted in her hair, but it was too late. Someone jerked her head back hard enough to bring tears to her eyes, and the pain intensified the fear flooding the room.

A low curse ended on a snarl as one of the men began to shift. Andrew yelled something, but the words disappeared in a cacophony of angry yips and howls as a second man shifted, tearing free of his clothing.

So fast. It happened so fast. One second she was staggering under the weight of her attacker's anger, the next she was on her knees and Andrew—

Andrew lay on the floor, his clothes rent and dark with blood. Bleeding, and so pale, clutching at his stomach with one hand and his throat with the other—

Dying.

Fear vanished. Pain followed, leaving sweet, icy numbness behind. Cold, cold, cold, she was so cold she should be shivering. So cold they should all be shivering.

She'd make them shiver.

She'd make them *crawl.*

The power had always been there, a burden and a nuisance. Shields kept it contained, but nothing could contain the protective rage gathering just under the surface.

She took Andrew's pain. There was so much it should have split her in two, but she took it. Her nails scratched against the rough carpet as she took his anger too, his anger at himself for not being able to protect her. She took the shapeshifters' rage and their fear and their determination to see her dead, she took her own breaking heart and the ice that would never melt.

She took it all, then took Andrew himself and imagined him safe in her arms, safe in the numbness making the world a distant dream. With him wrapped in her shields, she stripped her soul bare and let everything go in a terrifying thrust of power that hollowed her out and left her trembling.

Her pulse pounded in her ears. Throbbed in her temples. Everything was silent, so silent she was sure she'd failed—

And then the screaming started.

Chapter One

Someone was cooking waffles.

For one disoriented moment, trapped between sleep and waking, Kat thought she was home again. A teenager, safe in her uncle's house with her aunt making breakfast and her parents alive and the world at her fingertips. If she rolled out of bed, she'd find hot chocolate waiting for her in the kitchen, and her aunt would ask her about the boy in her math class and laugh when she blushed...

The bed shifted, and a solid arm settled over her waist, jerking her abruptly into the present. *Miguel,* her brain identified at once. He was warm, a comforting weight at her back, and as familiar as her favorite pair of slippers. Kat threaded her fingers with his and gave his hand a tug. "Hey, lazy ass. Wake up. Sera's making us breakfast before she goes into work."

He laughed but didn't move. "Score. I'm starving."

"Impossible. You ate a supreme pizza last night all by yourself." He'd eaten a few slices of her pepperoni pizza too, proof that his appetite hadn't waned after six months of being a full-blooded shapeshifter.

"Shapeshifter *and* psychic," he corrected aloud. "That burns a lot of calories."

Kat groaned and dragged a pillow over her face, spending a few careful moments reinforcing her shields. Not that they'd stop Miguel from picking up her surface thoughts any more than his mental shields kept her from reading his mood, but the practice never hurt. "If being a psychic burned that many calories, I'd be a lot scrawnier."

Miguel slapped her hip through her flannel pajama pants. "That'd be a crying shame. Zola's already worked too much of your ass off."

"There's plenty left." She tossed the pillow aside and leaned over the side of the bed until her fingers brushed the edge of her netbook. "And all of it off limits. Your new girlfriend doesn't strike me as the sort who wants to listen to explanations about why you were smacking another woman's ass this morning."

"Victoria," he said slowly, carefully enunciating every syllable, "does not own me. And I've done nothing wrong."

The tiniest hint of defensiveness echoed between them, sharp enough to ruffle his otherwise placid emotions. Kat didn't much care for How-Dare-You-Call-Me-Vicky-It's-*Victoria* and didn't give a damn if Miguel plucked *that* thought out of her head. She dragged her computer up onto her stomach and popped it open. "She's too prissy for you. And you know it, or you wouldn't have crashed in my sexless bed last night, Mr. Playboy."

"She had to work. And I like your sexless bed." He rolled to his side, propped his head on his hand and blew away the hair that fell over his forehead. "It's better than being at home until Julio finishes moving out. It's all politics, all the time since the coup."

A dangerous route of thought, especially with a psychic in her bed. Thinking about the coup always lead back to the men who'd led it. And one of those men...

She jerked her thoughts under control and wiggled her finger over the track pad on her computer until the screen came to life. "Politics get tiring," she managed, and it sounded like a weak attempt even to her. "Sera and I don't mind you crashing. She gets to cook for three, and I don't have to turn the heat above sixty-five because you're like a shapeshifter radiator."

"Uh-huh. And my sister says that's why I eat like a horse now. Increased metabolic function."

"Yeah, it takes a lot of dedicated eating to be a chubby shapeshifter." She'd left her browser open, and the endless row of tabs retraced the path of the previous night's research. Seventeen in all, ranging from Wikipedia to her Gmail, which now had thirty-seven unfiltered messages awaiting her attention. "Sera likes cooking for you. Maybe you should ditch Victoria and start putting the moves on her. She could use some damn fun."

He studied the bedspread and nodded. "She's not really my type."

The words were right, but empathy told her he was laughing inside, amused over some joke she was missing. "Is it because she's a coyote and not a wolf?"

He stretched out on his back and grinned. "Maybe it'd be more correct to say *I'm* not really *her* type. I'm not badass enough for your roommate."

"That's a shame." But easy enough to believe. The last time Sera had managed to get her hands on enough alcohol to make a shapeshifter drunk, she'd scrawled *No fucking alpha bastards!* across the bathroom mirror with a Sharpie. Kat had tried three different types of cleaner before giving up and repunctuating it. *No, fucking alpha bastards!* was a motto she could get behind, at least.

And speaking of alpha bastards... She actually had email from her boss. The timestamp was seven-thirty—eight-thirty in New York, where he was clearly already awake and busily messing with shapeshifter politics. Kat flagged it to check later and scanned the rest of the subjects. Junk, most of it, with a spattering of casual correspondence and a few messages from potential clients and colleagues at the university.

Then, third from the top, she stumbled across a sentence that made her heart stutter. *Regarding your mother's association with the Cult o...* The subject line was too long to display in full, but what was there stole her breath.

"Hey." Miguel laid a hand on her shoulder. "You okay?"

"I don't—" She rocked upright, spilling the netbook onto the covers in her haste. After a moment groping behind her back, she closed her fingers on her pillow and hauled it around to serve as a makeshift desk. "I sent out some emails last week. I just—I didn't really expect to get a reply."

He must have caught a stray thought. "Cult? Some kind of cult shit? Is this something you're doing for work?"

"Ancient history." Crossing her legs, she set the pillow in her lap and resituated the computer. It could be nothing or a scam or even a joke.

It could be answers.

Miguel hesitated. "Do you need me here, or do you need me gone? I can't tell."

Neither could she. Her hands shook like she'd mainlined espresso and chased it with Red Bull...and if she didn't get herself under control, she'd have two worried shapeshifters climbing all over her. "I think I need a few minutes. And Sera's going to all that trouble making breakfast—someone should eat it."

"*You* should eat some of it."

"I will, I promise. In a little bit."

"Kat."

She dragged her gaze away from the browser window and met his eyes. "I'm okay, Miguel. It's not like I can sneak out the window. I'll be out in a few minutes."

"All right." He rolled off the bed and snagged his shirt from the chair by the wall. "I'll grab some coffee and wait for you."

Relief and gratitude made her smile as real as her words. "You're the best."

"Hey." He stopped and rubbed his thumb over her cheek. "You're still my girl."

For one crazy second she wished she *was* his girl, that

she'd met him before her broken heart had healed wrong, before life had twisted her up until even a handsome, skilled lover couldn't keep passion from fizzling out. Maybe her empathy would always be a curse—she knew exactly what she had...and everything she was missing.

At least in Miguel she had a friend, and a friend was more important than a lover any day. "Go get some waffles before they get cold. I'm sure she'll still be making them when I get out there."

"I love this place." He rubbed his hands together. "Waffles and whipped cream in a can."

"Better than heaven."

Miguel ducked out of the room and closed the door behind him, leaving Kat staring at her netbook.

Regarding your mother's association with the Cult o...

She eased the cursor to hover over the subject before noticing for the first time that the email had an attachment. The tiny mouse cursor sat there, balanced on top of the apostrophe in *mother's*, and her resolve wavered for a moment.

Ancient history, she'd told Miguel, and she hadn't been lying. Whatever her mother had done, it had been over for at least a decade. She'd been dead almost that long, and maybe proof of her misdeeds needed to die with her. Ignorance was bliss, wasn't it?

Holding her breath, Kat clicked on the email.

From: 876@johndoeanon.com

To: kat@katgabriel.com

Subject: Regarding your mother's association with the Cult of Ariel

I have information about the Gabriel family's past and present involvement with the Cult of Ariel, and I'll trade it for protection from the Southeast council. I'll be in Mobile, Alabama tomorrow. Meet me at the USS Alabama at 10 AM.

Bring Andrew Callaghan or Julio Mendoza.

Kat ignored the way her stomach flip-flopped and read the email a second time. No signature, no name. Just the attachment which, judging by the extension, was an image. The virus scan seemed unbothered by it, but she still spent a few minutes double and triple checking before opening it.

When she did, she wished she hadn't. Her mother's face stared up at her, but not the mother she'd known. This woman couldn't be any older than twenty-five—not so long after Kat had been born. But it wasn't her mother's youth that made dread curl in Kat's gut—it was the wide, crazy grin and the way her hands gripped an automatic weapon.

So much for the waffles.

Kat stormed the Southeast council's newly acquired headquarters armed with a laptop, a printout of the offending email, and all of her arguments carefully marshaled. Then she went in search of Miguel's brother.

When she knocked, an unintelligible shout from inside beckoned her. She found Julio stirring a big pot of something on the industrial range, and he waved her over as she walked into the kitchen. "I guess those wards Mari put up work. Unless..." He eyed her as he wiped his hands on a towel. "You're not here to kill me, are you?"

She flinched, and hated herself for it. Julio was joking. He wasn't afraid of her—sometimes she thought the damn man wasn't afraid of *anyone*—and even knowing it in her bones, with the confidence only empathy could bring...she flinched. If she closed her eyes, she might see the office, echoes of the nightmare that still woke her in a cold sweat. Walls painted in blood, wolves howling in challenge—

"You hungry? I got a head start on lunch."

Kat dragged in an unsteady breath and used Julio's

confidence to ground herself. He wasn't afraid of her, and the easy strength that surrounded him was better than a warm blanket for a jumpy empath. "No, I was force-fed waffles before I left the apartment."

He laughed. "I know my brother was there, but I'm guessing he wasn't the one who made breakfast."

Of course he knew. Kat had rolled from her bed into the shower, but one shower wouldn't be enough to erase Miguel's scent from her skin, not when he'd spent the night hogging more than half of the bed. Kat felt her cheeks heat and compensated by dropping her laptop bag onto the wide island in the kitchen. "He kept me and Sera company last night and didn't want to drive home."

One dark eyebrow shot up. "Tell the truth—he didn't want to go home, full stop."

Kat eased her laptop out of its case and shrugged. "You know Miguel. He's not all that interested in the shapeshifter new world order."

"That's putting it mildly. Joke's on him, though, because I was here all night." Julio slid onto a stool and propped his elbows on the countertop. "What's up?"

She'd thought of all of the arguments to convince him to help, but the one thing she hadn't considered was where to begin. "You know my parents died a while ago, right? My parents and my aunt and uncle, all at the same time."

"Andrew told me about it, yeah. He said that's how Derek ended up taking care of you."

Andrew's name shouldn't make her heart twist, not after this long. "Derek came down to New Orleans when his parents died, because I was already living here. With his parents, I mean. My mother..." There was no good way to put it, though her father had always tried. *Your mother's not feeling so great right now, munchkin.* "My mom was a little nuts."

He was too polite to let his sympathy show, but she felt it all the same. "I think we've all had a bit of experience with that, but something tells me you're speaking literally."

"Psychic cults." The outside zipper of her laptop bag held the printout of the email and the photo. She dragged the folded stack of papers out and fiddled with the edge. "Sometimes when I can't sleep I poke around, see if I can find out what really happened. No one's ever replied before."

He rubbed his jaw. "I've heard of some. Anyone who's tuned in to the psychic community has."

Damn, she'd forgotten that Julio was psychic. Again. Miguel's telepathy was powerful, almost as strong as her own empathy, but Julio was a precog, and one whose gifts seemed more prone to evidence themselves in hunches than Technicolor visions. It was easy to forget he was anything more than a shapeshifter.

Of course, it might make him doubly useful now. She unfolded the paper, and handed him the email and printed photo without comment.

"Cult of Ariel," he read aloud. "Your mom?"

"Yeah." She reached out and touched the edge of the picture. "She cut all of her hair off when I was ten and kept it short the rest of her life, so this must have been before that."

"And this contact says he has information." Julio flipped through the photos and the rest of the papers. "Do you know who this person is? Anything?"

"Nothing concrete yet. But I should know in a few hours." Hopefully no one would ask how many laws she'd broken or asked others to break to get the information. "I know you wouldn't want to walk into it blind, but if I figure out who it is..." *Please, Julio.*

"Not asking for myself, 'cause I'm not going. But you shouldn't walk into it blind, either."

It took her a moment too long to understand what he'd said. "Julio, *please*. I can't ask Andrew. We're not—" *What, Kat? Friends?* "He wouldn't do it anyway."

"Can't ask Andrew what?"

Julio had to have known. He would have heard Andrew's footsteps, would have caught his scent. Would have seen him, for Christ's sake, which meant the bastard had set her up.

Kat pivoted and promptly forgot she needed oxygen.

She avoided Andrew as a general rule, and over the past year he'd seemed happy enough to return the favor. It was supposed to make dealing with him easier.

Instead, she felt like she'd taken a roundhouse kick to the gut. Sometime in the past month, Andrew had lost his razor. The reddish-blond beard made him look older. More intimidating. Not that he needed it—he was the tallest man she knew and looked like he'd been carved out of stone. The gun tucked into the shoulder holster was overkill.

Andrew Callaghan looked like he'd stepped out of an action movie, and her sluggish libido that felt so stunted around other men began to stir.

God, she hated him.

He had his arms draped across his chest and his hard green gaze fixed firmly on her. Waiting for an answer, so she provided one. "I can't ask you to take a road trip with me."

He studied her, his expression inscrutable. "Where are you going?"

"Maybe nowhere." She deliberately turned her back on him and fixed Julio with what she hoped was a nasty glare. "Why not?"

He met her glare with a bland look. "Because I'm busy. Gotta hold down the fort while Carmen and Alec are in New York, dealing with the rest of the Conclave."

It was a bullshit excuse. Andrew and Julio shared the same damn job, keeping the world running while Alec and his wife danced circles around the Conclave who led the wolves. If Andrew could take a few days off, Julio could too.

Unless he didn't want to.

Kat held out her hand. "Can I have my papers back, then?"

He turned them over readily. "You gonna do what the email says? If I can't go, that leaves Andrew."

Yes, it left the man who stepped out of the doorway and plucked the papers from her hand. "What's all this about, Kat?"

The human she'd known wouldn't have waltzed into a conversation and seized control of it. He wouldn't have assumed he had a right to know her plans. She'd avoided Andrew so successfully since he'd become a wolf that she had no idea who he was anymore.

Maybe it was only fair. The Kat *he'd* known wouldn't have snatched the papers back, but she had no trouble doing it. "Someone has information I need, but they won't give it to me unless I bring one of you along. They want protection from the Southeast council."

Something flashed in his eyes—a bit of frustration, maybe anger. "The council protects those who need it. This person wouldn't be trying to buy that protection unless he knew he couldn't reasonably ask for it."

She wanted to disagree, but how could she with the world *cult* plastered all over every page? "Yeah. He or she might not be a stand-up guy. That's why I've got a friend tracking them down."

Andrew rubbed the heel of his hand over his forehead, a gesture she recognized as one that meant he was thinking hard. Considering all the possibilities. "When do you want to leave?"

Just like that. No questions, no conditions. They'd barely spoken in a year, and the bastard was ready to climb in a car and drive across three states on what was, in all probability, a wild goose chase.

God, she *wanted* to hate him.

Chapter Two

Sometimes, Kat was impossible.

They'd already passed Biloxi and she still hadn't spoken to him, so Andrew took the next exit off I-10 and pulled over at a service station. "Can we talk now?"

"Sure." She typed a few more words and closed the lid of the tiny laptop balanced on her legs. "My friend wants to know if there's anything in particular you want him to track down about this lady we're meeting."

"I'm not talking about that." He squinted against the glare of the morning sun and sighed. "Does your cousin know you've been turning over rocks, trying to find information on your mom?"

"Derek's busy being married. And I'm not seventeen anymore. I don't need his permission."

"It isn't about permission. It's about someone having your back."

Kat turned away and stared out the window, though there wasn't much to look at beyond the whitewashed gas station wall. "He practically lives in Wyoming now. Even if he knew about this, there's not much he can do from there."

Not much, except help her find a way to navigate the psychological and emotional minefield she was tap dancing on. "Are you sure you want it? Whatever information this contact might have?"

"No, I'm pretty sure I don't want it. I'm also almost

completely sure I need it." Her voice held a rough edge. "There's something damn scary inside me, Andrew. You of all people know that."

His hands twitched into fists on the wheel before he could stop them, a reaction to the flashes of memory that punched him in the gut when he thought about that night.

They'd come for Kat, and he'd tried to stop them. *Tried*, in his own weak, ineffectual way, and they'd nearly killed him. So Kat had opened herself to darkness to save his life, and it had nearly cost her her sanity.

She stiffened and flashed him a guilty look. "Shit, I'm sorry. That wasn't—that has to be even worse for you. I shouldn't have brought it up."

"What happened with the strike team wasn't your fault." *It was mine.*

"It's not—" She sighed. "I don't want to play the shapeshifter blame game. You guys spend so much time fighting each other over who gets to be the biggest martyr. Isn't it exhausting?"

If only that knee-jerk alpha reaction was the only reason he claimed responsibility for that night. "It's like a marathon that never stops. Now, tell me about this woman."

"Peace Kristoffersen." Kat popped the computer back open and lifted one hand to shade the screen from the early-morning sun. "Forty-three, born in Seattle. Her parents dropped off the grid when she was five. Resurfaced in rural Alabama. From there it gets a lot less pretty."

"Survivalist stuff?"

"I guess. A lot of DHR reports, but I haven't read them all. That's most everything until she got a GED when she was twenty-four and went to college. Nothing to say if she's a psychic or spell caster or what, but that just means if she *is* one of us, she was smart about hiding it."

He glanced over as he started the car again. "What's DHR? Like child services?"

"Yeah. I don't know how much of use is in there." She still wasn't looking at him, though now her body language seemed more nervous than hostile. "Usually I could dig this stuff up on my own, but it's not as fast as some people think. So I called a friend. He said he could send anything you want, up to her bank records or last dentist's appointment."

Having the wrong person digging around like that could spell disaster. One bad move could draw the kind of attention no one wanted. "So she's involved—or has been—with this cult."

"I guess. Some of the reports make it sound like there was some crazy backwoods militia stuff going on, but I don't know what my mom would be doing running with a cult in Alabama. Maybe the growing-up stuff was the normal human variety of crazy and this lady got mixed up with the psychics later."

She needed to hear what this contact had to say, but she also had to prepare herself for what was to come. "It could be bullshit, you know," he murmured. "A wild goose chase."

"I know. It could be bullshit, or she could be crazy. I could be crazy for wasting your time."

The sadness in her voice made his chest ache, and he regretted his harsh words. "I'm sorry. I just don't want to see you disappointed."

If anything, sadness sharpened. "Disappointment's not the end of the world."

Plenty of people lived through that and worse every day, but it didn't ease the pain she'd feel—or the way his own traitorous instincts would react to it. "We've got time to stop and eat if you want."

"If you're hungry. I'm fine." She eased the netbook closed and set it on the floor between her feet before rubbing her hands against her jeans. "This is all kind of spectacularly awkward. I'm sorry you got stuck with it."

Because their relationship for the last year or more had been one of constant awkwardness. Once upon a time, she wouldn't have hesitated before coming to him for help, and he wouldn't have felt the bone-deep need to warn her away from potential pain. He would have seen it through and picked up the pieces.

He would have been her friend.

"Don't mention it." He pointed the car back toward the interstate on-ramp. "I ate early this morning, and I'd rather have the time to check things out."

"Sounds good." Silence fell, and they'd gone five miles before she spoke again. "Is there a reason Julio wouldn't come with me?"

None he could discern—except that he hadn't wanted to tangle with Andrew. Not that he was about to try and explain that to Kat. "Busy, I guess. I didn't ask."

She blew out a sudden breath. "Damn. You're still impossible to read." Sudden color flooded her cheeks. "Not that I was trying, I mean. It's just...you've always been in control, but now you're stone cold. Are you sure you're not psychic or something?"

"Nope." His parents had been remarkable people, but nothing about them had been the slightest bit supernatural. "No psychic powers, just me."

"Yeah, well, whatever secrets you have, rest assured they're safe from me."

"Don't have any secrets, Kat, least of all from you."

"A lot has changed since we used to share them." She hunched down in the seat, her posture defensive even though her next words sounded perfectly casual. "How's Anna doing?"

Andrew tensed, because there was nothing he could say that wouldn't piss her off. "Fine. She's fine." He changed lanes and chanced a glance at her. "Is that really what you want to know?"

She was staring straight ahead, expression blank. "I'm glad you're happy."

He snorted out a helpless laugh. "You know, you're so *sure* of everything, and you don't even—" He bit off the words. "Ask me if I'm with Anna."

"I take it back. I was just—I was trying to say the right thing."

"Ask me, Kat, so I can tell you what you should have already figured out."

Her sigh sounded equal parts exasperated and annoyed. "Fine, Andrew. Are you and Anna still seeing each other?"

"No." He clenched his teeth to keep from elaborating.

"I'm sorry." It sounded genuine. "That it didn't work out, and that I brought it up. I just... Hell, it's stupid."

"Tell me, please."

The sound of her heartbeat filled his ears, pounding too hard and too fast for her placid exterior. "It's the elephant in the room. It doesn't matter if we never dated. Everyone tiptoes around like you left me at the altar or something. I'm not going to make it all the way to Alabama with you, me *and* a couple elephants squeezed into this car."

It was the converse of his own experience. The flip side. For every time someone had threatened to kick his ass for breaking Kat's heart, someone else had comforted her. "Yeah, well. That big-ass elephant you were asking about? We broke up about five minutes after we started dating, and that's not much of an exaggeration."

"The elephant was less Anna and more..." She waved a hand in a vague gesture. "I don't know. The fact that this is the first time we've really talked in over a year? If you're with someone else, or you wanted to be, you don't need to tiptoe around me. I'm a big girl, even if no one else thinks I am."

"Don't worry, I get enough shit for the both of us. I'm the *last* person who'll go out of his way to spare you, out of sheer self-defense."

"It's not—" Her teeth snapped together. "Never mind. This isn't what we should be talking about anyway. We need to make plans or something."

They hadn't talked in a year, and this was why. There never seemed to be a good time or place to *start*. "If it looks like a setup, we can't stay. And you know why."

"Because my cousin married the werewolf princess and now I'm good hostage material?"

Because Andrew would get himself killed making sure she escaped any such fate. "You're not going to argue the point, are you?"

She sighed quietly. "No. As long as you acknowledge that I'm not helpless."

Andrew fought to hide a smile. "Hell no, you're not helpless."

That seemed to mollify her. Her stiff posture eased, though she kept her arms crossed over her chest. "I know I don't look like I went all soldier of fortune like you do, but I've been getting my ass schooled five days a week by Zola and Walker. I'm a ninja with a taser."

He nodded solemnly. "I'm sure you would be, if you owned a taser instead of a stun gun."

"Thanks, Alec Junior. And by the way, I told him the next time he corrected me, I was going to *stun gun* his balls."

"Carmen might object to that."

Kat laughed, a clear sound he hadn't heard in far too long. "Carmen likes me. Though maybe not enough to forgive me for assaulting her husband, even if he does have it coming."

He flashed her a grin. "Something tells me she'd stop you, no matter how fond she is of you."

"Uh-huh. Won't stop me from doing the same to *you*."

The words may have been a threat, but they made him think of her tugging at his belt, passionate fire lighting her eyes. "I'll keep that in mind."

"Good." Laughter subsided, but the strangling awkwardness didn't return. After a moment Kat sighed. "I missed this. Laughing. You always made me laugh."

"You laughed *at* me. That is not the same thing."

"You did your share of laughing, too."

"Well, it was only fair."

"Yeah." She lapsed into silence.

They drove for a few miles, and Andrew tried again. "Derek seems happy."

"He is. He's so happy I don't have shields strong enough to block it out." She sounded satisfied—and a little sad. "He and Nicole have crazy epic love. I think epic love is an epidemic. Seems like everyone's coming down with a case of it."

And it left her feeling lonely. Her isolation prickled at his heart and conscience. "Always when they least expect it. That's something, anyway. It could happen to anyone."

He caught her looking at him out of the corner of his eye, but she turned away too fast. "I'm not sure empaths are cut out for epic love. Not the strong ones. It's not really all that safe."

Another elephant, this one ten times bigger than the specter of Anna. "It doesn't have to be too dangerous either."

"Yeah, maybe not." It was too fast and too bland to be remotely convincing, and she must have known it. "How far to Mobile?"

"Another hour or so. Maybe less."

"I should check my email. See if Ben's found anything else. He's a technopath—they're pretty fucking rare, which means no one really knows how to protect against them."

She had her hair up, and when she leaned forward it exposed a complicated pattern of dark ink on the back of her neck. He reached out before he thought about it, brushing his thumb over the tattoo. "When did you get this?"

Goose bumps rose under his hand, and she shivered, her breath catching in a soft gasp he might not have heard if he'd still been human. "Six months ago. I went to the Ink Shrink."

"You did *not*."

"Did so." Her T-shirt shifted as she reached for her

netbook, proving that the ink continued down toward her shoulder blades. "I got it after I finished my thesis. My life needed punctuation. Or a chapter break."

"Or a tattoo." He'd been to see the Shrink himself, several times over the past year. "What's it mean?"

"Hell if I know." She sat back fast enough to dislodge his hand. "He twisted a little magic into it for me, and you don't get to pick those. They pick you, whatever that means."

"I get it." He certainly hadn't wanted a giant flaming bird across his back, no matter what the Shrink said about his totem animal being a phoenix instead of a wolf. "The damn man pretty much puts whatever he wants on you."

"I suppose shapeshifters don't have a lot of options. Derek said normal tattoos heal."

With the attack that had caused him to change, he'd gone from half-dead to prowling around in only a few hours. "That goes doubly so for me, I guess."

"So you have some? Tattoos, I mean."

She sounded interested in spite of her studiously casual tone, and he couldn't help teasing her. "I've got a few, Kat. Want to see them?"

Her cheeks turned pink. "No."

He didn't blame her for lying. "Let me know if you change your mind."

The gesture she made was sufficiently rude to end the conversation, and she pointedly opened her computer. "Anything else you want me to look up before we get there?"

"Yeah." He gave her a mild smile. "What's the architectural and combat history of the ship? I'm curious."

"You're such a freak." But fondness laced the words, and in a few seconds she'd pulled up a page and started to read. "The USS Alabama's a South Dakota-class battleship..."

She continued to talk, sometimes reading and sometimes paraphrasing, as they drove. Andrew listened, not so much to her words as to the flow of her voice, familiar and soothing.

In an hour, they'd make it to Mobile. In two, if everything went exactly as planned, the meet would go down, and Kat would get her information. The problem was what he knew—and she did too, down past all her hope.

Things never went exactly as planned.

Chapter Three

Andrew had been spending too much time with Alec.

They arrived for the meeting early enough that Kat had every intention of waiting in the car while Andrew did whatever reconnaissance made him feel more secure. Instead she got dragged out into the crisp January air and glared at until she bundled up in her jacket, hat *and* scarf.

Andrew, it seemed, had no intention of letting her out of his sight.

The wind coming in off the bay didn't bother him. He looked perfectly comfortable in his stupidly hot leather jacket, and glaring at his back wasn't nearly as satisfying when she kept getting distracted wondering what sort of tattoos he might be hiding under his clothing.

He'd offered to show her.

Stupid, stupid, stupid. She was always stupid about Andrew, but she'd never seen him like this before. Focused. Intense. The humor and intelligence that she adored tempered by a dangerous edge. A couple of years ago she wouldn't have liked that edge.

A couple of years ago she hadn't had edges of her own.

He stopped outside the visitors' center and shook his head. "I don't like it."

"Don't like what?" She glanced around at the sparse crowd, but nothing seemed out of place, and she'd locked her empathy up behind her tightest shields the second they'd stepped out of the car. "Is something wrong?"

Instead of answering, he cursed and peered down at her. "Where exactly are we supposed to meet this woman?"

The email hadn't been specific, and her attempt to clarify had gone unanswered. "I don't know. I assume she was planning on finding me. Or you. You're not exactly unknown in supernatural circles."

"Right. Alec Junior." Andrew turned in a slow circle. "It's open, but not open enough. See how this building and the pavilion both block off this area by the waterfront?"

She glanced at the pavilion, then turned and squinted toward the far end of the ship. "We could go wait down there by those planes or something? Or hell, back in the parking lot if you want. She'll come to us. And if she doesn't..."

He hesitated. "If I had to pick a spot, it'd be back by the Vietnam War memorial. Not too much elevation, plenty of cover. But it's almost a quarter-mile, and your contact might never find us."

Closing her eyes, Kat tried to consider the situation rationally. Possible information against acceptable risk. Not just risk to her, but risk to Andrew. His willingness to throw himself between her and danger had never been in doubt, after all. "You decide. I trust your instincts more than mine."

For a moment, he fairly trembled with energy and tension. Then he held out both hands. "Here's fine. Just keep your eyes peeled, and if I tell you to hit the ground—"

"Then I'll kiss asphalt." She blew out a breath and glanced around again. Not too many people seemed eager to brave the morning chill, but enough milled about that it might not be easy to spot one face in the crowd. "I learned a few new tricks from that hotshot English empath. If someone's watching my back, I can pinpoint hot spots of specific emotions. Nerves, anger, whatever."

"How close?"

For one moment she hesitated, her teacher's words coming

back to her. *Strong psychics survive by keeping their abilities a secret. Unless you plan to find an employer so terrifying no one dares touch you, you're safer if no one knows just how much you can do.* Good advice, and she'd taken it to heart. But it was Andrew—and Andrew already knew. "I'll have to concentrate to keep from getting hits all the way back to the Civic Center."

The corner of his mouth kicked up. "Good." He pulled her closer with an arm around her shoulders, the pose deceptively casual, considering their conversation. "You don't know anything about this group at all? What they're after? If they like guns or magic?"

"Derek and I always knew that she was messed up in psychic-cult shit, but I don't even remember when I first found out. I heard my dad and Derek's dad talking once..."

The memory was fuzzy, painted in fear and worry that she'd later realized was coming from the adults. They hadn't known she was nearby, listening, or they'd never have spoken so freely. "My uncle said the Gabriel women had a history of being powerful. It was a *thing*. Legacy. That's why my mom wouldn't change her name when she got married, and why she gave me hers. Being a Gabriel psychic was supposed to be a big deal."

He nodded slowly. "Guess we just have to be ready for anything."

Kat let her eyes drift shut and leaned into him. "I'm going to see if anyone around us is really nervous. Can you make sure I don't topple over?"

"I've got you."

Andrew was so tall that the back of her head rested easily against his shoulder, though she wasn't particularly short. His body behind hers provided the perfect grounding, made it less of a challenge to find a quiet space inside her.

Her teacher had talked about trances, but Kat had never liked that word. *Trance* summoned images of chanting and drug trips or, at the very least, serious and dedicated meditation. Finding a quiet place was more like daydreaming, something she'd always been good at.

Of course, if settling into place was easy, preparing to scan the area was anything but. Dropping her shields in a sea of humans was asking for insanity, but a bit of concentration redirected the power, burning it through the sheer effort of changing the way she perceived emotions.

The waking dream, Callum had called it. *Temporary synesthesia,* she'd retorted, annoyed by his fondness for shrouding everything in vague, mystical metaphor when science provided a serviceable definition.

Whatever the trick was, it was useful. And disorienting. Five minutes later, she opened her eyes to find the world transformed. "Whoa."

Andrew's hand closed on her shoulder, strong and sparking purple flecked with silver. "What is it?"

If she turned around, she'd see him bathed in purple flames edged in inky black and glittering in the sun. Purple for strength, the silver of protective instincts and black for worry.

"Colors," she whispered, letting her gaze drift over the rainbow-shrouded crowd. "I see the emotions as colors when I do this."

"A pro might not be nervous or upset," he murmured. "Bear that in mind as you look around, okay?"

"Pros are your territory. I'm looking for a jumpy psychic."

"Then let's hope that's what we get." He went back to scanning the sparse crowd.

Kat did the same. Colors danced in the sunlight, some a thin mist, some so vivid they nearly obscured the person they surrounded. The first time she'd done this, Callum had taken her to the Skydeck at the Hilton. The idea of dropping her shields in the crowded business district had made her stomach flip-flop, but any hint of nerves disappeared in a rush of wonder when Poydras Street lit up in her own private light show.

Not just Poydras, either. Spikes of emotion had twirled up for blocks in all directions. In the fall she'd gone back during some big football game and watched sports fanatics light up the sky above the Superdome with a thousand shades she didn't even have names for.

She didn't have names for all of the colors surrounding her now, but she knew what they meant. Glossy red with marbleized black streaks around a nearby man showed intense stress, but the soft red cloud obscuring the couple half-hidden around the side of a building held sparkling glitters of gold so bright it made her heart ache. Passion, and giddy love.

Plenty of emotions twisted around them, but nothing seemed unusual. Not until she turned and saw a column of thick, shiny black shooting up into the air, inky nothingness streaked with the ice blue of terror. Her body stiffened, and she leaned back into Andrew without thought, so fixated on the colors that she could barely see the person beneath them. "There."

He slid his arm around her. "The woman in the green?"

"I can't—" *Breathe, Kat. Breathe.* She slid her hand down and clutched the hard arm locked around her waist, letting the solid strength of him flow through her. Another deep breath and she managed to fight back the instinctive panic.

If she'd opened her shields and felt this woman's fear, she'd be on her hands and knees, puking up her breakfast. As it was, she could barely fight past the writhing colors to catch a glimpse of her face—a pretty face. Blonde and freckled, with clear blue eyes and a perfect complexion, like a beauty queen who'd slid gracefully into middle age. Only the nervous pinch of her lips ruined the idyllic picture, and even that was nothing compared to the seething turmoil hiding just beneath the surface.

"She's scared." Kat kept the words to a whisper. Andrew's shapeshifter hearing would pick them up easily enough, but no one else would be able to eavesdrop. "She's so terrified I don't know how she's standing upright."

His jaw tightened, and he lifted her half off her feet. "Let's go find out."

His body was an unyielding wall of heat at her back. She hadn't been this close to him since the day he'd been changed, since he'd risen from near death and snatched her to him. Sometimes she'd close her eyes and remember how safe she'd felt in those first moments, clutched against his bare chest, the wildness of his new instincts curled around her with two needs. Keep. Protect.

He'd chosen the latter. Protected her from his uncertain strength and the turmoil of his adjustment. That first day he'd hurt her, held her so tight she'd had bruises around her waist for weeks. Not this time. His arm didn't move when she pushed at it, but there was a fine edge of control in his unwavering grip. "You can let go."

He did, immediately, dropping his hand to brush hers.

After a moment she twined her fingers with his. A practical thing to do when the empathic vision might leave her wobbly, but it wasn't practicality that made her heart skip like a teenager's. "Let's do this."

"Remember what I said," he murmured. "If I give the word…"

Then they were in deep shit. "I know."

The capitulation seemed to ease him, and he squeezed her hand.

The woman didn't look surprised by their approach. White-hot relief cut a swath through the cloud of fear for a few trembling seconds before they slowly began to cancel each other out.

"You're them," she whispered. "Thank you, Jesus."

Andrew's paranoia must have been contagious, because Kat felt too exposed. "I'm Katherine Gabriel. This is Andrew Callaghan. If you have requests for the Southeast council, you'll have to ask him."

The blonde licked her lips nervously. "I—I don't know how these things work."

"Why don't you start off telling us what you know?" Andrew suggested.

She laughed, the sound bordering on hysterical. "How much time do you have? I know too much, that's the problem. I can't hide forever, no matter how good I am at it. They'd find me eventually, so here I am."

Kat clutched at Andrew's hand and braced herself. "You knew my mother?"

The woman's expression evened. "Yes. Yes, I knew your mother. We were part of the same—the same group."

Standing in the bright January sunlight, it was impossible to force the word *cult* past her lips. "Your email said you have information about the Gabriel family. It wasn't just her?"

A sliver of doubt spiked out from the woman. "They never told you."

Those words never heralded good news. "I know that being a Gabriel psychic was such a big deal to my mom, and I know we were both strong."

"And your grandmother and aunt, and all the women before them."

"So? Lots of people are strong."

"Not like the Gabriels." The woman took a half-step back. "Not so strong it drives them—it—"

Crazy.

Andrew didn't let her say it. "Enough. You said you had *information.*"

He couldn't protect her from everything. He sure as hell couldn't protect her from whatever genetic legacy had been handed down to her. Kat squeezed his hand. "That *is* information, Andrew."

"Helpful information," he growled.

Kat drew in a breath, deep enough that the cold air burned her lungs. "Give us something. Something that satisfies him that you're not trying to take advantage of me. Then we can go somewhere safer to talk."

The woman nodded and reached into her pocket, jerking when Andrew's growl grew in volume. "Just this. Your mother gave it to me to hide." She pulled out a small brass key and held it out to Kat. "Safe deposit box at Winchester Bank & Tru—"

A high-pitched whine filled Kat's ears a moment before red bloomed on the front of the woman's shirt. Kat's fingers clutched tight around the key, an instinctive reaction to pain she didn't notice until the woman started to fall.

Andrew grabbed Kat before the body hit the ground.

The world shattered into agony. Callum's ruthless training kept the synesthesia in place while her mind fractured. Her arm throbbed, worse when Andrew began to move.

She stumbled along next to him because there wasn't a choice. Her feet remembered how to move, which was good because the rest of her was replaying the scene over and over again.

A shot.

A bullet.

Blood.

Andrew's boots kept getting under her feet, because he was so close to her that she bumped into him with every step. Shielding her, she realized belatedly. Someone had shot at them, and Andrew wasn't going to let it happen again.

Probably a good idea. She got one hand up to her injured arm and felt something warm and wet. Blood, but maybe not so much that she was dying.

God, she had better not be dying, or Andrew was going to kill her. Then Derek would kill *him*—

Shit, she was losing her mind.

Andrew jerked her behind a building and covered her with his body as he looked around. "Where is he? Where the fuck is he?"

Kat leaned her forehead against his leather jacket and focused on breathing through the pain. "I'm bleeding. I don't know how bad."

"Shh, I know. Let me see." He didn't wait for her to act. Instead, he got her jacket off, tore her shirt and swore again. "Press your other hand to it," he told her as he ripped at the bottom of his own shirt. "I know it hurts, but try to do it anyway."

She obeyed because he sounded confident, and she couldn't focus. Tears stung her eyes as she pressed her fingers over the spot that hurt the most. "I'm a wuss. I'm not a shapeshifter warrior."

"Don't think about it." He wound a strip of fabric from his shirt around her upper arm. "There's no safe cover here. We have to head for the car. You ready?"

Kat lied. "Ready."

His hands slid around her body and coaxed her away from the wall, and Kat choked back a moan and gathered every scrap of nerve and will she had.

Then she walked.

She *tried* to walk. Andrew's long legs ate up the ground, and she struggled to keep pace without attracting more attention than they'd already garnered. Most of the people were running toward the water—toward the body, she was sure, to gawk and stare and tell everyone they'd been there when a woman had been shot.

Two women. Blood stained Kat's shirt, and she spent a moment hoping no one had gotten a camera phone out quickly enough to take pictures of her stumbling and bleeding. That was all they needed—to go viral online as a crazy couple escaping the scene of a crime.

She *was* losing her mind. Shot and bleeding and possibly stalked by a sniper, and she was thinking about the internet.

This had to be what shock felt like.

Andrew must have noticed her distraction. Closer to the lot,

41

he practically picked her up off the ground. "Come on. Not far now."

It wasn't until he dragged her past a startled woman that she realized the most terrifying truth. The old woman's confusion rippled through the air in bright yellow and black, a swarm of angry bumblebees. The pain from her arm hadn't disrupted the synesthesia—it was still going strong.

And Andrew was...nothing.

Blank.

Colors faded around him. By the time he got her to the car he was etched in black and white, an old-fashioned action hero cast in terrifying shadows. She couldn't see the green of his eyes or the color of his clothes, just a thousand unrelenting shades of gray.

He didn't ask why she was staring, just unlocked the SUV and urged her into the passenger seat. "Can you buckle up?"

She had the key clutched so hard in her right hand that uncurling her fingers revealed a deep imprint of the damn thing. She lifted her hips to shove it deep into the pocket of her jeans, then fumbled with the seatbelt.

"*Kat.*" His gaze was riveted to the strip of cotton wrapped around her arm. "Talk to me."

The seatbelt buckle clicked, and she squeezed her eyes shut. "Get me out of here before my empathy implodes. I can't hold this much longer but I can't let it go, either. Not while I've got enough energy left to project."

"I'll try." The door slammed, and the driver's side opened so quickly he must have run around the vehicle. "Just hold on."

She had to. Whatever Andrew had done to her arm might have staunched the bleeding, but she clearly lacked the badass shapeshifter gene that kept them all running with bullets in them. If she let go of the empathic synesthesia, she'd shove her pain into every driver they passed. They'd be lucky to survive.

The engine rumbled, and Kat concentrated on breathing. Slow, deep breaths, while she tried to decide how best to describe the feeling of being shot. Throbbing pain was too mild, stabbing was too...sharp. Though when Andrew spun them out of the parking lot fast enough to shove her against the door, *stabbing* became a serious contender. So did blinding. Agonizing.

"Sorry." Andrew kept his eyes on the road, but the first hints of panic began to creep into his voice—and his aura. "Shit."

"It's okay." That was the least convincing lie ever. "I've got two choices here. I can let go of this empathic trick and try to shield, but I don't think I'll be able to. Not while I'm hurting this much."

"What's the other option?"

"Controlled burnout. It's already starting. It won't *hurt* me, but I'll be useless until tonight. Maybe tomorrow morning." Though the giddy euphoria and vaguely stoned feeling might make being shot a little more tolerable. "You'd have to feed me and find me a place to sleep it off."

He ground a curse between clenched teeth. "Is that safe for you?"

"It won't hurt me," she repeated, putting more strength into it. "But I'm going to be even more of a burden than I already am."

He cast her a quick, disbelieving glance. "I can take care of you. If burning it out won't hurt you, do it. You can trust me."

Trusting him had never been the question, but she didn't have the energy to argue the point. Instead she closed her eyes and fought to find the half-trance again.

It was harder this time. She could smell her own blood, and if the scent bothered her, God only knew what it was doing to Andrew. Her arm ached, and it was getting worse instead of better. Fear formed a sick knot in her belly, and beneath all of it a wild, terrible excitement gathered.

They'd found something. Something big, something *real*. Later she'd be horrified that a woman had died and she'd been shot and Andrew had been placed into danger, but for the first time in her life, answers were within her grasp.

Or maybe she'd just found more questions. She dropped her hand to her hip and traced the outline of the key in her pocket, using the slow, repetitive motion as its own sort of ritual.

Once she found the quiet place, it was easy to lock her mind into a carefully controlled spiral. Callum might have been obsessed with a mysticism she didn't care for, but he'd earned his reputation for being the most powerful empath on the planet. Not through strength—he'd happily acknowledged that she outstripped him in raw magic—but with a skill and control that bordered on artistry.

He'd also been a brutal teacher. Burnout was the first defense he'd taught her, and the one she'd been most motivated to learn. A nice, safe recursive loop that drilled down to the heart of her gift and exhausted her too much to hurt anyone.

With her eyes closed, she could almost see her empathy, its usual raging flames winnowed down to a cheerfully flickering campfire. Soon it would be a candle. Smoke.

She could only hope that half-drunken numbness would give way to unconsciousness before she did anything truly humiliating—like tell Andrew the truth of why she'd spent so much time avoiding him.

Chapter Four

It took him far too long to find a suitable motel, because he couldn't drive more than three miles without checking to make sure Kat wasn't slipping into unconsciousness.

Andrew gripped the steering wheel until it groaned in protest as he pulled into the parking lot of a small, run-down motor inn. It was impossible to tell when it had last been painted, but the white blocks and bright aqua of the doors had faded to grimy beige and pale green.

He chose it because it wasn't a chain, which meant they might get away without giving any real personal information—including credit cards—and because it was an utter *dump*, which meant they might not have to answer any questions.

Which brought him to another problem—what the hell to do with Kat while he paid and retrieved a key.

He thought about leaving her in the SUV. She could climb in the back and hide until he returned, but his instincts balked. She'd be alone and bleeding, and he couldn't leave her like that.

He actually literally *couldn't*.

Andrew parked and stripped off his jacket. "Sit up, sweetheart. Can you slip your arms into this without it hurting too much?"

She held up her injured arm and leaned toward him without unbuckling her seatbelt. The canvas snapped tight across her chest, and she frowned, glanced down and wrinkled her nose. "Seatbelt."

Christ, she was completely out of it. Panic threatened again, and he swallowed it with fierce determination as he unbuckled her safety belt. "We're going to put this on you, go inside and check in. Everything's fine, you just had a little too much to drink."

"Got it. I'm a lush." This time she lifted her arm more slowly, and the pain of easing it into his jacket showed on her face. By the time she'd gotten her other arm into the sleeve her eyes were too bright, and she had to blink away tears. "I'm a wuss. I'm sorry I'm such a wuss."

"Quit it. You're doing fine."

She nodded and lifted her good hand. Her fingertips barely cleared the end of the sleeve, and the sight seemed to amuse her. "Sometimes I forget how huge you are."

"Uh-huh. I'm a real mountain of a man, sweetheart." He zipped the jacket and buckled the top for good measure. "Ready?"

A nod. A smile, sweet and unguarded in a way he hadn't seen from her in a year or more. "I like it when you call me sweetheart."

The smile *hurt*, more than he'd believed anything could. "Pull this off, and I'll call you anything you want." He hurried around to her door and opened it.

Kat was wobbly at first, but once she had both boots on the ground and one hand around his arm, she steadied. Enough to make it inside, and if she pressed a little close to his side, it looked more like affection than necessity.

They could pull this off.

When the bell above the door chimed, the clerk inside barely glanced up from the small television behind the desk. "Fill out a registration card. Room's forty-three fifty a night."

Kat kept her feet while he filled out the card and handed over the cash. Under the harsh lights she looked pale and worn, but her expression stayed blandly pleasant until he got her back out into the parking lot. "I'm starting to feel woozy."

"I've got to get the first aid kit from the truck, and then we're right here. Room number five."

"Can we get my bag too? My computer?"

"Yeah, sure." He propped her against the side of the SUV and grabbed the three bags, including the duffel he'd brought along, in one hand. "Just a little farther."

"I can do it." And she did, though it seemed like stubbornness might be the only thing that kept her moving. As soon as he got the door open, she crossed to the sagging bed and slumped on the mattress. "Wow. It's not even noon and I think I need a nap."

"You need food first." He locked the door and grabbed the takeout menu hanging on the back of the knob. "Can you look at this while I check out your arm?"

"After." She tugged at the zipper, working it down in uneven jerks that made her wince. "I think you're gonna have to help me get this off. And the T-shirt, too, if it needs to go."

He pulled off the jacket and wished again that he had something to give her for the pain. The makeshift bandage around her upper arm was soaked through with blood, and the sight and the smell combined made him want to *rage*. "Good thing Carmen gave me a crash course in creative first aid."

Her eyebrows came together. "I didn't know you were taking lessons from her too."

He couldn't tell Kat the truth—that he'd done it for himself, but he'd been thinking of her. Shapeshifters healed quickly, but the most important person in his world wasn't a shifter at all. "Pays to know how to patch people up."

"Guess so." She closed her eyes, and some of her earlier giddiness seemed to have vanished under tense lines of pain. "So how bad is it?"

"Could be way worse." He probed at her arm. The angry furrow angling up the outside of her biceps was bleeding but sluggishly, and it looked shallow. "I don't think it hit anything important. Doesn't look like anything I can sew up, though.

Maybe just some butterfly bandages."

"Oh, good. That suturing shit looks hot in the movies, but I think I'd probably puke on your boots. I'm not exactly Lara Croft."

He had to find some way to put her at ease, or she might puke on him anyway. "Your pop culture references are getting dated. What the hell have you been doing with yourself?"

"Getting a PhD and becoming a psychic ninja." She trembled under his touch. One hand rested in her lap and the other fisted around the covers so tightly her knuckles were white. But she kept talking, kept *trying*, even when her voice shook as hard as her body. "Oh, and letting Zola and Walker kick me around their dojo five days a week. My PlayStation has cobwebs."

"Okay, so you've been busy." He dug a bottle of antiseptic and some gauze pads out of the first aid kit.

"Mmm." She listed to the side, and he gently righted her. "Had to. Busy's better than brooding."

"So I've been told."

Her voice dropped to a whisper. "Busy's better than missing you."

No amount of activity had kept him from missing her. "I know what you mean."

Kat laughed, though it broke off when he dabbed the antiseptic on her wound. "We both kept so busy to keep from missing each other, and now the people we were missing are gone."

"I haven't changed that much," he lied.

"Don't need empathy when the lie's that stupid."

It hurt to acknowledge the truth, so he'd forced himself to do it a long time ago. It hadn't occurred to him that she would do the same. "All right, those people are gone. No laid-back architects or happy-go-lucky programmers here."

"No." The pain in her voice cut deep. "But you found a new

place. You're on the Southeast council and you're changing the world and I'm—I'm practically unemployed and stuck on shit that happened before I was born."

And if the stuff about her mother hadn't been kept from her, maybe she would have already dealt with it. "You had more to work through than me."

"Yeah. And it got me shot. It could have gotten you shot." She flinched as he fixed the first bandage in place. "And all because I don't want to be Alec's pet hacker for the rest of my life."

"Who *would* want to be? The man's a terror to work with."

"He wants me to be nineteen still. But I'm *not* nineteen."

"If you were, he'd still have a reason to protect you."

She choked on a hysterical laugh. "Guess I just proved I need it. Way to go, Kat."

"Quit it," he ordered. "You can't blame yourself for a fucking sniper."

"It's not about blame. It's about—" She hissed in a sudden breath, her hand opening and closing helplessly on the thin coverlet. "Okay, I really am going to puke on you. Are you almost done?"

He placed the last strip and sat back. "Yeah. It wouldn't heal pretty, but it'll hold you together until we can do better."

She said nothing for a long time, her gaze fixed ahead and her jaw tight with pain. Then she unclenched her hand and lifted it to swipe at a stray tear. "That's all I really need."

Don't do it— Andrew slipped his arm around her and bent to put his mouth close to her ear. "You're all right. You think you're not, but you are."

Another tear slipped down her cheek, a salty sharpness undercutting the scent of her vanilla lotion and the spicy cinnamon of her favorite shampoo. "Maybe. Or maybe crazy really does run in my family. Maybe I can spend ten hours a day with the world's best empath and it won't matter, because

I'm a ticking time bomb. Aren't you even a little afraid?"

He *was*, but only of himself and what would happen if he had to walk away from her again. "I'll never be scared of you, Kat."

"You would be if you could remember."

"Remember what? The attack?" He urged her chin up so she had to look at him. "I *do*."

Her blue eyes were chips of ice. "Alec's scared of me. *Alec.* The crazy fucker that shapeshifter moms tell stories about to terrify their kids. They all try to hide it. They try to make me a hapless stupid kid so they can pretend it's not there. But I feel it, Andrew. Every damn day."

He had to make her understand. "Are you scared of me, Kat? I could kill you right now, in a heartbeat. Crack your neck before you had a chance to think about liquefying my brain or whatever. Does that mean you're pretending I can't just to get through the day?"

Kat fisted her good hand in his shirt. Her eyes narrowed, her jaw clenched. "You've never been afraid of hurting me?"

"That's not what I'm saying. I'm just saying there's a lot of scary going around, and if you're going to condemn yourself for being dangerous, move over. There are a lot of us who belong on that bench with you."

"But I couldn't—" Her teeth dug into her lower lip. "I didn't do it on purpose. I was scared, and I was mad, and I *snapped*, and I could have melted your brain too."

And so she'd gotten help, the best to be had, and Callum had spent six months teaching her to harness that power. To control it, instead of letting it control her. "A year ago, you never could have done what you did this morning."

For the first time, the anger and fear in her eyes wavered. "No. No, I couldn't have. Of course, if I hadn't, you wouldn't be trapped in a crappy motel room with a burned-out empath who's kinda high and has the munchies."

It was enough—for now. Andrew released her and snagged

the takeout menu. "Screw the munchies. Ever had steak delivered to a shitty motel room?"

She made a face at him. "Crappy. If it were shitty, there'd be an hourly rate."

"Oh, is that how we judge these things?"

"Uh-huh. Trust me, those places are sketchy."

He didn't bother holding back his groan, though his playful words would hopefully hide his tension. "Where the hell has that Mendoza kid been taking you?"

Her cheeks turned pink, and she busied herself with the laces on her Doc Martens. "Miguel took me wherever I wanted him to."

Julio had been reluctant to discuss anything having to do with Kat and his brother, but the supernatural community in New Orleans wasn't big enough for Andrew not to have heard things. "Good for him." He almost meant it too.

She jerked one boot off. "I keep trying to hook him up with Sera, but neither of them will take the bait."

He snorted. "If you think that slick little Casanova is what Sera wants, you haven't been paying attention."

"Hey." She struggled with the other boot, tugging at the laces with one hand. "Be nice. He might be a tiny bit of a man whore, but he's still my friend. If I can be nice about Anna when she was screwing the love of—" Her teeth snapped together. "Are you ordering steak or not?"

He wrapped his hand around her arm and held her still. "Look at me."

She didn't. "I'm wasted. I can't even untie my damn boot. Just feed me and let me sleep it off."

He released her and dragged her foot into his lap to unravel the knotted laces. "You're not nice about Anna. You might not hate her or wish she'd die a horrible death, but you're not *nice*. You don't like her and you never will and that—" The heavy boot hit the floor, and Andrew sighed. "That's how I feel about

Miguel."

Kat finally looked at him, her face lost to bewilderment. "You really think it's the same thing, don't you?"

"I guess you don't."

Uncomfortable silence filled the space between them before she looked away. "I need to eat, or I'll be sick."

He snatched the menu off the bed. "I'll order a bunch of stuff. In the meantime, there's an energy bar in my bag. Grab it, okay?"

She obeyed without a word, and her stubborn silence continued until the food arrived. She ate with the same quiet determination, every movement mechanical. Methodical. All her attention seemed turned inward, even when she pushed away from the rickety table with a quiet sigh. "Thanks, Andrew. I'm just hurt and tired and need some sleep."

"How bad's the pain? I don't have anything too strong, but there's some over-the-counter stuff in my bag."

"Maybe tomorrow." She smiled wanly and crawled onto the bed. "I'm about to be unconscious whether I take drugs or not. Don't be worried unless I sleep more than twenty-four hours."

"Got it."

He stared at the remains of his sandwich until her breathing deepened and steadied. Then he retrieved his phone and slipped out the front door.

He'd need to tell Sera, at least, that they weren't coming back right away. As Kat's roommate, she would be the first person to raise the alarm, and he didn't know if they could afford that right now.

Best-case scenario, that sniper had been targeting the dead woman. Worst case, he was a lousy shot who only winged Kat...or missed Andrew entirely.

Both possibilities sucked.

Burnout dreams were the worst.

Kat struggled her way into consciousness, guided by the throbbing ache in her arm. Her dreams had always been vivid, but after a controlled burnout, the deepest, darkest corners of her psyche turned her brain into their playground.

She'd dreamed of pirates. The sexy, swashbuckling kind with ambiguous sexuality and a historically improbable lack of STDs. Miguel was their leader, and she'd been balanced on the precarious edge of a plank over the deep blue ocean, everything inside her screaming to close her eyes and jump.

Her psyche wasn't subtle.

Neither was the pain, which her groggy mind identified as the delightful aftermath of being shot. Far less sexy than in the movies, where a few gunshot wounds never seemed to stop a determined heroine from dirty sex in a dingy motel room. Sticky blood had mostly dried on her T-shirt, and the fabric stuck to her skin as she rolled over. She was groggy, hungry, sore and distinctly sketchy. Sex had never seemed less appealing.

Then she sat up, and remembered what it felt like to want.

Andrew was doing pushups. Shirtless. The muscles in his shoulders and back flexed with every effortless movement, which made the tattoo on his back flex right along with them. Thick black ink cut across tanned skin in a style she recognized all too easily. One of the Ink Shrink's creations, an intricate phoenix with a vaguely tribal feel, so large the bird's wings spanned Andrew's back and curled around his shoulders.

The Ink Shrink wasn't always subtle, either.

"Almost done," he said without looking up. Two more pushups and he rocked back on his knees, stretching his arms. "Feel better?"

He had a tattoo on his arm too, and finding it fascinating kept her from dwelling on his chest. "Uhm, I feel less drunk. More like I got shot."

"Stiff and sore?"

Yeah. Those were two very important things to remember,

especially if Andrew was going to stay half-naked. "Pretty much. And I should have taken my shirt off last night, I think. There's blood on it. I could use a shower."

"Bath," he corrected. "And keep that arm dry."

She hadn't brought a change of clothes, and the bathtub looked so questionable she opted to do the best she could with a towel and some warm water. The grimy mirror reflected an unpleasant picture—pale skin, tangled hair, bruised-looking eyes. She did her best to avoid her own reflection as she washed, then dragged her fingers through her shaggy hair and gathered the mess up on top of her head.

Trying to rinse her shirt in the sink proved pointless, and the effort just made her left arm burn. She abandoned the garment in the garbage can and pulled on the closest thing to a shirt that she had—a black hoodie with the word *meh* emblazoned across the front in all its apathetic glory.

Meh pretty much covered it. She eased the sweatshirt on over her bra and zipped it up as she returned to the main room. "I really need to buy some clothes."

He rose and passed her on his way to the small bathroom. "We'll take care of that as soon as we figure out—" His words cut off in a curse.

Kat jumped and regretted it. "What?"

He backed out of the bathroom and turned, his eyes shadowed. "You left your stuff all over."

"My T-shirt? Why would it..." *Shit.* Sera was addicted to one of the thousands of procedural crime shows that cluttered the airwaves every Wednesday, which made Kat a captive audience. "You mean I need to clean up the evidence?"

Andrew averted his gaze. "More like it's a damn hard thing to look at."

"Oh." He'd been acting so restrained that she'd forgotten the main reason alpha shifters drove her insane—the stifling, oppressive protectiveness. Even Sera, the most submissive shifter Kat had ever met, got downright testy when she thought her human roommate was in danger. The fact that Andrew hadn't dragged her into the bathroom to bathe her himself probably evidenced the kind of self-control people gave medals for.

Against her better judgment she reached out and touched Andrew's shoulder. His skin was hot under her fingertips, and she traced the swooping whorl of one of the phoenix's stylized feathers before she could stop herself. "I'll take care of it."

"Kat." He tensed, and his voice dropped to a rasp.

"Sorry." She leaned into him, pressing her forehead to his shoulder as she snuck her good arm around him in an awkward hug. "Thank you. For not flipping out and getting neurotic bossy alpha on me. But if there's something I can do that'll make it easier, you can ask."

He smoothed her hair. "Help me figure out what comes next."

No commands. No plan, already outlined and fixed into place. She swallowed hard and held him tighter. "My technopathic friend lives in Birmingham. If we need to keep off the grid, he's the guy to see. I think it's farther than going back home, but he could probably figure out where this key belongs."

"The harder we are to track without magic, the better. Hell, the harder we are to track *with* it."

"I can email Ben before we leave. He could have IDs and credit cards for us by the time we got there." Which would mean a real hotel, with a bath she wasn't afraid to climb into and sheets she'd let touch her body. "Ben will know the local magical community too."

"Good. We might need that."

Kat didn't want to ask the next question, but she had to. "My life's boring right now, but you have things to do. Important things. Do you need to—"

Both his eyebrows shot up. "Are you about to say what I think you're about to say?"

Stepping back gave her space. "Someone should say it."

"Does someone also want her cousin to find out she got *shot* before she gets what she came here for?"

Not so reasonable after all, then. Kat could read between the lines. Andrew would let her pursue any leads she felt the need to, as long as he got to watch her back. "That's a little bit like blackmail."

"It's a little bit like self-preservation," he argued. "I don't want Derek to murder me."

Whatever the reason, she didn't have to do it alone. "So we go to Birmingham?"

"We go to Birmingham." He backed toward the bathroom. "I'll clean up in here. You get on the line with what's-his-name."

"Ben." Kat reached out and caught Andrew's hand, and damnable butterflies fluttered to life in her stomach at the simple touch. "Thanks. Even if you're only doing it for Derek."

He looked down at her, his mouth set in a firm line. "I'm doing it for *you*. I'm just not above blaming Derek."

She couldn't look away. "It means a lot. More."

He pulled away with a quick nod. "Shouldn't take more than four hours or so to get there. We'll hit 65 and head north."

"Got it." Kat checked her wrist out of instinct before she remembered she'd lent her watch to Sera twenty-four very long hours ago. She circled the bed on the way to her bag and caught a glimpse of the cheap bedside clock. Bright red numbers informed her it was just after six in the morning.

Way too early. If she knew Ben, he'd only fallen into bed a few hours ago. She'd never actually called him before—she'd never *needed* to, considering how much easier it was to use voice-chat—but his number was stored in her address book along with the numbers to every takeout restaurant within ten miles of her apartment.

She dug her phone out of her bag and plugged it in to charge before calling Ben. After four rings, she was directed to his voicemail.

Sorry, Ben. She left a brief message, then began the systematic process of annoying him awake with a series of text messages. The first was her phone number, followed by a string of abrupt notes typed as fast as she could manage.

Got shot.

Need papers.

Coming to town.

I thought you always answer text messages.

Even if your phone is on vibrate.

Or if you're asleep.

Or drunk.

Wake up, lazy ass. Or I'll stop using punctuation.

BTW, I'm stuck in a crappy motel room.

With Andrew.

She was seriously considering a few messages filled with creative obscenities—or offenses against the English language—when "The Ride of the Valkyries" filled the room. Kat jabbed at her phone to answer the call. "Ben?"

"You got *shot?* What the fuck?" Ben's voice was groggy with sleep, but familiar enough from long hours of gaming to bring the stark absurdity of her present circumstances into sharp focus. The residual warmth from her quiet moment with Andrew faded, leaving her cold and scared as she outlined the story to Ben.

Just as well. A little fear was probably appropriate for her first foray into fake identities. And if she concentrated on that, she wouldn't have to dwell on why she needed one, or who might be out to get her. Or Andrew.

Chapter Five

They hit Montgomery right at rush hour, so Andrew circled the city to avoid traffic. The rest of the drive to Birmingham went smoothly, though it took forever to park.

"That's it," he told Kat as he opened her door. "The Watts building."

The sun was bright overhead, but the air still held a cold bite. Kat shivered and pulled up the hood on her sweatshirt as she stepped onto the curb. "He's on the fourteenth floor."

She started to lift her bag onto her uninjured shoulder, but Andrew took it from her. Let her get pissed off about it if she wanted. "Up there, almost at the top. That's where the condos are."

She only nodded and studied the building. "Looks posh. Ben's a hotshot software designer, though, so I guess he can afford it."

"Maybe not as expensive as you think. Stuff like this in Birmingham is a lot more reasonable than in New Orleans." Her friend had probably managed to pick up this place for half what Andrew himself had paid for his old condo on South Peters.

"Yeah?" She reached the door and tugged it open. "I forget you're the real estate smartie. Maybe when this is all over you can help me find a place, one Sera can afford too. I keep telling her she doesn't have to pay rent since she actually cooks and cleans, and I wasn't so great at that, but she's pretty stubborn about it."

"It can't make her feel very independent, not paying rent or anything."

Kat's eyes shadowed. "I know. I keep telling myself not to say anything, but then I see her mending her work clothes because she can't afford to replace them. I feel how worried she is, and I *have* money."

The fact that Kat had the money to spare wouldn't be any easier on Sera's pride than if they'd both been scraping by. In fact, it robbed their situation of the camaraderie it could have had. "She needs to do it on her own as much as she can. I can respect that."

Kat's boots scuffed the lobby floor as she crossed to the gilded elevator and jabbed her finger at the button. "Her ex-husband makes me glad all the controlling bastards in my life have always meant well. I used to say it didn't make much difference, but I was really, really wrong."

"Yeah." His own limited experience with alpha bastards—knowing them and being one—had taught him that. "There's no avoiding instinct." Then he proved it when the elevator door slid open and he urged her inside with a hand at the small of her back. "Sorry."

Her gaze caught his for a moment and then skipped away. "Just don't get protective and weird because of Ben. Or his girlfriend, since she's probably more dangerous than he is. She's some sort of priestess. Pretty sure she can smite people, though she probably wouldn't do it in downtown Birmingham."

He forced a smile. "Now why would she smite me?"

Kat's expression stayed deadly serious. "Because I'm hurt, and Ben's a stranger to you. And *you* are an alpha bastard, no matter how hard you're choking it down. I don't want anything to explode."

"Least of all me?"

Her hand snuck into his. "I'd be sad if you got smited. Smote? What's the past tense?"

Smitten. He squeezed her fingers. "Don't know. You'd better

59

Google it."

Because she was Kat, she shook her hand free, pulled out her phone, and did just that. She was still muttering under her breath when the elevator doors slid open, and she stepped forward without looking up. "Fourteen-C."

"Got it." The hallway was clear and the door solidly closed, so Andrew knocked.

Kat laughed her triumph just as the door opened. "Smite, smote, smitten!"

The pretty brunette on the other side of the door tilted her head. "You pretty much have to be Kat, which makes you Andrew. Come on in, Ben's finishing up in his office."

The front room of the condo was packed with expensive electronics. A longsword that looked like it had seen some use stood propped in the corner, and it drew Andrew's eye. "Nice sword."

The woman gathered her hair up into a ponytail and rolled her eyes. "His brother's," she said in a voice that made her disapproval clear. She picked up a badge and clipped it onto her scrubs, then braced both hands on her hips. "Now, Kat. Ben told me you're hurt. Do you mind if I take a look?"

Kat glanced at Andrew, a quiet question in her eyes, and he swallowed the protest that rose automatically. "Bathroom?" At least if there were windows, they'd be covered, with no easy visual access from someone perched on a neighboring roof.

"All right." Kat slipped her bag from her shoulder and held it out. "Admiring the weapons should keep you entertained until Ben comes out."

He took the bag, and she disappeared with the brunette, leaving him alone in the room. Aside from the sword, he found two guns, a taser, a collection of knives, and a scuffed set of brass knuckles.

Soft footsteps warned him before the loft's owner appeared. Ben proved to be a lanky redhead with a neatly trimmed beard and sharply intelligent eyes. His gaze fell on the brass knuckles, and he grinned. "My brother keeps some of his shit here."

"So your girlfriend said." He held out his hand. "I'm Andrew."

"Ben. I take it Lia dragged Kat off to look at her arm?"

"Yeah. She's wearing scrubs. Is she a doctor?"

"She's a chief resident at UAB." Ben jerked his head toward a smooth wooden table. "But she's also an acolyte of Panacea. They're a healing order of spell casters, and she's good."

"Couldn't ask for better credentials, I guess."

"Kat'll be fine." Ben dropped a folder to the table. "So, she finally jumped your bones, huh? Took her long enough."

The last thing he wanted to deal with was five minutes of stammering apology or, worse, Kat killing the guy. "Yeah. Your brother's really into weaponry, huh? What's he do?"

"Bounty hunter, kind of. Takes care of dangerous witches and the occasional rabid beast. He's over in Georgia, tracking down a rogue shifter who's been causing trouble."

Andrew was surprised he hadn't run across him yet, since he sounded like exactly the kind of person Alec and Jackson would know. "What about you? Kat said you design software."

"Mmm." Ben slipped into a chair and flipped open the folder. "Not as cool as my monster-chasing big brother, but at least I can talk about my job at parties. Well, my day job." He pulled out a piece of paper with a driver's license and a credit card paper-clipped to the top. "This one, not so much."

It looked like solid work, just from the glimpse he'd gotten. "Will the license records check out, or are they just for show?"

"Oh, they'll check out. You're Andy Normanson. Construction foreman from California. Kat picked the job and place, relevant details are attached." He pulled out a second set of IDs, these with Kat's photo attached. "Kate Normanson. Congratulations on your recent elopement. Elvis officiated."

Andrew studied the dossiers. Similar backgrounds to their own, similar first names. "You do good work."

"Sure, and I do it real quiet, just like Kat with her brain-scooping lie-detector thing." Ben's eyes narrowed. "Psychics are the underdogs of the supernatural world. We have a habit of disappearing down rabbit holes if we prove too useful."

"Is that a warning?"

"It's a fact, that's all. Kat's got a serious blind spot when it comes to her empathy. She's so busy angsting over the sort of damage she can do accidentally that I'm pretty sure she's never considered the sort of havoc she could cause if someone made her do it on purpose."

Painful because it was true and far too close to home. "If you know that much about Kat, you must know how many people would die before they let anything like that happen to her."

Ben held up both hands, making a vaguely placating gesture. "I don't know about Kat's life outside of what she tells me. I know you two have a Lifetime Original Movie going on and that her cousin used to smother her a lot. I've always assumed she's just fine over there, but if people are shooting at her..."

"I don't think she was the target." It was the conclusion he'd finally reached during the long hours of waiting for Kat to sleep off her exhaustion. "Whoever was doing the shooting was trying to silence Kat's contact."

"Who gave you guys a key. Listen, I started to do the research, but there are a ton of cities called Winchester, and a bunch of them have a Bank & Trust. So I got frustrated and cheated." He tapped the side of his head.

Technopath. He'd almost forgotten. "What'd you uncover?"

Ben lowered his voice, even though Kat was safely behind the closed bathroom door. "In 2002, an Alyson Gabriel got a safety deposit box at Winchester Bank & Trust in Huntsville, Alabama. Two weeks later, she died in a car crash in Boston."

It sounded right. Andrew swallowed hard. "That'd be it, I think. Could you do some more checking, see if you can find out what she might have done during those two weeks?"

"Sure thing, man. Kat has my cell number now. Anything you need, call. I'm used to being the geek on tap."

"Thanks, Ben."

A shrug. "I owe Kat. She got my brother out of a jam once when I was laid up in the hospital with a very unheroic case of appendicitis."

He had a surgical scar of his own, though it seemed like a few lifetimes ago. "Happens to the best of us."

"All worked out okay." The unmistakably goofy smile of a man in the grip of serious love curved Ben's lips. "That's when I met Lia."

By complete and utter chance. Andrew had seen it over and over, events that spun off a single moment where one changed detail would have changed *everything.* "Fate, right?"

"On the days I remember to put the toilet seat down. The rest of the time I'm a test from her Goddess."

"That just means you're a typical guy."

"Who can ask nicely and have computers do things for him." Ben flipped the folder shut and shoved it across the table. "Kat can handle reservations for wherever you end up, but I was thinking I could make a few too. In Atlanta, maybe. I can ask the system to let me know if anyone else goes looking for you."

Andrew nodded. "It'd be helpful. Whoever shot Kat and that woman is scared of what's in that safety deposit box. If they knew where it was, they would have taken it already."

"Atlanta, it is. Course, no one may be looking, but if they are, doesn't hurt to have a false trail."

Ben seemed like a nice guy, and Andrew was surprised his sword-wielding brother hadn't already taught him the most important lesson of all. "Someone's always looking."

Kat didn't have to beg. Andrew drove them to Huntsville

and straight to the Embassy Suites, where he stretched out on the couch while she dragged a couple hundred bucks of Target loot into the bedroom. The king-sized bed was vast and immaculate, with a plush comforter and a stack of fluffy pillows that took up the top half of the mattress. Pretty enough, but nothing compared to the clean bathroom with its shiny counters and polished metal fixtures.

The tub was big enough for two, and she was pretty sure she could happily die there.

It took an hour of soaking before she felt clean, and another thirty minutes with the scented shampoo and body wash before she was sure she'd got every last bit of dried blood and covered the pungent scent of the dye Lia had used to turn the purple streaks in her hair brown again.

Scrubbed and buffed and smelling of almond and vanilla, Kat twisted her damp hair into a braid before pulling on her new flannel pajama bottoms and the first tank top she'd been able to find in her size—a baby-blue number with an absurdly cheerful butterfly embroidered on it in sparkly silver thread. It left her arm bare, and she ran her fingers over the mostly healed scar where the bullet wound had been that morning.

Magic. The serious business kind that knit human flesh together with a speed normally reserved for shapeshifters. Lia had confessed, almost apologetically, that healing minor wounds was the extent of what a priestess could do on her own. To Kat it had seemed like a miracle, and she'd expressed miracle-level gratitude at the absence of pain.

A peek into the other room proved that Andrew still slept, so Kat killed another two hours trying to catch up on her email and sending both Sera and Miguel reassuring but vague notes insisting everything was fine. Then she made herself filter through the responses from her latest round of queries in her unenthusiastic job search.

Job search. As she clicked listlessly through the emails, she decided she needed a better description. Obligatory resume exportation. Unwilling employment makeover. "Going through the motions" seemed to fit best.

Whatever she was doing, it wasn't active enough to be called searching. Her qualifications and her thesis had earned her attention from researchers. Her gender had gotten her courted by every guilty tech company with a quota to fill. One of her professors had even tried to push her toward the NSA, and she'd enjoyed an evening of near-hysterical laughter trying to imagine Alec's face if she announced she was going to work for the government.

She went to the interviews. She wore combat boots and T-shirts that were trying too hard to be witty and outrageous. Her hair stayed purple, and sometimes she twisted it into styles that should have been impossible outside of a comic book. She played edgy hacker and social misfit with a dedication that deserved an Oscar nod. Sometimes her passive-aggressive self-sabotage worked. The truly desperate offered her jobs anyway, and she'd started "forgetting" to call them back.

Career suicide in slow motion. That was what it had come to, since the restless need to do *more* had invaded her life. Maybe it had come from watching Julio navigate New Orleans' supernatural community under Alec's guidance, or from seeing Carmen and Alec sacrifice everything but each other for the chance to save the world. Things were changing—for the better, *finally* for the better—and she wanted to be a part of it.

Maybe. Somehow...if only she could figure out where. All she knew for sure was that her college trust fund—left untouched for years by scholarships and then grants—was starting to trickle away. The money would run out eventually, if she didn't get out of her own way.

Whatever happened with the safety deposit box, it had to be her last self-indulgence. After this, she'd force herself back into the real world. Put the past behind her. Get a haircut, maybe a suit and a couple of nice blouses. She'd stop going to interviews in sweatshirts and steel-toed boots.

She'd get a job.

She'd grow the fuck up.

By nine, her stomach was starting to rumble. For about two seconds, she considered leaving the hotel room in search of a vending machine. For another five, she considered calling room service without waking Andrew.

Ten seconds after that told herself to stop being a baby and made her way into their suite's sitting room.

Andrew lay sprawled out in nothing but his jeans. Comfortable as the couch looked, he was too damn tall for it, and a dangerous tenderness stirred inside her. He was exhausted because he probably hadn't slept a damn second of the fifteen hours she'd spent unconscious. Two straight days of driving, fighting and worrying, and the stubborn bastard wouldn't even claim the bed when she was short enough to fit on the couch just fine.

Kat smoothed blond strands of hair from his forehead and smiled. "Hey, sleepy. Why don't you get up and pass out someplace where your feet don't dangle off the edge, huh?"

He mumbled something unintelligible and rolled over, almost pitching himself off the couch in the process. Kat planted both hands on his shoulders and pushed him back to the cushions. "Wake up, Andrew."

His hands latched around her arms, and he lifted her clear off her feet and dropped her to the couch. The breath whooshed out of her, stealing her squeaked protest. When he loomed over her, his eyes were blank, dark. Unseeing.

Three heartbeats stretched out to a lifetime. Her stun gun was in the other room, but even if she had it in her damn hand she wasn't sure she could have forced herself to use it on Andrew. Knowing it was futile, she couldn't stop her hands from flying up, bracing against the dangerously hot skin of his chest. Pushing him was like trying to push a brick wall, and the first hint of real fear uncurled inside her. "Andrew—"

His eyes cleared, and a roar of fear eclipsed that tiny thread inside. His fear, not her own, though it vanished in the space of a heartbeat as Andrew released her. "Sorry, that was—sorry."

She hadn't expected her powers to recharge so quickly. After a burnout it could take days for them to come back online at full strength. Kat reinforced her shields to be safe, but didn't move. She barely breathed. "I know better than to poke a shapeshifter when he's asleep. It's my fault."

"No, it isn't."

Something inside her broke at the utter lack of self-forgiveness in his eyes. He looked exhausted. Worn out. "I was just going to let you know that I'm ordering some room service...and that you can take the bed. I'll fit on the couch better than you do."

He rubbed both hands through his hair and stood. "It's a king. Plenty big enough for both of us."

Share a bed with him? If she'd had a masochistic streak, maybe. Or if he was going to sleep in a parka. Fear had a funny way of waking up all of her nerves, and a lot of them seemed to be tracing the memory of his chest under her palms.

Which made her feel warm—and she could only hope it wasn't an obvious kind of warm. "We'll figure it out. You need to eat something before you go back to sleep. Wanna look at the room-service menu?"

Andrew shook his head. "Whatever you get is fine. I'm not picky."

Kat swallowed and eased herself upright, then rose to her feet. "Okay, but if you leave me to my own devices, I'm ordering like, every expensive dessert on the menu."

His smile didn't reach his eyes. "Two for me."

Maybe that was how she looked when she was shaking and scared that her empathy was a weapon that would destroy the people she loved. Not the mirror she'd expected to look into, but a powerful one.

So she did what he'd done. Reached up and framed his face with her hands, and shivered at the texture of his beard against her palms. "I will never be afraid of you, Andrew Callaghan."

His chest heaved with shaking breaths, and he groaned as he grabbed her wrists. "It's dangerous, Kat. *I'm* dangerous."

"So am I." She swiped her thumbs over his cheeks and willed him to believe the same words he'd told her the day before. "Andrew, I'm still mostly burned out, and you've got strong shields for someone who's not a psychic. But I couldn't just hurt you—I could destroy you. I could drive you to your knees and make you crawl for me. I could take away everything you are."

He closed his eyes, but he didn't release her. "Then that makes this a doubly bad idea."

Andrew was going to walk away from her again, and the tense parts of her that had started to unwind over the last few days would shatter. The only way to save anything was to let him go before he came up with a polite, stilted reason. "I understand."

"No. No, you really don't."

He bent his head and kissed her.

The world stopped.

His lips were warm. Firm. As firm as the fingers locked around her wrists, holding her hands to his face. She'd played out this moment in a thousand girlish daydreams and more than one guilty adult fantasy, and imagination hadn't provided the little details. The heat of his body, the strength of his grip, the way she melted, like chocolate left in the July sun, and from nothing but that innocent contact.

His lips, on hers. Parting, and oh *God*, he knew how to kiss, like he was hungry, like he loved the taste of her, and Kat became mortally certain that her knees were going to give out if he got his tongue in on the action. Her body throbbed with the rhythm of his mouth moving on hers, until she was one exposed nerve, and she would have begged him to touch her anywhere—everywhere—if she wouldn't have had to stop kissing him.

When he released her wrists, it was only to grip her hips and lift her, mold her to his body, and she moaned her gratitude. He was harder than he looked, an unforgiving wall of muscle and smooth skin, so distracting and arousing that she didn't realize they were moving until he stepped over the threshold.

Into the bedroom.

"Open," he rasped, and lowered her to the bed.

Her back touched the mattress—gentle, so damn gentle—and Andrew stretched out over her, shirtless and beautiful, and her brain fritzed out like a fried circuit board as she obeyed and parted her lips.

He touched them with his tongue, a soft sweep of one lip and then the other, and kissed her again, deeper, one hand winding in her hair. That stirred old memories, brought to life every unacceptable fantasy she'd had of their anger and hurt and longing all coalescing into a dark passion that would satisfy her body even as it cut her heart to pieces.

But there was no darkness in the grip of his hand, just a gentle control, a sweet hint of dominance that barely deserved the description, but thrilled her anyway. The throbbing was back, magnified into an ache that pulsed in time with the stroke of his tongue. Every time she tried to catch a breath it escaped in tiny, helpless noises that would have embarrassed her if she hadn't been burning alive.

He dragged his mouth to her chin and then her throat, nipping lightly when she tilted back her head. The scrape of his teeth curled her toes, and the sheer insanity of the way her body reacted splintered fear through her.

She fisted both hands in his hair and dragged his head back, panting for breath. "What are we doing? Are we—"

He panted too, his eyes glazed with pleasure and need. "Are we what?"

If she let him keep touching her, she'd fly apart before she got her pants off. "We can't do this without talking about it. Sex with an empath as strong as I am—it's not that simple. I could hurt you. Hurt *both* of us."

Andrew's chest rumbled, as if a growl formed that he didn't quite voice. Then he rolled away. "I didn't think."

Disappointment made her voice shake. "You shouldn't have to. It wouldn't be that bad if you were anyone else...but with you I'm—I've got—" She covered her face with her hands, and now she was disappointed and embarrassed. "My empathy might as well be hardwired into my sexual responses. Is there a girl version of premature ejaculation?"

He choked on a snort. "I don't think anyone minds it, usually."

Maybe her violent reactions had nothing to do with magic and everything to do with chemistry. Maybe wanting Andrew so long had built a tension that would make even innocent touches feel fantastic. Maybe she was in denial.

Maybe she didn't care.

The room seemed too warm as she rolled to her knees. Andrew had his hand over his face, which made asking the question a lot easier. "If it gets too overwhelming...can we stop?"

He rolled to his side, propped on one elbow, and studied her, his expression intense. "We can stop whenever you want. Whenever you need to."

Christ, she was a teenager, making rules about where her prom date could touch her while they groped in the back of his car. Except she'd never gone to prom. She'd been sixteen her senior year, struggling with the violent surges in power that made puberty a worse nightmare for a psychic than for the average hormone-riddled teen.

And Andrew—Andrew was *not* a teenage boy. He was six-foot-something of shapeshifter alpha bastard who had to have his share of instinctive needs. "That's not going to drive you crazy?"

"I have two hands, Kat," he reminded her. "I can take care of things myself."

It was not remotely okay to pause and savor that image, but she couldn't stop herself. Andrew, stretched out, his face slack with pleasure, the muscles in his arm flexing as he curled his fingers around—

She slapped her hands over her face and actually whimpered. "That was mean."

"Was it?"

Anything else she said would reveal her newly formed and overwhelming need to watch him and his two hands take care of things. So she leaned down and kissed him again.

He held the back of her head and fit his mouth to hers, slow this time. Easy. A gentle kiss from a controlled man trying to make her feel safe, with no clue that his tender protectiveness turned her inside out.

If her empathy had been at full power, she would have come when he stroked his hand from her hair to her collarbone, and then down to her breast. She moaned, imagining how much hotter his callused fingertips would be against her suddenly tight nipples.

Not that the silly butterfly tank top offered much protection. Kat shuddered and tore her mouth free of his, then shoved at his shoulders until he rolled onto his back. Sliding one leg over his body was reckless, and straddling his stomach was *insane*. "You're too hot. My brain is going to overheat."

Muscle flexed under her as he shifted slightly and gripped her hips. "Isn't that the point?"

The fine hair on his arms tickled her palms as she touched him, sliding both hands up until they passed his shoulders and she was stretched over him, clutching the blankets on either side of his head. A position of power—if you were fool enough to think an alpha shapeshifter couldn't dominate a lover from flat on his back.

She might be on top, but the need pulsing through her answered to him. Her body answered to him, held captive by empathy and her growing suspicion that some of the arousal turning her inside-out was coming from him, in spite of her shields.

He held her gaze and thrust up, and suspicions and shields were the last thing on her mind as the hard ridge of his erection rubbed against her. Instinct had her moving before she could stop, grinding down to chase the too-perfect pleasure that couldn't possibly be twisting inside her already.

But it was. Her elbows gave out, and she sprawled across his bare chest, open mouth pressed to his shoulder. Moaning, she clenched her eyes shut, afraid to move. "I can't come before you've barely touched me."

He flipped her onto her back and stretched out over her, one knee between her legs. "You can come whenever you damn well please."

It was permission, though she doubted he realized how imminent it might be. She drove her fingers into his hair and dragged his mouth to hers, kissing him with open-mouthed desperation, as if she could drown her terrifying lack of control in physical sensation.

Even as he kissed her in return, his knee pressed closer, rocking hard between her legs, and he murmured something into her mouth.

She couldn't understand. She didn't *care*. Her mouth fell away from his as she arched her head back, digging it into the mattress. She was practically riding his damn thigh, and opening her eyes was the final mistake. Andrew stared down at her, intense and hungry, eyes heavy-lidded and face flooded with passion.

For her. He wanted to see her pleasure. He wanted her to come.

Critical mental processes shut down as she dug her heels into the bed and lifted her hips. She arched one last time and gasped when his muscular leg rubbed against her clitoris in the perfect, *perfect* rhythm, right in time with the blood pounding in her ears.

Her empathy twisted sharply inside her, taking in his satisfaction in her responses and drowning her in it. She came with a scream, an honest-to-God cry that mixed surprise and pleasure, and she couldn't find the wit to be embarrassed about it. Not when empathy had triggered a physical response so intense she wanted to scream again. All that was missing was touch, skin on skin, or—*fuck*, the actual act of fucking, him driving into her, taking her, claiming her.

Andrew groaned and buried his face against her shoulder, his body shaking. "Fuck—God—"

White-hot ecstasy slammed into her, surreal because no physical reaction accompanied it. His orgasm, a desperate, intense fulfillment that fed her empathy, and realizing that he'd come roused her body until she trembled on the knife's edge. One strong thrust of his hips set her off again.

She twisted. She writhed. She came hard, so damn hard her whole being shook with it, even as she ached, empty, craving him inside her to make this complete and beautiful and *real.*

"*Fuck!*" He rolled off her and hit the bed, still shuddering, one arm thrown across his eyes. Relief and loss tumbled end over end as Kat gasped in a helpless breath that made the stars in her peripheral vision dance.

Slowly—too slowly—the chaos faded, leaving her limp and wrung out, sprawled across the bed fully clothed and more naked than she'd ever been in her life.

Suddenly, Andrew shot upright, leaving her staring at his rigid back as he spoke. "You okay?"

"I'm—" Humiliated. "I'm sor—"

He cut her off. "Stop. You can't apologize to me for this. It's not right."

Kat covered her face with hands that trembled. Too much, too fast, and now she had to confront the reasons why such an insane feedback loop could have happened with her shields locked firmly in place. "You don't understand."

"Which part?" He laughed, a little desperately. "The empathy overload, or the part where I just came in my jeans?"

"Both. More. It's..." Her body hummed as she sat up, her hands falling to her lap. "We need to talk. About a lot of things. Things I should have told you before we—before this."

He shook his head and eased off the bed. "I'm going to change. I'll be back in a minute."

As soon as the bathroom door closed behind him, Kat rolled from the bed and fought to smooth her clothing back into place. Her loose braid was disheveled, half-undone from his fingers. Tiny tingles danced up her spine at the memory of callused fingertips sliding against her neck as he tilted her head back and kissed her—

Pleasure stirred, sluggish but terrifying in its quiet insistence. Andrew called to her body. He'd flipped her on. Short-circuited the gate governing her libido. Every input came back *TRUE*, and he didn't even have to be in the damn room.

She couldn't begin to fathom the reasons, but her terrified brain whispered one word, over and over in an endless loop. *Imprinting.* The only thing that made sense, and she didn't know what was worse—imagining that it could be true, or having to tell Andrew.

Her gaze fell to the rumpled bedspread. If she *did* have to tell him, she couldn't do it here. So she gathered the shreds of her courage, dragged herself to the marginally more innocuous territory of the couch, and waited.

He needed time more than anything else, so he jumped in the shower.

A cold one, since his body didn't seem to have gotten the memo about recovery time and how he shouldn't have a throbbing erection right after an orgasm, even if he was relatively young and virile.

That's what you get for dry humping an empath, dumbass, he told himself viciously as he chattered under the frigid spray.

A change of clothes and a cold shower. It sounded like the punch line to a bad joke, the kind that didn't make anyone laugh.

His arousal had subsided by the time he climbed out, toweled off and dressed in clean clothes, but he took a moment anyway, because what came next was more unappealing than leaving the bathroom to talk to Kat.

He stared into the mirror and forced himself to go over the possibilities. She could tell him that it was a mistake, that a moment of horny weakness had made her stumble into his arms. Or—*oh God*—even worse, that it wasn't right because she was still tangled up with Miguel Mendoza, though she'd talked like that shit was over.

Do it or quit, but you gotta pick one. Alec's words, echoing in his head. Sound advice, except that he was pretty sure Alec would kick his ass for about a dozen different things he'd done in the last two days.

"Fuck it," he whispered, and shoved open the bathroom door.

Kat was huddled on the couch in the other room, one leg tucked under her and the other foot bouncing nervously on the floor.

Her gaze landed on him for a split second before skittering away. "There's so much stuff, I don't know where to start. I don't know how much you know about the creepy dark side of the psychic community."

"What you've told me, or Derek."

"Derek doesn't know much of it. He *couldn't*, or he really would have locked me in a closet until I was twenty. Empaths..." She dragged in a deep breath and let it out in a shaky sigh. "Lots of psychics are in danger during their formative years. Lots of us have powers that people would love to exploit. But empaths who don't have fully developed protections are...vulnerable."

It sounded like Ben's warning. "Are you talking about the

fact that there are people who would use them?"

"I'm talking about *how* people use us. If you get ahold of a strong receptive empath when they're young, or you can manage to break an adult, we're trainable. A patient person can make us love anyone, or anything. And I don't mean make us *think* we love it. It's real."

"I don't understand."

Kat met his gaze. Held it. "They call it imprinting. Not like baby ducklings or anything, though. They're not going for filial loyalty. Not usually. Because people are perverts and most empaths aren't really useful as weapons. But if you strip an empath's shields and flood them with pleasure, after enough time they'll associate whatever the hell you're doing to them with pleasure. Custom-built sex slaves."

Andrew dropped to a chair. "People don't really do that shit, do they?" Even as he asked, he knew it was a stupid question. If there was a way to do what she described, of course people would exploit it.

A weak smile curled her lips, and it looked forced. "Supernatural world kinda blows, doesn't it? So much power, and people misuse it to find creative and more disgusting ways to get laid."

"Yeah." And that didn't explain why she was telling him any of it. "You're not trying to say this has something to do with me, are you?"

The smile faded. "That's the scary, bad side of imprinting. The malicious side. But it can happen naturally too. We can grow around someone who's important to us. Become what they need...and need what they want."

"Oh." He leaned back instinctively. "You think that might happen with me."

Pain tightened her eyes, and she looked away. "No, I've got solid training now. Good shields. Someone would have to break me first. But I didn't have those shields when I met you, and I was young. Infatuated. In love."

How could hearing that still hurt so much? He was so busy quelling that pain he almost missed the import of her words. "When you met me."

"I don't usually have crazy porn-worthy orgasms from making out." Her voice twisted, turned dry. Morbidly amused. "And trust me, it wasn't because Miguel sucked in bed. But it didn't matter how well he brought it, he was never..."

You. Andrew rose and took a step back. "When? When did this happen?"

Kat slashed a look at him, eyes narrowed and mouth tight. "I don't know if it happened at all. There's no test. It's not a switch or a spell. We all change because of the people in our lives. I just...change on a more fundamental level."

"It's got to be reversible."

"Yeah, maybe with a time machine," she snapped.

He'd hurt her feelings, and he didn't know whether to laugh or cry. "Don't get snotty, Kat. I'm not worried about myself here. This isn't fair to you."

She crossed her arms over her chest in a blatantly defensive gesture. "Yeah, I was scared before you started backing away like you're afraid I'm about to rape you. How much scarier do you think this is for me when you act that disgusted?"

The fear he'd been holding inside exploded in an unstoppable rush. "I'm not disgusted, I'm fucking freaked out. Can you give me a goddamn minute to process this?"

Kat rose stiffly. "You had a right to know, so I told you. But I don't know if that's what this is, or if I'm bent in some other way. Maybe I have a kink for shapeshifters who blew me off."

She couldn't have meant to marginalize what they'd shared, but he closed his eyes and turned away anyway. "Thanks a lot."

Her breath hissed out. "I'm sorry. My shields aren't—I didn't mean—" Moments passed in silence. Then, "Sometimes pride is all I have left."

"After *what?*" he asked. "Did I take that much from you? Did I hurt you that much?"

"I loved you. I *killed* for you. And I was never what you needed."

It stopped him cold, and he turned to face her again. "If that's what you think happened between us, then you don't get it at all, Kat."

"Maybe not." She looked tired. Older than her years, her blue eyes numb. "But you needed time. Space. Alec to help you adjust, and Derek to be your friend. Anna, even if it was only for a while. You never needed me. Not once."

He'd needed so many things from her, but one most of all— her safety. It had just turned out to be the one thing he couldn't personally ensure, the one reason he'd had to push her away. "You're so sure of that, and there's nothing I can say, is there? Not a single damn thing."

"You don't *say* you need someone. You just do, or you don't." She rubbed at her face and dropped back to the couch so fast the springs creaked. "We can drown in words, and it's never going to help. We're both wrong, and we're both right. That's life. A big fucking mess."

"You're right about one thing." The admission came grudgingly, but he forced it out. "Talking isn't going to get us anywhere, not now. Not like this. So we may as well order room service and rest up for tomorrow."

"Okay." She looked down. Her fingers closed on the hem of her baby-blue tank top, folding and unfolding it over and over. "I should have told you before. I would have, if I'd thought it was a possibility. And it might not be it, but if it is..." She swallowed. Cleared her throat. "I'm not your responsibility."

He tried to stay silent, but it didn't work. "Bullshit."

Kat didn't look up. "I don't want to be your responsibility."

It didn't change the facts, not for either of them. "I get it."

"Do you?" Her hands stilled. "I don't want to be your *responsibility.*"

"Yeah." He understood better than she knew. "You don't want that to be *why*. I get it."

"Okay." She rose without looking at him. "Would you order me a cheeseburger? I need to check my mail and see if Ben's found anything else."

A big fucking mess. "Yeah, okay. Cheeseburger."

Her eyes met his for just a moment. There was longing there, and pain, a weary resignation he could almost feel as she turned toward the bedroom.

Andrew snatched up the room-service menu and cursed viciously. A big fucking mess, just like she'd said, and nothing but time would help.

If anything does.

Chapter Six

The safety deposit box looked mundane—until you touched it. It zinged with energy, and the lock refused to yield, even with the key.

Andrew sighed. "If it weren't practically vibrating with magic, I'd say maybe we had the wrong key."

Frustrated, Kat twisted the key again. "Do you think it's a spell? A charm?"

"It has to be. The question is, what's the trigger?"

Whatever it was, the knowledge had died with the woman who'd given them the key. "Words, maybe? Or...well, it couldn't be anything I wouldn't have access to, unless my mom expected me to find a spell caster." Abandoning the key, she ran her fingers along the metal edges of the box's lid, tracing every irregularity until she found a small indentation.

She tried to wedge one finger under the edge, but a quick tug proved that the metal was unyielding—and unforgiving. Pain zipped up her hand as her fingertip slipped over a sharp spot.

Magic crackled through the small room and then vanished.

The lock clicked, and Andrew reached over and lifted the lid. One edge bore coppery traces of her blood. "I guess that answers it. Are you okay?"

Kat winced as she checked her hand. "Yeah. Just looks like the world's ugliest paper cut."

He poked at the contents of the box—a lone manila envelope. "Want me to open it?"

She almost said yes, but felt like a coward. "No, let me see."

He handed her the envelope. Kat opened the top and upended it, spilling out a black square of plastic. She stared at the blocky Iomega logo, confusion warring with abject disbelief. "A zip disk? Are you kidding me?"

Andrew eyed it with raised eyebrows. "It *has* been in here a while."

Somewhere around a decade, which she supposed explained the outdated method of data storage. "Yeah, well, my netbook isn't going to read this. And I doubt Staples is selling external zip drives these days."

"There's always eBay, or maybe your friend Ben has one lying around."

"Maybe." Kat tugged off the scarf Sera had knit for her and wrapped it around the disk for extra padding, then tucked it into her bag. "Figures none of this could be easy."

"Finding the place was pretty damn painless." He cast his gaze around the tiny room, with its bare desk and one-way mirror. "Is that all that's in there? Clean it out and let's go."

The box looked empty, but Kat ran her fingers along the inside, as if she might find a hidden catch or secret compartment. Instead she felt the smooth metal of the box and not a damn thing else. "That's it."

His hand grazed the back of her shoulder. "Then where to now?"

Warmth followed the path of his touch, streaking through her to settle low in her belly. Kat closed her eyes and thought of ice, of the vast snowy expanses of Antarctica, Alaska, or—hell, a walk-in freezer. Cold. Safe. She used the brutal training Callum had given her and wrapped herself in chilly quiet.

It was enough. Barely. God help them both if he touched more than her shoulder. "If we get to the car, I can use my phone. I was thinking of checking Craigslist. Maybe I can find someone who wants to unload some old computer parts. I'm better with hardware than Ben is, anyway."

"Local's quicker than an online auction," he allowed as he guided her through the door.

Outside the sunlight seemed too bright compared to the chill in the air. Not so cold—the red LED display on the bank's sign put the temperature at a reasonable fifty-two, but a decade in the South had thinned her Boston-born blood. Kat let Andrew herd her toward the SUV, forcing her brain to stay on the puzzle of the zip disk and how she'd retrieve its contents.

If she concentrated on that, she could pretend the previous night had never happened.

"What are you thinking?"

"Zip drives." Only a little lie. "And what might be on the disk. I mean, I don't know what file types they might be, or what sort of software I'd need to read them. It's got to be important though, right? If people are killing over it?"

"Important to someone." He unlocked the SUV and pulled open her door. "I don't know if it'll give you your answers, but it was important to your mom."

Inside the vehicle, Kat tucked her bag between her feet and fiddled with her phone as Andrew climbed in. "This is all crazy, isn't it? Us, acting like we're in the supernatural version of *National Treasure*. Safety deposit boxes and snipers... This is crazy. Nuts."

He buckled his seatbelt and shook his head. "The crazy part is that I'm getting used to it."

It was hard to get out the words, but she needed to ask one question. "You still want to see this through?"

"Hell yeah. I'm not going anywhere."

Relief. Confusion. Andrew had her twisted in knots so complex she couldn't begin to see how to unravel them. Talking to him about anything serious felt like the first time she'd tried to understand recursion. Maybe *they* were recursive, cycling back through the pain they'd caused each other, each hurt built upon the last. He hurt because she hurt because he hurt because she hurt...

Back and back until they hit the base case. The night she'd lost control and nearly destroyed them both.

She had to say something. To find some rapport, casual small talk to fill the time between awkward moments that were too real. "I'm glad you've got all that new training then. If we're about to embark on a caper adventure, I'll need an action hero."

His brows drew together. "That isn't who I am, Kat. Why I train."

So much for light hearted. "I know. I'm just... It's a joke. Laugh."

His mood didn't change. "I'm not a hero."

"Who gets to decide that? Is there a guild? A committee?"

Finally, a hint of a smile appeared. "You can't take my word for it?"

"Don't see why I should," she retorted, then smiled. "You're not taking mine."

"Fine, you got me. I'm a hero, and this is a big damn grand adventure full of thrills and spills."

It was exactly the way they'd always talked to each other, but the ease was gone. She might as well be writing her own dialog in script format. Smile here. Laugh there. Insert pithy pop-culture reference. She was a walking, talking parody of the girl who'd died the night she'd killed.

So she broke script. "You're here. You're helping. Right now, that seems pretty heroic to me."

He stared straight ahead, even as he reached out and grasped her hand. "I always will, no matter what happens between us."

Callused fingers against her skin triggered a rush of need totally out of proportion with the gentle touch. She knew the pleasure of his touch now, and her body wasn't going to let her forget it. Her cheeks heated, and she squeezed his fingers once before easing her hand away. "Maybe we shouldn't touch while you're driving."

"Good plan." He started the engine, backed out of the parking space and angled the vehicle toward the main road. "Back to the hotel, then, and we'll figure out the next step."

A solid enough plan, but even she could tell that Andrew was headed in the opposite direction from their hotel. *Back to the hotel* apparently involved complicated evasive maneuvers, another piece in the overall puzzle of the new Andrew.

Carmen had taught him first aid. Zola and Walker had taught him how to fight. Alec... The Devil himself might prefer not to ponder Alec's skill set, which had always seemed geared more toward covert ops than private investigation. They were surrounded by dozens of supernaturals with unique skills, and Andrew had been collecting them like a kid with Cracker Jack toys.

That isn't who I am, Kat. Why I train.

Not to be a hero. She couldn't imagine any other reason. *So ask, dumbass. Just ask.*

"Andrew—"

"Check your seatbelt and stay low in your seat."

The words were calm. Composed. The faint buzz of background nervousness that she'd barely noticed faded until the SUV was a quiet pool of emotional silence. Not the terrifying blankness from before, but a studied focus that reminded her of Alec at his most calculating.

It scared her enough to obey without question. She tugged her seatbelt until it pulled tight across her chest, and hunched down for good measure. "What's going on?"

"Someone's following us." He'd realigned the rearview mirror earlier, but she'd thought nothing of it. Now, he seemed to be watching the road and the mirror simultaneously. "Tried to shake them, but they're persistent."

Fear made her skin prickle. Kat curled her hand around the door handle and fought not to twist and look behind them.

"This is why you made me pack everything up and bring it with us, isn't it? Because you knew we might not be able to go back."

"Looks like Andy and Kate Normanson had to leave town on the spur of the moment." He tightened his hands around the steering wheel. "Do you need to go anyplace in particular?"

There was only one thing she could say for sure. "Not back to Birmingham. We can't lead them to Ben and Lia."

"Someplace no one else knows, then."

Her brain wouldn't settle long enough to think. "How do you think they found us? Ben's IDs are always flawless."

"Maybe we were followed. From Mobile, even, and they've been waiting for us to lead them to the box." He glanced over at her. "Better warn your friend."

Ben's line rang five times before sending her to voicemail, so Kat left a brief message, then powered her phone off, just in case someone was using the GPS to track them. "Maybe we need to go back to New Orleans and regroup. We've got resources there. And backup."

Andrew nodded. "How long will it take from here? Seven or eight hours?"

She reached for her phone before she remembered it was off. "If we go back the way we came? Yeah, I think so. Maybe a little longer?"

He hadn't sped up or made any turns, and now he looked at her, his face tense. "There's still some morning traffic left on the interstate. I'm going to try again to lose our tail. If I can't, it could get rough."

"If you can't..." Kat drew in a breath. Let it out. Trusted him. "There's something I could try. It's dangerous...but I'm a human, Andrew. My survival probability for a high-speed chase isn't as high as yours."

"If I can't pull this off, it'll be time to break out whatever we can use."

This proved to be waiting until they'd reached a crowded

part of the interstate. Andrew maneuvered the SUV in between two trucks while Kat focused her attention on reinforcing her shields. Brick by brick, piece by piece. She'd had two good nights of sleep since the burnout, but it would take one more before she would be at full strength again.

All the better for this. No matter how much she'd trained with Callum, the idea of unleashing her empathy as a weapon made her queasy.

Not as queasy as the idea of a broken neck, though. She clutched at the door handle until her knuckles turned white as Andrew signaled for the next off-ramp. The wheels of the SUV were seconds from touching it when he whipped back across traffic, cutting off a red pickup that laid on its horn until they were in the far lane.

She didn't dare look around. "Did it work?"

It took him a minute to answer. "I think maybe so."

Kat blew out a relieved sigh and released her death grip on the handle, one finger at a time. "So where'd you learn defensive driving? Is someone in New Orleans giving Car Chase 101 lessons?"

"That?" He laughed, the sound only mildly shaky. "I learned that from your cousin."

"Derek? Damn, I would have guessed Mackenzie. Have you ever been in a car with her when she's late? I'm surprised she hasn't had to take out a second mortgage on her dance studio to pay all the tickets."

"I should teach her how to flirt her way out of those."

Kat almost choked. "The officers of New Orleans love you lots, huh?"

"Sure, they—" The mirror drew his gaze again. "God damn it."

Relief melted away. Terror took its place. Her stomach twisted into a tense knot, and she ignored it and tried to keep her voice steady. "Before I can do anything about it, we need to get to a place where there aren't so many other cars."

"Hold on." He jerked across the lanes again, his jaw tight with concentration, and took the next exit, tires squealing on the ramp as it circled around. "How remote?"

"The fewer people, the less chance that I'll hurt a bystander."

"I'll try." The intersection was clear, so he ran a red light, though several horns blared in protest. "Damn it, I wish I knew this town."

Kat twisted just enough to peek behind them. A dark car with tinted windows darted through the red light, almost sideswiping a station wagon. "I'm going to try to read them. Get a sense of what they're feeling." How big a threat they were.

"Go for it, but keep hanging on."

Some of Callum's lessons she'd excelled at. Burnout, synesthesia, building shields that could withstand the pressure of a thousand frantic hearts. This one, though... Well, strength came with its own drawbacks.

Callum could pick out people in a crowd and touch their auras with the precision of a sniper. Kat felt more like a grenade, sending shrapnel flying in every direction. Trying to narrow the scope of her gift was difficult enough under calm, stationary conditions. In a high-speed car chase, there was no way to narrow her reading to the car behind them.

Still, she'd endured worse. Kat closed her eyes and opened herself, fighting to keep the gap in her shielding focused on their pursuers. It didn't work, of course. Andrew was a quiet knot of tension at her side. They zipped past someone who echoed shock and outrage so sharp it tasted metallic.

Two distinct sets of emotions filtered through. One, fierce concentration cut through with satisfaction and determination. The other, ruthless, unabashed pleasure.

Déjà vu made her dizzy. For one terrifying moment she wasn't in the SUV. She was in her old office, watching a shapeshifter pound a fist into Andrew's stomach over and over while ruthless pleasure drowned her.

"Kat?" Andrew took his hand off the wheel for a moment, dropping it to her knee for a little shake. "Kat!"

His fingers burned. The heat skittered up her skin, flames licking over her, struggling to find a way past the ice living inside her. Andrew was fire and passion and animal instinct, but nothing could eclipse the desperate need to protect.

Protect. It resonated with the darkest places inside her. Tiny, weak girl, fragile psychic playing with the big bad shifters. They could break her body into a thousand pieces, but they'd have to get to her first.

It was easier than breathing. Stopping would have been harder. No need to worry about Andrew this time. He lived inside her. She could feel him under her skin. Her power would flow harmlessly past him, because he was already a part of her, whether she wanted him to be or not.

"You're scaring me," he whispered, just before she let go.

Not all the way. Not even that much, just a little of the pain that had lived inside her, a little of the rage that built at the thought of someone hurting Andrew. She braided them into a shining arrow of psychic power and sent it twisting back.

Distance was meaningless in the vastness of her gift. The heart traveled at the speed of light. She felt her attack slam home, slicing through the driver's mind like a well-honed blade. When he lay open and vulnerable before her, she called up the one memory that would never fade.

Andrew, on the office floor. Her hands clutching at his abdomen, holding things inside that she'd never seen before outside of a biology textbook. Bright red blood everywhere, on her face and her hands and his clothes, and his life pumping out through her fingers as she sobbed and he flooded her with loss and pain that faded to numbness. A thousand missed opportunities slipping away, and her lips too numb to form the words she should have said. *I love you, I love you, I love you—*

Pain. Pure, unrelenting terror. More than a year and she could still smell the metallic stink, feel the slick heat of blood drying tacky on her skin. Even with Andrew's hand gripping her leg, for one endless moment she felt the loss of watching him die.

Her heart broke in two.

So did the driver's mind.

Tires squealed behind them. Kat opened her eyes in time to see the dark car fishtail. It momentarily righted itself, then spun out. Gravel flew in every direction as it swerved onto the shoulder, then back, narrowly missing a giant red pickup truck. The driver of the truck wrenched his vehicle out of the way as the car careened through an intersection and into the ditch, rolling out of sight.

Kat.

The small things came back first. Fingers on her leg. A firm grip. Steady, considering the fear dancing up and down her spine, a wicked tickling like bugs over her skin.

"*Kat,* I swear to God, if you don't answer me, I'm stopping right here."

She followed the thread of his voice back to sanity, even though her own came out rusty. Hoarse. "Andrew?"

"Jesus Christ." He was driving up a ramp, getting back on the interstate. "Are you okay? Do I need to stop?"

Her mouth was so dry that swallowing hurt. "They wanted to hurt us." He had to understand. He had to believe her.

"I know." No hesitation. No doubt. "We're headed toward New Orleans now. I think we'll be all right if you need to rest."

She felt naked, laid bare to the world. She'd spent more power than she should have, certainly more than she should have had to spare. Rebuilding her shields and gathering the shreds of her self-control would take most of the endless drive back. If she concentrated on the ritual of it, the trancelike beauty of Callum's waking dream, she wouldn't have to face the stark, ugly truth.

Darkness lived inside her. Thrived, even. The slightest hint of danger to Andrew, and she lost her grip on morality. She maimed. She killed. Worst of all, she *regretted* it, felt the pain she'd caused, felt dirty and sick...and then she did it again.

All that training, and she was right back where she'd started. A broken girl with too much power and an unraveling grip on reality.

"Hang in there." Andrew moved his hand back to the wheel. "Just hang in there if you can."

"I'll be okay." Carefully phrased to avoid an outright lie, but maybe one anyway, if only because she didn't really believe it.

"We'll have to stop eventually, for restrooms or gas," he murmured, "but we can take precautions."

"Okay." A shiver claimed her so hard her teeth knocked together. "I need to find the quiet place for a while. It's like a trance, I guess. I need to rebuild my shields. As long as my breathing stays steady, I'm fine."

The fear in the car spiked. "If you say so."

Some tiny piece of her shattered, and her heart bled from it. "I won't hurt you." *Don't be afraid of me.*

He answered as if he'd heard her silent plea. "I'm not afraid of you, Kat. I never have been." He glanced over. "I'm afraid *for* you."

The hardest thing she'd done in months was hold out her hand. He took it and breathed a shaky sigh of what felt like relief.

Her body was too conflicted to stir with desire, her mind too fragmented. She moved their joined hands to rest on her leg and closed her eyes. "You can let go when you need to," she whispered. "But it's...nice. It makes me feel like I'm not alone."

His answer was concise—and anything but simple. "I'm here."

Waking Kat seemed like a bad idea, so Andrew drove. He drove for nearly two hours, straight down the interstate, and pondered taking the exit ramp into downtown Birmingham—and back to Ben's condo. But he couldn't guarantee they'd lost the trouble following them, couldn't guarantee the safety of Kat's friends.

He kept driving. The best thing to do would be get them home.

Home.

He finally had to stop just outside of Montgomery, and he reached over to shake her shoulder gently. "Kat, wake up."

At least she didn't seem too deeply asleep. Her eyes fluttered open, and she squinted against the early-afternoon sunlight. "Where are we?"

"A place called Prattville. On the way back home."

"Gas station munchies?" A ghost of a smile curved her lips. "I could use some chocolate. Three or four pounds of it."

He could pay for the gas at the pump, but the only way to grab food was if she went in with him. "Got your land legs yet?"

"I'm fine." She unbuckled her seatbelt and stretched. "I didn't need that much sleep to get past it. The drain was more...emotional."

He stuck close, even hovering outside the women's restroom while she was inside, but the station was deserted, save for the bored clerk behind the counter. They piled its surface high with drinks and snacks, enough to keep them going until they'd reached New Orleans.

Outside, Andrew hustled Kat back to the SUV. "I'm not going to be able to rest until we get home."

She must have had some sympathy, because she tolerated him opening her door and holding it as she climbed back in. When they were headed toward the interstate again, she dug through the bag and surfaced with a bag of Twizzlers. "Home, New Orleans? Or home, like your place?"

She sounded tense. "Got a preference?" he asked quietly.

"Do you?" Not just tension now, but a challenge.

"Makes sense to stick together until you get the information you need."

Her fingers tightened around the Twizzlers until the plastic crinkled loudly. "So we're just being practical?"

He made a concerted effort to breathe, to relax his hands on the steering wheel. "It would make me feel better—more secure, I mean—if we went to my place."

"Okay." The tips of her fingers barely brushed his shoulder. "I'm sorry. I shouldn't have pushed. You've had a shitty couple days, thanks to me, and hardly any sleep."

Admitting as much felt like weakness, and something in him railed against it. "Just need to get you safe, that's all."

"Then go home, Andrew. To your home, if I'm invited."

Having her there would soothe him. He knew it because he'd wanted it a hundred times over the last year. A thousand. "You're always welcome." *Wanted.*

"Good." Plastic crinkled again as she stored the candy and retrieved her phone. "I need to call Sera, then. If I were with anyone other than you, she'd have tattled on me already."

He believed it. The young coyote tended to think every human belonged to the strongest shapeshifter with a claim. "Who would she tattle to? Julio?"

Kat actually laughed. "Hell, no. She wouldn't go within ten feet of Julio if you paid her. She'd tell her dad, who would tell Alec, who would fly down here just to call us idiots to our faces."

Maybe he would have, once upon a time. But now he had the Conclave to deal with, a million problems more pressing than Andrew and Kat getting themselves offed on a fool's errand. "She could always call Derek, I guess."

"I think I'll keep her updated and happy." Kat started to dial, then froze with her thumb hovering over the screen. "Unless you think she's not safe in my apartment. They have to know where I live."

"Wouldn't hurt to get her out," he admitted.

"Okay. Shit." Guilt laced the words. "Damn it, after everything she's been through... I was supposed to give her somewhere safe to crash. This went so wrong, so fast."

Andrew could think of only one good option. "Send her to Anna."

Kat stiffened, enough to be telling. "Yeah, you're right. Anna's tough. She can take care of anyone who needs help."

Shit. "You said she wouldn't go near Julio. What about Miguel?"

"Anna," Kat said, her voice careful and precise. "Sera needs a break from male shifters bossing her around. Anna makes sense, and my tender little feelings don't get a vote."

"I'll call her." He reached for his phone without taking his eyes off the road. "Want to give Sera the heads-up, maybe get her out to the bar?"

She made the call and laid out the situation for Sera in a calm, clear voice. Judging by the coyote's reaction, Kat's previous updates had glossed over all of the details involving danger and violence.

The conversation lasted through Montgomery and another ten miles past, both sides clearly audible in the silence of the car.

Kat hung up looking ragged around the edges. "Wow. Shapeshifters don't like it when people shoot at their friends."

"That can't be news, sweetheart."

"Maybe you're throwing off the curve. You kept it together okay."

She never seemed to understand how hard he worked not to freak out at the slightest hint of danger to her. "Still a work in progress, but I figure you should have one alpha bastard in your life who doesn't flip his shit every time you get a paper cut."

Kat swallowed and looked away from him. "You haven't

been in my life much lately. I kind of figured you weren't comfortable there."

The bare truth, Callaghan. Too late for anything else. "I haven't been comfortable much of anywhere lately."

"Is it the wolf stuff? I thought—I mean, when you joined the council with Julio and Alec, I thought you had a place."

"They *made* a place, Kat. There's a difference." An uncomfortable one.

"I suppose there is. Prejudices don't change overnight." She sighed softly. "I remember, from when Derek was turned."

"Yeah, Derek's smart." He'd done what he had to for Nick and her family, and then he'd walked away.

"Andrew?"

"What?"

"Do you want to be on the council?"

Want had never much figured in to it. "I'm needed. Before Alec brought me on, I had no idea things were as fucked up as they are. I barely believed it."

"Does helping out at least make you happy?"

He had to think about that for a moment. "Not happy, not exactly. Content." Satisfied in a way he still didn't entirely understand.

Out of the corner of his eye, he could see her staring at him. Studying him. "Instinct," she offered after a moment. "Taking care of people. If I thought the shifters could help it, I never would have put up with it all these years. But it was something I could give them, something that made them feel content."

"I need it," he confirmed. "I never understood that. Before, I mean."

She wet her lips, a gesture as nervous as her sudden quickened heartbeat. "You can take care of me, if it helps. I mean—if you want to."

Of all the things she'd never wanted, that was king. The

ultimate cap on her own self-sufficiency. "I know how much it means to you to stand on your own, Kat. I get it."

"I wanted to stand on my own." She hesitated, and her breathing sounded too loud, raspy and hoarse. "I didn't want to be alone."

He didn't take his eyes off the road, but he held out his hand. "You're not alone."

"I know." Her fingers trembled as she curled them around his.

Part of him wished they were in New Orleans already, locked away in the confines of his home, safe and untouchable. The rest of him was glad for the drive and grateful for the tentative truce they'd reached.

Chapter Seven

Andrew stopped at her apartment long enough for her to pack some clothes and trade her netbook in for a more powerful laptop. Sera had already cleared out, but she'd left a plate of freshly baked cookies and a note with her work schedule for the next week.

Kat tucked the folded paper into her jeans pocket and let Andrew wrestle her bags down the stairs. The drive to the new headquarters was short, and soon they parked beside the old building in the Warehouse District. It looked like it had once been a factory, and even the service-style elevator remained, though Kat had always taken the stairs.

Andrew slid shut the metal grate behind them and pushed the button for the third floor. "I haven't done much decorating at my place. I spend most of my time now traveling or fixing up the other units."

Decorating had never been her priority. Her apartment had been disorganized college-geek-chic at best before Sera, who did domestic, grown-up things like sew curtains and pick color schemes for the bathrooms and kitchen.

Even her efforts at chaotic comfort seemed impressive compared to the stark emptiness of Andrew's loft. A small kitchen sat to the left, separated from the rest of the room by bar counters. The closest thing to decoration was the fact that he had punching bags hanging from the ceiling. An open door showed an equally Spartan bedroom.

Kat swallowed and glanced toward the television stand. Game consoles were stacked neatly, cords organized instead of tangled like they were at her apartment. "I guess if I can't sleep, I can catch up on my gaming." The lamest joke she'd ever made, but it helped cut the miserable sadness of imagining Andrew living every day in an empty, lonely loft.

"Feel free." He dropped her bags by the couch. "There should be stuff in the fridge."

He didn't sound sure, and she didn't want to look. It wasn't like she could cook worth a damn anyway. "I've still got gas-station junk food. And the cookies Sera made."

"I can cook later, if you stick around. We could even go downstairs and make a family-style meal, hope Julio shows up. Right now..." He swayed. "I think I should take a nap."

As far as she knew, he hadn't slept much in forty-eight hours. Not impossible for a shapeshifter—but not comfortable, either. "Get some rest. I need to catch up on my mail anyway."

He kicked off his shoes. After a moment, he pulled off his shirt, as well. "Can you stay close? I think it might be the only way I can sleep."

Her heart ached so much that not even miles of naked skin could stir lust in her. Just sadness, and protective anger simmering at a low boil. People had known. Alec, Julio—they'd *known* that Andrew was living some empty shadow of a life, and they'd left him to stew in it for God only knew what reason.

He was so tired, and she could help him. She eased off her shoes, then her sweatshirt, stripping down to the sweatpants and tank top she'd purchased in Huntsville. "Can I lie down with you?"

Something flashed in his eyes, something almost like gratitude. "Will you?"

It wasn't just a random hotel bed this time. It was Andrew's bed. A place where he slept, where his scent would curl around her. She didn't always understand shapeshifters and their instincts, but she'd never met one who issued an invitation to their bed lightly.

Most of her half-formed sexual fantasies had started with Andrew's bed. Innocent ones from years ago, when he'd been human and she'd been virginal and basing her knowledge entirely on fiction and dubious web searches. Then the darker ones, fueled by anger and bitter longing and the desperate need to be the one thing Andrew wanted more than perfect control.

So many fantasies, and none of them eclipsed this moment, with him looking at her like she held the secret to peace in her hands. He was showing his weakness to her, and it melted her heart.

She didn't need to sleep. She probably couldn't, not after dozing most of the way back to New Orleans—and it didn't matter a bit. "Let's take a nap."

Once in the bedroom, he didn't pull back the covers, just crawled on top of them and held out his arms. Kat went to him. She couldn't have stopped herself, and it wasn't until she'd settled against his chest that she worried about her empathy and the feedback and the miserable way her body heated at the slightest touch.

It hadn't faded, which scared her, but it wasn't as bad this time, which made it easy to rationalize. They'd both been excited before. Years of wanting and not having had pushed them over the edge, no imprinting necessary. Now he was tired, and she felt more protective than sexy. Without the echo of his desire feeding into hers, she could enjoy the comfort of just being held.

They'd be okay. She believed it.

Liar.

He stroked his hand down her arm. "Relax."

Closing her eyes helped, so did taking a deep breath. Pushing away worry, Kat focused on the present. On the things she could control. On *him.* "We're kind of cuddling."

"Kind of." His voice had already slowed, begun to slur. "It's nice. I've missed stuff like this."

So had she. Andrew's breathing evened out, and Kat let herself ease into the pleasure of being in his arms. It felt foreign. New, even though it shouldn't have been. Once upon a time they'd had casual touches and moments full of maybes.

They'd had her twenty-fourth birthday, when she'd gotten tipsy on tequila and he'd never commented on the fact that she'd landed a drunken kiss or two on his jaw before he managed to pour her into bed.

Five days later the world had ended. He'd almost died, and she'd killed two men, and all of those maybes had turned to dust.

Starting over felt like traversing a minefield. Every time they took a step forward, something blew up in their faces. Misunderstandings. Assumptions made in anger and left to fester over fourteen months. Andrew's time with Anna, her relationship with Miguel.

She'd brought trouble down on herself. On both of them, maybe, and the irony of it was that trouble might be the only thing that could keep them stepping forward long enough to get to the other side of their respective pasts.

Of course, to do that, they'd have to stay alive. Metaphorical minefields seemed a lot less terrifying when people started trying to kill you for real.

Andrew woke in a dream, with Kat draped over him, her head on his chest and her hips snug against his.

He didn't think. He didn't *want* to think. He wanted to roll her underneath him and kiss her, so he did, sliding his fingers into her hair to hold her still. Her lips parted on a sleepy murmur that turned to a moan as borrowed heat zipped up his spine. Her pleasure, vast and needy and wrapping around him until he had to admit it, even though he didn't want to.

This wasn't a dream.

Next on the agenda was figuring out if he cared. Andrew

nipped at Kat's chin and groaned. "You want me to stop, tell me now."

She was breathing fast already, gasping little breaths as her fingers opened and closed on the covers. "I don't want to stop, but I'm afraid I'll ruin it again."

"Make me come again, you mean?" Maybe, if he said it like that, she'd realize how ridiculous it was to worry.

Color flooded her cheeks as she squeezed her eyes shut. "My experience is limited, but most of it has led me to believe that guys don't like coming in their pants."

"It's not the most convenient thing in the world." He kissed her closed eyelids. "Wouldn't call it ruining anything, though, not by a long shot."

"Oh." Her hands found his shoulders, tentative and shy. "Everything is all tangled up. I've wanted you for so long, before I even knew what I wanted."

He had his own tangles, ones that twisted tighter at her words. "Don't think so hard for once, Kat, and neither will I."

"Even if it means crazy orgasms in under five minutes and you having to take a shower?"

His lips grazed hers. "Even then."

She kissed him, hard and fast, clumsy with speed, like she was trying to squeeze in every touch she could before her hunger swallowed them both.

And it would. Already, he trembled on the edge of control. She was in his bed, her scent entwined with his, and it sparked to life the banked hunger that lurked inside him.

So he licked her lips and sighed. "Open."

She made a quiet, aroused sound and obeyed. He took his time fitting his mouth to hers, letting every sensation shoot through him. She'd feel it, and maybe she'd know how much he needed her.

There was nothing slow about her response. He felt her thrill at the stroke of his tongue, felt hot need twist when she shifted her hips and he settled more firmly between her thighs.

Kat tore her mouth from his with a gasp. "Andrew, it's too much. I'm projecting—what if I *hurt* you?"

"How are you going to do that?"

"I don't know." Her eyes fluttered open, glazed and uncertain. "Promise me you won't let me."

So hesitant, so terrified, and it was all because of him. "You won't hurt me. I promise."

"All right." She touched him then, slid her fingertips along his jaw and smiled. "I like your beard."

"Yeah?" He tilted his head and closed his eyes to focus on her gentle caress.

"Mmm. If you were an action hero, you'd have to shave it off in a dramatic moment of renewed dedication." Her lips brushed his cheek. "There might even be a montage."

So carefully slow. "What if I want to keep it? Can it be a training montage instead?"

A tiny hitch in her breathing, and that control wavered. "I don't think I should watch. You getting all sweaty and badass sounds a little pornographic."

"Really?" He teased her with a quick nip of teeth on her earlobe. "That's hot?"

"B-blame biology. Human evolution." The words trembled, and she arched her hips, rubbing up against him with a soft moan. "I can't hold it together much longer."

Neither could he. Andrew gripped her thigh and ground against her, a low growl vibrating free before he could stop it. "Relax, baby."

"Oh—*oh*, oh God." Pleasure returned, twisting tighter with every desperate rock. Kat's fingers clutched his hair, guiding his mouth to her throat as she arched her head back.

Biting her would send them both spinning, but he had to. He *had* to. He closed his teeth on the delicate, pale skin at the base of her throat.

She cried out. Not just with physical enjoyment, though that thrummed through him strong enough to shiver pleasure up his spine. In that moment, underneath sensation, he caught a hint of *her*, open and vulnerable and so relieved to be wanted.

So relieved to be his.

It tripped instincts he'd fought so hard to wrestle under control. Possessive, protective ones that demanded he close his arms around her, keep her safe from everything, including herself. *"Kat."*

She came with a gasp, all of her frozen for one breathless moment when she stretched taut beneath him. Then her empathy slammed into him, bringing with it the blinding echoes of her release.

It was easier this time to lock it down, to ride the waves of her pleasure without letting them sweep him away. He distracted himself by stroking her hair, pressing his mouth to her cheek, her ear. "Beautiful."

"Andrew..." Just a whisper, husky and low. "I think I'm floating."

Purely masculine satisfaction offset his own physical tension. "Good. That's how it should be."

"But you're not—" She blushed. "Was it not so bad this time?"

When she looked at him like that, nervous and shy, it was as if the last year never happened. The trauma and hurt feelings melted away, leaving it easy to smile. "It was good."

The sweet innocence vanished as she wet her lips and rubbed her foot against the back of his calf. "Are you going to take care of things on your own, then?"

She wanted him to, and she wanted to watch. Arousal spiked again, his blood roaring in his ears. "You'd like that, huh?"

"Maybe." Her toes crept higher, and she was stroking his arm now too, fingers drawing tiny circles on his skin. "Maybe if we've both taken the edge off, we can work our way back around to the kissing. It's backwards..."

"No such thing." He rolled to his back, bringing her on top of him. "You want me to come?"

The uneven tips of her hair tickled his cheek as she nuzzled her nose against his ear. "Yes."

Control. She needed it, and she needed him to have it—up to a point. He raised his arms and folded them under his head. "Make me."

Kat lifted her body slowly and ending up straddling Andrew's thighs. Her perch afforded her the perfect view of his chest and arms. All jokes about training montages aside, he was doing *something* to look like he'd been chiseled out of the side of a mountain.

Ten months of private lessons with Zola might have slimmed some of the extra padding off her hips, but Kat was still soft. Soft all over, but Andrew didn't seem to mind, and she couldn't feel self-conscious with him watching her like the slightest move could strip away what was left of his self-control.

He didn't touch her, but he spoke. "You're gorgeous."

God, she loved his voice. She loved his eyes, green and a little gray, and the way his eyebrows rose when he was deadpanning to make her laugh. Of all the things she'd missed without him in her life, the biggest had been laughter.

The way her heart fluttered when he smiled might be a close second. She dropped her hands to his chest and stroked down, tracing the well-defined ridges of his abdomen. "You're just stupidly hot."

He grinned. "Stupidly? Not ridiculously?"

"Stupidly." She slid her fingers lower, until her fingertips found the edge of his jeans. "Ridiculously." The cool metal of the button made her shiver. "Absurdly. Unbelievably."

He arched under her, and his voice went husky. "Any more adverbs you want to add?"

"I wasn't very good at English classes..." Her heart skipped a beat as she pressed her hand to his jean-clad erection.

Andrew dropped his head back with a groan. "Harder."

More command than request, and part of her liked it. Not a small part, either. Disobeying felt like an illicit thrill, but she didn't want to grope him through his jeans. Instead she tugged open the button and eased the zipper down. "Can I touch you?"

"Are you going to ask, or are you going to take?"

Her hands shook. She took a breath, and smelled sweat and his aftershave. "I think I like asking. I like the way your voice sounds when you tell me what you want."

His eyes flashed, and he tensed beneath her. "Touch me. Open my pants and put your hands on my cock."

Oh, he liked it as much as she did. It thrilled through her, an echo of his instinctive pleasure, sharper when she reached for the waistband on his boxers. "Lift your hips?"

He did it easily, bearing her weight as well as his. Shapeshifter strength, and her hands were unsteady as she hooked her fingers under the edge of the fabric.

Unsteady didn't begin to cover how she felt while she eased his boxers over his cock. From ten feet away, she was sure he'd look proportional. Up close and personal...

Kat swallowed hard and braced herself for the jolt as she curled her fingers around the undeniably impressive length of his erection. He hissed in a breath and wrapped his hand around hers, pressing her fingers more firmly against his hard flesh.

If the sight hadn't scrambled her circuits, the echo would have. Her eyelids drooped, and she struggled to keep her gaze focused on his large hand enclosing hers, on the sound he made as she slid her fingers slowly toward the crown.

Hot skin, soft over steel, and she was going to come again without anyone touching her. Kat tore her attention from their hands and sought his eyes instead. "How do I make you come?"

He laughed, a strangled, hoarse noise. "Keep breathing?"

"Might be a problem, actually..." She closed her eyes and concentrated on the pulses of pleasure coming from him, on finding the rhythm that twisted him up and the pressure that made him groan.

His arms dropped, but he only clutched at the bedspread as he thrust into her grip. "Fuck, Kat."

Empathy wasn't all bad. Not if she could use it to put *that* look on his face—jaw clenched, fingers gripping the comforter as if it was all that kept him from grabbing at her. So close. They were both balanced on the edge, an edge sharp enough to slice her open.

It might, if she didn't let it go soon. "Come on, Andrew. Please. Come and take me with you."

He did grab her then, reached up and dragged her down to his chest as the first pulsing wave of ecstasy shuddered through the room. He kissed her, open-mouthed and needy, groaning her name as his teeth scraped her lip.

Kat kissed him as his orgasm washed over her. He'd trapped her at an awkward angle, with one of her arms pinned between them, but she couldn't bring herself to relinquish his mouth long enough to find a comfortable position. Everything was hot and desperate and *now*, and it didn't matter that he'd come on her stomach and they couldn't seem to get out of their clothes.

Her back hit the bed, and Andrew loomed over her, his eyes bright with lust. "You don't understand how sexy that is, do you?"

She told him the truth, and it came out a breathless gasp. "No."

"Not the empathy or the orgasms," he rumbled. "*You.*"

No. Miguel had made her feel attractive. He'd given her anything she wanted from the start, though he'd known her heart was tangled up in someone else. But even at their best, when she'd been caught up in the novelty of sex and pleasure, he'd never looked at her like this.

They'd never *been* like this. Wild and out of control, her empathy overriding everything but base instinct. Kat lifted her hand to Andrew's bare chest, over his heart. "This is... I don't know what this is. It's like you're inside my skin. You're inside *me*."

His thumbs stroked over her jaw. "Isn't that where you want me to be?"

The joke was there, inviting her to laugh it off with dirty innuendo. Maybe he'd meant it that way. Old Kat would have clutched at the chance to lighten the moment with a suggestive smile and naughty words.

Instead she held his gaze. "Do you remember my twenty-first birthday?"

He nodded. "Everyone got drunk, so we went back to your place to play video games."

The memory was so clear, even now. She could remember the dress she'd worn—one of the cheerful, pastel ones her aunt had bought just before her death. Blue flowers and butterfly clips in her hair, and she'd been so *young*, barely into her belated sexual awakening.

It hadn't been so long ago. Four and a half years, but she hadn't felt young for a long time. "I was in love with you by the time you left. I had a crush on you from the first day I met you, but that silly, geeky girl I was... After that night, she loved you with all of her silly, geeky heart."

"That's what kills me." His eyes went dark. "That girl doesn't exist anymore. Because of me."

Always shapeshifters and their blame. Their guilt. "That girl doesn't exist anymore because life sucks sometimes. People suck, Andrew. They do bad things, and the rest of us have to choose between stopping them or not. And sometimes we can't win either way."

"No, we can't. We just have to keep going."

"We *did* keep going. In different directions, because that

was what you needed." She closed her eyes, because she couldn't let him see how much the next words hurt her. "I'm trying really hard to pretend that I'm not worrying about you waking up tomorrow and needing that again."

"That depends." His breath feathered over her cheek. "I didn't know I was killing you all over again by staying away."

"Everyone knew. They've treated me like a broken toy ever since. 'Poor, stupid Kat got her heart broken and can't move on.'"

"I'm sorry." The words were thick, agonized.

"No, it's not—" She took a breath. Her throat felt tight with tears, but she refused to cry. She *refused*. "It was never that simple. I know it, and you know it. It's easier to blame ourselves and each other."

"I never blamed you."

A lie, whether he knew it or not. "Andrew."

"I *didn't*. I don't."

"Why not?"

He sighed and propped up on one arm, traced the side of her face until she looked at him. "You saved my life. You did what you had to do, and you've tormented yourself over it. You don't deserve to have me wondering if maybe you shouldn't have done it at all."

Her heart might have stopped beating. "If I should have let them kill you?"

Andrew hesitated. "Maybe."

"I don't—" No. No talking without thinking. Maybe it was cowardice that drove her back from the edge, but it was too big. Too much, and she wasn't ready to traverse a path that could well lead them back to the ugliest truths of that night.

Instead she lifted her hand and touched his cheek. "I'm glad you're alive."

Amazingly, he smiled. "So am I, now. But it took a while, and I didn't want you to feel that."

She couldn't find it in her to smile back. He didn't know that she was the reason their attackers had changed forms to begin with. He didn't know that she'd lost control and brought violence down on them.

For all her mockery of shapeshifter guilt, she was as bad as they were. Worse, because she didn't even have the courage to own her mistakes.

"Stop." There was a cajoling lilt in his voice, one she hadn't heard in a long time. "Come on, smile for me."

She didn't have the guts to charge forward. But she didn't retreat, either, and at least it was something. A step.

Smiling, she turned to kiss his palm. "You should go back to sleep. Sera's pulling an early shift at Dixie John's tomorrow, and if I don't turn up and let her yell at me, she's going to be unlivable."

Andrew brushed a kiss over her chin. "We can stop by for a late brunch."

"Good. And after that..." The zip drive was buried in one of her bags, wrapped in a scarf for safekeeping. "You have a key to Alec's place, right?"

"Course I do."

"Instead of hitting the parts store or Craigslist, I thought we could head over there. He's the only person I know who still uses a computer with a zip drive." Though *use* might be a generous term. As far as Kat knew, the last time anyone had booted the damn thing up had been when she'd done it a year ago just to see if she could. "It's worth a shot."

The corner of Andrew's mouth twitched. "You're brilliant. If anyone's going to be stuck in 1995, it's Alec."

"Then all I have to worry about is platform and software and encryption..." She closed her eyes. "Andrew, can I ask you something?"

He wrapped a lock of her hair around his finger. "Sure."

"Are we sticking together because I'm in danger? Or are

we...starting something?"

He stared at her for a long moment, considering. "Starting something, or picking up where we left off? Either one works, I think."

"Except we didn't leave off with crazy orgasms." She settled her cheek against his chest, mostly because it was easier to say the words when she didn't have to look at him. "We were so close to starting something. Or maybe we weren't and it only felt that way to me because I wanted it to be true."

He combed his fingers through her hair. "We *were*, but...something wasn't right yet. Me, I guess. People around here don't exactly have nice, uncomplicated relationships, you know? Being comfortable, being friends... It felt so good I didn't want to let it go."

His heart thumped under her cheek, just fast enough to prove his casual words a lie. He'd been scared, and she could feel the echoes in him, as clearly as she could feel the pleasure he took in touching her. "You were human," she said softly. "I never was, not entirely. It *would* have been complicated."

"It seems stupid now," he admitted. "It feels like I wasted so much time."

"No." At least there was one thing she could reassure him about. "I skipped grades, a few of them. I graduated early, went to college early. I was never really around people my own age, so I missed out on the social stuff, and the empathy only made it worse. I was young a few years ago, Andrew. I wasn't ready. But I would have been so afraid of missing my chance, I couldn't have said no. Not to you."

"And with both of us not ready..."

Maybe it would have worked. Maybe it would have been a mess, and ruined any chance they had. Either way, there was no going back. "I know we keep saying we're not going to talk about the big stuff, and I don't want to, not yet. But I need something to hold on to."

"I'm here," he said simply. "I'm in it, Kat. Not going

anywhere, and we can figure it out together."

"So we have a thing." It brought a goofy-feeling smile to her lips. "Can I wear your letter jacket?"

Andrew laughed. "They don't let you letter in being a giant dork, remember?"

"Depends on where you go to school." Peace settled over her, following the path of his fingers as he stroked her hair. She yawned and snuggled closer. "If you don't have a letter jacket, we're going to have to rethink this whole thing."

"Obviously I'm worthless without one."

"Obviously." Another yawn, and this time she didn't try to fight it. "Except you're warm. And surprisingly cuddly, for a big mean council member."

"That's exactly what it says on my business cards."

Chapter Eight

If there was one thing Andrew had never expected Alec Jacobson to master, it was videoconferencing. The man avoided technological advances with singular dedication.

Still, necessity compelled even the most drastic changes, and it looked like it had dragged Alec into the twenty-first century. At least, it seemed so until the blurry picture on the laptop screen slid into sharp focus to reveal not only Alec, but his smiling wife as well. "There," Carmen said. "I think that should work."

Alec made an annoyed face, his lips tugged down and his eyebrows pulled tight together. "I gave up ten minutes of my life so Andrew could *see* how pissy I am over the fact that I can't just use a fucking telephone. How is this progress?"

"Don't be grumpy." Carmen waved. "Hi, Andrew."

He waved back. "Is this a bad time?"

"Not at all." She kissed Alec's cheek as she rose, and paused to smooth the frown from between his brows. "I'm going to make French toast for breakfast. Don't forget we have that thing this morning."

When she was gone, Alec sighed. "She's bribing me so I don't choke anyone at our ten o'clock meeting."

"Must be damn good French toast."

"Not that good." Alec ran his hand over his disheveled hair and shook his head. "It is not a good time up here. John Peyton's got some upstart on his council poking at him, and things are...unsettled."

Knowing Alec, it was the understatement of the decade. "I wouldn't have bothered you, but I ran into trouble in Alabama. Car chase that ended badly for the other guy, but someone might have gotten a license plate. I thought maybe you could call McNeely—"

"Hold up." Alec ducked out of view and reappeared a moment later with his cell phone in hand. "I thought I gave you McNeely's number. Maybe Julio has it."

"Well, I have it, but..." But he wasn't really in charge, wasn't the one with the authority to call up a lieutenant in the New Orleans Police Department and ask for favors.

"Oh Jesus, kid." Alec leaned forward until his face all but filled the screen. "Okay, listen to me. I've been letting this slide because you need to find your footing, and we've been between crises. But shit's liable to hit the fan any day now, so the training wheels are coming off. You know what to do, and you need to start doing it without checking with me first."

Andrew choked back a growl. "It might be that simple for you, Alec, but my situation's a little more complicated."

"Yeah, on the subject of complicated, have you heard from Derek this week?"

"No." Andrew tensed. If he'd somehow heard what happened to Kat...

Alec sighed again, something that was starting to sound like a nervous tic. "Great. Okay, I'm telling you this because the rumor's spreading so fast you're probably going to hear it before he calms down enough to call you. Nicole's pregnant."

"Holy shit." It seemed like the sort of thing Derek would want to shout from the rooftops, and the fact that he hadn't made Andrew's hands clench into fists. "Is something wrong?"

"Nothing life-threatening, but Nick's not feeling well. Sicker than usual, I guess. Carmen's tried to tell him it's all manageable, but Derek watched his wife's twin sister go through a miserable pregnancy and premature labor, so panic has set in pretty hard. He's calling Carmen at all hours, damn near every time Nick twitches a toe."

They were going to have a *baby*. "He hasn't told Kat yet, either. She'd have mentioned it."

Alec's eyebrows climbed up. "I thought you and Kat weren't talking."

It was stupid to feel as though he'd gotten caught smoking under the bleachers. "That was the situation. I was helping Kat with some stuff about her mom."

"Uh-huh." Alec scrubbed his hand over his hair again, leaving it half sticking up this time. He looked ragged around the edges in general, as if it'd been a few days since his last shave—or his last full night of sleep. "Shit. Okay, you've got to handle this, Andrew. Derek can barely handle himself and his wife, and John Peyton's got a daughter to worry about and that cagey little shit on his council who's stirring up trouble. Can you and Julio keep Kat safe and get this shit done?"

"Yeah, I'll get it done." For the first time, Andrew caught a gleam in Alec's eyes, a satisfaction that belied his apparent frustration. For all his exasperation, he was in his element. "This thing with Kat's mom might be big, Alec."

"I don't doubt that. I know Derek's never thought her mother's death was really an accident. Is she digging around again? She was obsessed with it for a few months when she was nineteen and had just gotten access to our list of contacts at the detective agency."

"Yeah, she was digging." And she just might have broken the whole thing wide open. "What do you usually buy McNeely to say thanks when he's just saved your ass? Scotch?"

"Not anymore. McNeely's on the wagon. Get him some music. A CD or two."

"Done. Thanks, Alec."

"Hey. If shit gets so bad you can't figure out your next move...call me. But if you know the next move, take it. You've got the instincts, kid. Time to start trusting them."

"Right." Julio had undoubtedly already been taking care of business while Andrew kept his head in the sand, but that was going to change. "I'll keep you posted."

"You do that." Alec paused. Frowned. "Tell me one thing. Are you tangled up because it's Kat?"

"Yes," he replied readily. "And also because her contact was looking for protection from the Southeast council. It had to be me or Julio, and Julio wasn't touching it."

"No, I didn't mean—" He made an amused noise. "Is your head tangled up? And your instincts? That girl has never made it easy for you to think."

"My brain's working fine, Alec." It was even mostly true.

"Uh-huh. It's the rest of you working just fine that I'm worried about."

Andrew couldn't resist an arrogant grin. "That's working all right too."

Six months in New York had perfected Alec's exasperated peevishness. "God help us all. Don't be an idiot."

"No more than usual, you have my word on that."

"Good." Alec's finger rushed toward the screen, diverting at the last moment to crash into the keyboard, judging by the sound. He looked back up at Andrew, cursed, then pounded another key before bellowing, "Carmen, how the fuck do I turn this thing *off?*"

The call dropped, and Andrew muffled a snort as he closed the laptop. Things may have changed a hell of a lot over the last year, but some things never would. It was comforting, in a way.

Not that he had time to sit around and ponder it. He had to get on the phone with McNeely and clean up his mess, and then he had to figure out what to tell Kat about her cousin's impending fatherhood—and what it could mean if she chose to pursue her investigation.

Dixie John's was the sort of restaurant tourists would have driven miles out of their way to visit, if they'd had any way of knowing the place was there. Once in a while, a tourist wandered in and enjoyed a meal, utterly oblivious to the fact that they were surrounded by witches and priestesses or psychics and shapeshifters.

Not that everyone who visited the place was a supernatural, but the humans who tended to return were the sort who didn't mind the rumors that Dixie John dabbled in voodoo. If patrons saw the regulars acting oddly, they shrugged it off and went on about their business.

They probably didn't imagine that the pretty redhead taking orders turned into a coyote sometimes, or that the bartender wasn't just skilled at anticipating their orders—he really *could* read their minds.

Kat loved Dixie John's. During the worst months after Andrew had been attacked, John had given her sanctuary within the walls of his restaurant. At Mahalia's, she always felt compelled to paste on a smile and pretend she felt healthy and happy, or the staff would tell their boss—and their boss's husband. Derek had enough to worry about without reports that she was moping about, even if she was.

John never tattled. Kat had written her thesis in a cozy corner booth, sustained by coffee, music and some of the best damn cooking in the state. John had even given Sera a job, one where she made decent enough money to feel independent as she struggled to find her place. There was something soothing about the big man's steady presence, an odd mixture of determination and utter belief in fate.

It had done wonders for Sera, that was for sure. Kat pushed through the front door and found her roommate bent over a table, making faces at a toddler whose shrieks of laughter hit Kat a moment before the wave of youthful glee.

The few minutes it took to settle her psychic barriers firmly in place gave Sera time to cross the room. Even in jeans and a

T-shirt, Sera attracted the gazes of most of the men she passed. Her curvy, pin-up girl looks made Kat feel like one of Cinderella's stepsisters, an insecurity not soothed when Sera nodded to the back booth. "Anna's waiting for you. I've got to get a couple orders in before I take my break."

Time alone with Anna. Fabulous. Kat managed a smile. "Okay."

Sera sighed, clearly exasperated by the lukewarm response. "Be nice, Kat. Be nice, and I'll bring you coffee, okay?"

"I'm nice." But the admonition reminded her of a blurry moment in a motel in Alabama. Andrew, holding her foot and whispering that he'd never be nice about Miguel.

As she started toward the booth, Kat forced herself to admit that it was hard to be nice about Anna. Blonde, petite, practically a damn *bounty hunter*—Anna was everything Kat wasn't. Including a shapeshifter, one who'd been able to handle Andrew's strength in the first months after his transformation. With a shapeshifter's instincts, she'd understood him, probably in ways Kat never would.

Every time she looked at Anna, all Kat could see were the ways she hadn't been enough.

Even now. Anna was halfway through one of John's omelets, and she waved at Kat as she lifted her coffee cup. "This place is insane. Did you know John mixes his own andouille?"

"Is that the sausage?" Kat slid into the opposite side of the booth and dropped her bag onto the seat next to her. "He's a great cook." See, she could be nice. She was the damn queen of polite, meaningless chitchat about breakfast foods.

"Yeah, the sausage stuff." Anna eyed her and shook her head. "Did you tell Andrew you didn't want me anywhere near you or your roommate?"

Kat froze, one hand suspended over the table in the act for reaching for a glass of water. "I—what?"

"Come on, Kat. I'm not a rocket scientist or an empath, but I know when people wish they didn't have to be looking at me."

There it was, blunt and so unrepentant that it took a few moments for Kat to realize that the emotion churning through her was relief. The truth had been festering, an ugly emotion that shamed her so deeply she'd never given it voice. She was Kat—nice, sweet Kat, and she wasn't allowed to be petty and jealous.

Kat dropped her hand to rest on the table. "It's hard sometimes," she admitted, and the truth felt like dropping a heavy bag full of schoolbooks at the end of a long walk home. Light and freeing, even if her words carried the ghost of pain. "He ditched me and picked you. Not your fault, but it didn't make it easier. Especially since you're not that easy to hate."

"You'd be surprised how many people manage it," Anna told her. "But you're wrong about one thing."

According to Andrew, she'd been wrong about *everything*. "What's that?"

"He never ditched you."

"Yeah, he tried that line too. He disappeared from my life and never talked to me. That's my definition of ditched." Kat gripped the edge of the table and met Anna's gaze squarely. "If this is some shapeshifter thing I'm not getting, I wish you'd tell me. Because no one else will."

The blonde laid down her fork. "It's not human emotion, for starters. It's not that sentimental. It's *visceral*. Andrew damn near ripped out his own heart to protect you, but not because he had some macho, noble idea that it was better for you. In our world, if you don't know how to take care of someone, you have to walk. Make room for someone else, someone who can."

Well that was...typically egocentric shapeshifter bullshit. "Because obviously that's your choice to make, right? I mean, what say could *we* have in it?"

Anna snorted. "I hope that's a rhetorical question, because you should know the answer by now."

This time, she said it out loud. "Well, it's bullshit. You can't trade the rest of us around like baseball cards. And if it's such a universal truth, why the hell has Alec been giving Andrew such a shit time over it?"

"He's an alpha shifter," Anna reminded her. "We're hypocritical assholes."

Apparently. Kat laid both hands on the table. "So let me get this straight. If Andrew sticks around and I get hurt, it's his fault. If he sticks around and hurts me, it's his fault. If he leaves and I'm sad...it's his fault. If he leaves and someone else hurts me..." She trailed off and tried to come up with a polite way to ask a question that didn't feel polite at all. "Could you all *be* any more self-centered or condescending?"

"Nope."

Yelling about it was less fun when Anna agreed with her. Slightly perturbed, Kat sat back. "I don't know how shapeshifters survive, if almost all of you are like this. How do you stand each other long enough to have babies?"

"You think we're all like this?" Anna tossed her head back with a laugh. "Sweetie, if that were true, we'd definitely all have killed each other by now. I'm only talking *alpha* shifters, and it just so happens that New Orleans is lousy with us. Lucky you."

As many times as she'd noticed that all of the shifters in her life—save Sera—seemed obnoxiously dominant, she'd never stopped to consider why, or if that was unusual. "Why is New Orleans different? I mean, I know Alec's made it into the safe place, but if shit is so bad everywhere else, wouldn't the submissives *want* to live here?"

"You think all the subs run away from home like Nicky Peyton?" Anna shook her head as she drew one leg up to rest on the vinyl seat. "Hell no. Even if they want to, they stay put. Right where their more dominant relatives or spouses want them to be. Usually," she added with a nod toward Sera.

Kat glanced around to where Sera was leaning over the bar. She said something Kat couldn't hear, and the man on the other side burst out laughing.

Sera had run away from home at seventeen. Walked off her

high school campus one day and climbed into a car with Josh. They were across state lines before anyone realized she was gone. She hadn't told anyone, hadn't tried to talk her friends and family around. Not that Franklin would have been talked around, and Sera would have had to obey.

So she'd run. And she'd regretted it.

Shivering, Kat turned back to Anna and lowered her voice. "Josh made my skin crawl. He treated her like a princess, but it was never right. It was like...deathless love that you knew was going to end badly. It was Romeo and Juliet." If Romeo had been in his midthirties and had a mullet.

Something feral and angry sharpened Anna's gaze for just a moment before vanishing. "Sometimes you think someone's being treated like a princess, but what they're really being treated like is a favorite pet or a doll. Property."

Harsh words for the possessive interest Kat had never been able to put into words. Maybe she'd been too innocent to understand then. Now she knew better. "Thanks for looking out for her. I didn't want to drag her into another mess. Not when she's getting back on her feet."

Anna picked up her cup again. "She's a good kid."

"For what it's worth, Anna, I never hated you. Maybe I wanted to, and maybe I hated myself for the urge, but I never hated you."

"Believe me when I say it's understandable." Anna finished her coffee and propped her elbows on the table. "Now, are you ready for the good news?"

That depended on if their definition of *good* diverged as sharply as their definitions of *ditched*. "Lay it on me."

"He's figured it out. That he's the one who can get it done."

"Oh." Maybe to Andrew, it was that easy. Walk away when he couldn't handle it and come back when he could. It was *instinct* after all, and humans weren't allowed to hold instinct against shapeshifters, no matter how much they'd hurt you. Derek had pulled that one on her for years, smothering her like she was a kid and blaming instinct every time she tried to push back.

Before she could frame a more meaningful response, Sera appeared, squeezing into the booth next to her. "Y'all playing nice over here?"

"Mostly." Anna tilted her head and sighed. "It's hard as hell trying to explain some of this crap without losing a lot in translation."

Sera flipped her ponytail back over her shoulder and pushed a cup of coffee toward Kat. "If you thought coming in here smelling like you spent the night under Andrew is going to distract me from the part where you got shot, you're going to be massively disappointed."

Kat flinched, heat filling her cheeks. She'd forgotten—again—and her conversation with Anna seemed a hundred times more awkward now. "Shit, Sera."

"Don't 'shit' me. You got *shot*."

Relating the story from the start took most of Sera's break, and earned Kat a blistering lecture on communication and asking for help that only ended when the bartender flagged Sera down to pick up an order.

When she was gone, Kat took a sip of her coffee and grimaced when it turned out to be lukewarm. "Do they teach that speech about protecting your people in shapeshifter school?"

"Closest thing to shapeshifter school is Conclave training, and you don't want to know what they teach you there."

Kat had more guesses than she wanted. "How to rip up men and torture psychics?"

"For starters. And hey, maybe they've expanded the curriculum since I left." Anna prodded at her cold omelet. "What's this shit you're mixed up in that's got people trying to off you?"

"I don't even know." The zip disk was a foot away, tucked safely in her bag, and it took effort not to reach out and touch it. "Someone who doesn't want me knowing why my mother was so dangerous she ended up dead."

"Got any leads?" She shook her head without waiting for an answer. "Of course you do, or they wouldn't be after you. Dumb question."

"Yeah." Kat folded her arms and watched as Sera stopped at the table with the toddler again, bending down until the girl got a fist full of Sera's ponytail. Kids loved her, and Sera loved them back with an outward pleasure that masked the echoes of pain that Kat caught in unguarded moments.

Glancing back at Anna, Kat tilted her head toward her roommate. "She's doing okay, right? Is she staying with you?"

"Mmm, over the bar. I tried to get her to take the bedroom, but she insists on sleeping on the couch."

It sounded like a Sera thing to do. "As long as she's safe. If there are shifters after us..." Anna bristled with power as dominant as Andrew's. Sera was a quiet submissive who could be bent to a stronger shapeshifter's will no matter how viciously she fought. "I don't want to drag her into my crap."

Before Anna could answer, John dropped onto the booth beside her with a heavy sigh, a kitchen towel slung over one shoulder. "You around next weekend, Kitty Kat? Jimmy Aucoin's gonna play here Friday night."

One week, and it seemed like a decade away. She already couldn't begin to make sense of the events that had transpired—open an email on Monday, wake up in Andrew's bed on Friday.

By next week she could be married. Or dead. "I don't know. Things are hectic right now, but if they settle down, I'll be there."

"How about you, Lenoir?"

"I don't make plans, John. You know that."

He laughed. "Course not. Little rambling Anna."

"Plans aren't the best idea in New Orleans," Kat pointed

out. "Making them is lots of fun until you realize someone or something is always going to come along and break them."

"Those days are over," John insisted. "The place is finally calming down—and I, for one, am gonna enjoy it."

Yeah, that was a guilt-punch to the gut.

"Don't you have shit to do?" Anna asked him. "Chef-type things back in the kitchen? Make me another omelet."

He said something in response, something no doubt both creative and obscene. Kat heard the sounds, but the words drifted away into meaningless noise as Andrew stepped through the front door.

For a moment, he stood in the late-morning sunlight, and Kat held her breath. The flutter was back, the one she'd had in her hapless innocence, when his mere presence had filled her with imagination with possibilities. Not just the flutter, she had *tingles*, the kind that came with high school crushes and the driving urge to make out in dark corners.

She had no idea what they were or where they were going, but sometime in the last week he'd resurrected her ability to hope. To imagine something between them besides pain and loss. It was exhilarating.

It was terrifying.

It was kind of turning her on.

Her heart beat too fast, and Anna would hear it. So would Andrew, and Sera, and probably any number of patrons who were shapeshifters she didn't recognize. There was no subtlety in the world of supernatural senses, and no privacy.

Half the people in the room knew she wanted to jump on Andrew, and the rest could probably make a pretty good guess.

He stopped beside the table and smiled down at her. "I got things squared away with Alec. How's it going, Anna? John?"

They murmured their hellos as Kat oh-so-carefully didn't touch him. Considering what had happened last time, being within five feet of him seemed risky enough. Instead she gripped her bag as a reminder to keep her hands to herself. "Sera yelled at me until she felt better, so I'm ready to go when you are."

"I'm parked right outside." And he seemed eager to go.

John grinned and slid out of the booth. "Y'all take it easy." He disappeared back toward the kitchen.

Anna spared a glance for Kat as she refilled her coffee cup from the small carafe on the table. "Let me know if you need any backup, okay?"

That the offer had been made to her, and not to Andrew, was a gesture Kat appreciated. "I will. Thanks, Anna."

"You're welcome."

Outside, the crisp January morning had her digging a scarf out of her bag. "Sera seems okay. I think Anna is really good for her."

"I think so too." Andrew rested his hand on Kat's shoulder, drawing her closer. "I didn't clear the trip out to Alec's house, after all. He gave me a lecture about independence and initiative, so I said fuck it."

"Go us. Breaking and entering." Leaning into his side felt nice. Fuzzy, but nice. "It's not like we're going to trash the place or anything."

"Unauthorized entry," he corrected. "I have a key and security codes."

"Spoilsport."

"Would you feel better if we were likely to get arrested?"

Kat stepped off the sidewalk. "I guess not. So how was Alec? I haven't gotten any email from him in a couple days. Not even the profanity-laced ones when he breaks something."

"Up to his ears in Conclave crap." He unlocked the doors and opened hers. "There's some stuff going on right now."

"Uh-oh. Worse than usual?"

"No, just—" He climbed in and slid the key into the ignition before falling still, his hands on the wheel. "Derek and Nick are going to have a baby."

Kat froze, the seatbelt clutched in one hand. "Derek and Nick—" Oh *shit*. The faint hurt of not hearing it from her cousin personally was swallowed up by a far more intense emotion—sympathy. "Nick is going to kill him before it's over. Derek has turned overprotectiveness into an extreme sport."

"Apparently, she's fine but doesn't feel great, so he's freaking out."

That was Derek. "The first time I got the flu after he became my guardian, he took me to the clinic three times. Franklin finally had to tell him he was doing more harm dragging me back and forth than he would be by letting me puke my guts out at home. And that was *before* he got turned and got all the crazy shapeshifter instincts."

Andrew closed his hand around hers. "He'll call you after he settles down. Alec only told me because there are rumors floating around already, and he only knows because Derek's been asking Carmen for advice."

This time the spark of need was quiet enough to give her hope. Touching Andrew was magic, but maybe there'd come a time when it wasn't too much magic. "I know. Derek doesn't call me when he's worried."

"'Worried' might be putting it mildly. I talked to Derek after the problems Michelle had with her pregnancy. I know he was concerned, especially since Nick and Michelle's mom died in childbirth."

It probably didn't help that Nick was tiny. Kat towered half a foot over her, and Derek was even taller. Child-birthing hips had never sounded like a compliment, but it suddenly didn't feel so bad to have them. "Nick's going to be okay, though, right?"

Andrew fastened his seatbelt and started the engine. "From what I could gather, Carmen seems to think it's no big deal."

"Okay. Then I guess that can go on the worry backburner. Except I *really* can't call him and tell him I'm getting shot at by possible cult members."

"Which is why I didn't bring that part up. If this thing gets to the point where we can't handle it, we'll get some help. Until then, we're on our own."

The moment of truth, then. Time to deal with her shit like a grown-up, without having to worry about everyone she knew tripping over themselves to shield her from unfortunate truths. Sliding her hand to the bag, she traced the hard edge of the zip disk. "Then let's go find out what we're dealing with."

Chapter Nine

They found the zip drive and appropriate cable in a stack in the corner of Alec's home office, but one thing was conspicuously absent. "No power cord." Andrew's frustration boiled up. "Do you see one anywhere?"

Kat lifted a tangled mess of cords in her fist. "Only about twenty of them. I'm guessing he puts every cord he finds in this box and forgets it."

"Damn it." He angled the blue case toward her and tapped the front. "Check for the logo first."

She glanced at him, both eyebrows raised and her head tilted at an angle that almost screamed, *No, really?*

It felt good because at least it wasn't guarded, and he choked back a laugh. "Okay, Ms. Expert. You've got this. What do you need me for?"

"Just stand there and look pretty," she muttered, taking the drive from him. Two minutes and nine cords later, she let out a whoop of victory and shifted to her knee. "Got it, just have to plug this in now..."

He stepped back to give her room. "If it doesn't work, are we heading back to Birmingham to visit Ben?"

"Mmm. We could, but he's really better if the data's encrypted or corrupted. He won't be able to pull it off a disk that's not connected to anything." She plugged in the drive as she talked, every movement quick and efficient. "Honestly, I don't really know how it works, and God knows I've tried to figure it out. Something with electricity though. Having a signal. He needs a way in, like a network or an access point."

It made Ben sound like a comic superhero. "He's wireless?" Andrew asked, amused.

"Uh-huh." Kat scrunched up her nose, the look she always got when she was trying not to laugh. When she leaned forward to reach one of the cords at the rear of the computer, her ponytail slid away from the back of her neck, revealing the vivid black ink twining up toward her hairline.

He stared at the ink for a moment before dragging his gaze away. "How likely is this information not to be somehow encrypted?"

"No clue." Powering up the computer resulted in a buzzing whir, clearly loud enough that even Kat heard it. She frowned as she turned on the monitor. "I guess it depends on if my mom put the data on there, or had someone else do it. She was okay with computers, but I was fixing her hosed SMTP settings by the time I was nine. I doubt she was messing with data encryption."

Apparently, she'd been tangled up in a lot of things Kat hadn't known about. "Only one way to tell, I guess." He gestured to the drive. "Look and see."

Kat made a noncommittal noise as the screen came to life, the boxy operating system at least five years out of date. Instead of navigating the windows, she pulled up a command line and stared at the blinking white cursor, her fingers hovering over the keyboard.

Her heart beat too fast, and the shallow, quick breaths she drew spoke of real fear as well as nervousness. Andrew slid his hands over her shoulders and leaned down to speak. "I'm right here. I'm with you."

"Thank you." The words trembled, almost as badly as her hands as she began to type. Slowly at first, then with growing confidence, too fast for him to follow what she was doing as blocks of text scrolled past in response to her short commands.

It took a few minutes, her shoulders growing tenser under his hands. Finally she cursed softly. "There are a ton of files. No extensions, no fucking clue what they are. But I can get at them, at least. Transfer them and send them to Ben. The only one that's different..." She typed something, and a plain text file popped up.

A letter.

Katherine,

If your father gave you this letter, it means I didn't survive to see you turn twenty-one.

What I'm doing now, I'm doing for you. I need you to understand that I believed in this cause. Our world is broken. Spell casters and shapeshifters scorn us, use us, hurt us and discard us. Psychics have huddled together and bowed their heads for decades, as if our powers mean nothing. They told me they were working to change that, and I believed them. I fought for them. I killed for them.

I know that can't be easy for you to see. What you are is why I have hope for you. The more powerful you grow, the more you understand the suffering of those around you. Maybe your empathy will keep you from denial. I convinced myself I wasn't hurting people who didn't deserve to hurt. I believed I was building a world where you could be powerful without needing to be brutal. Instead I helped create a world where your power can be used against you.

If I die, it's because I fought to stop that. I can't look in your eyes and know I helped make a weapon that could turn you into a killer.

I know the lessons I've already taught you seem harsh, but your life will be hard. Maybe I shouldn't have taken the risk of passing this legacy on to a daughter. Your uncle's too afraid to have another child, afraid that he'll have a daughter and pass the Gabriel curse on to her.

But I can't regret you. I love you more than anyone or

anything on this earth, and there's nothing I won't do to keep you safe from my mistakes.

Your heart is so big, I still have hope you'll forgive me for them.

Mom

An emotional bomb, with so much that could either hurt Kat or set her free, and Andrew's eyes zeroed in on one word: *weapon*. No time to feel guilty about that, not when Kat drew in a shaky breath and came to her feet in a jerky, uncoordinated movement.

She ducked under his hands and took a few steps away, leaving him staring at her back as the sound of her heart pounding thundered in his ears. "Whatever I am is so terrifying that Derek's father wouldn't have more kids. And Nick's pregnant."

If he let her continue down that path, give in to those thoughts, he'd lose her. "Kat, stop. You don't know that's true. Even if it is, your mom..." He struggled to find the right words without hurting her even more. "Your mom had shit going on. Do you blame him for being scared? It had nothing to do with you."

"I don't blame anyone for anything. I can't." She pivoted so sharply her hair whipped around, and the gaze she fixed on him was just short of wild. "Don't you get it, Andrew? I get all the noble suffering of a martyr and all the guilt of knowing I wouldn't be so damn selfless if I could keep everyone from shoving their pain down my throat until I give them whatever they need. I'm a fake. I *want* to be selfish."

"You want a *choice* in the matter. It doesn't make you a bad person."

Color filled her cheeks, and the room pressed in on him. Anger—helpless, bitter anger, and not his own. "Why not? Why doesn't anything make me a bad person? Not being selfish, or petty and jealous? I killed people, and all anyone can do is rush to tell me I'm not a bad person. Am I a bad person if I'd do it again?"

He didn't stop to think, to analyze. "Maybe it does. Maybe that means you're just as low as the rest of us, and that's the part we can't stand."

Silence. Her fists clenched, and she shook her head. "I can't live up to that. You want me to be happy and loving all the time, and no one can be that."

"It's not about not wanting you to bum me out, Kat." Everything between them had always been so fucking hard to explain. "If you think people aren't worth saving, *I believe you.* You see inside them, know what they're hiding way down at the core. You of all people have to think there's something good here, or what the hell are we all scrambling so hard for?"

"Oh, Andrew..." For a moment she seemed at a loss. She crossed her arms over her chest—not an aggressive stance, but a defensive one. "It's not... People are worth saving. They're petty and confused and so many of the horrible ones are only afraid. Like me. I'm petty and confused and afraid."

"I don't need you to be perfect," he said again, the words a harsh grind in his throat. "I need you not to think it's all a total loss, including—no, *especially* you."

Her gaze slid past him. Fixed on the computer. "I need to know what I am. What's in my genes that turned my mother and all the other women in our family crazy, and whether it's going to do that to me. Or Derek's kid."

"You need to know," he agreed, "but don't give it too much power. Everyone's different."

"I'm not so different." She eased around him to settle in front of the computer again. Flexing her fingers, she took a deep breath and began to type. "I'm powerful. Callum taught me *how* powerful. I'm not a floppy little puppy who knows a neat trick. Empathy makes me vulnerable to the people I love, but it makes me dangerous to everyone else."

"Believe it or not, there's a middle ground between floppy

puppy and psychic warrior."

"There's a middle ground between laid-back wolf and stone-cold alpha badass too."

A middle ground he couldn't, for the life of him, seem to find. "Point taken."

"Really?" She bent over, slipped a flash drive from the side pocket of her bag and plugged it in without looking at him. "I don't even know what my point was. Maybe my point is that we would have already gotten to the middle ground if we could. Maybe we should get used to being a psychic killer and a warrior alpha."

They used to be just Kat and Andrew, and now he wondered if he'd fucked everything up a long, long time ago. If sitting on his ass and waiting her out had cost him everything. "I guess."

Her fingers danced over the keys, the *clacks* coming so close together they sounded like one continuous noise. "I can send these to Ben once we get close enough to the city to get a decent signal with my aircard. Then, I guess we wait? See if anyone tries to kidnap or kill us?"

It wasn't funny. "We try to get back to some semblance of normal."

"Do I—" Her voice cracked. She swallowed and stared straight ahead. "Do you want me to go back to my place tonight?"

She sounded so scared. "We shouldn't split up." He didn't know how recently Jackson had buffed up the wards around her apartment, though part of him almost relished the thought of someone coming in to start a fight. "We can stay at my place again."

"At the council headquarters?" She jerked the flash drive free and twisted to look up at him. "I guess there's plenty of room there. And good protections."

And an extra well-trained fighter. "Julio will be glad to have company for a few days. He can cook for more than just us."

"Julio likes to cook?" The thought seemed to amuse her, at least enough to tease her lips up into a half-smile.

"Firehouse food. Gigantic pots of chili and spaghetti, stuff like that."

"Of course." Sighing, Kat rose and began packing up her things. "After this, I think I should swing by the dojo. I've missed four lessons in a row. If I don't drag my ass in there, Zola's going to kill me before any assassins get a chance."

"You've been shot," Andrew said firmly. "If she doesn't understand why you might need to miss a few more sessions, I'll set her straight."

But Kat shook her head. "No, the healing spells worked. My arm's fine. And if things are going crazy, training's more important than ever."

She was determined, he had to give her that. "Okay. After we talk to Julio and get him up to speed, we'll head to the dojo together."

"Good." The letter from her mother was still up on the screen. She spared it one last look, then cut the power to the computer. "Let's go."

Time. She needed it for everything right now—decrypting the information on the disk, dealing with her mother's letter. Dealing with him.

He took her bag and slung it over his own shoulder. "It'll work out, Kat."

She smiled, and he couldn't tell if she was lying when she said, "I know."

Andrew was building things.

Fresh from the shower, Kat followed the faint noises down the stark, undecorated corridors of the Southeast council headquarters' third floor. Cleaning up and converting Alec's newly purchased warehouse had taken second priority after reestablishing the supernatural clinic last year, but signs of renovations were everywhere. She hadn't wandered during her last stay, but now she passed several clean rooms with fresh coats of paint before finding Andrew and Julio.

Julio was nodding along with the music undoubtedly playing on his earphones while he sanded a spot on the wall, and Andrew wiped his arm across his forehead as he picked up a damp rag. "Want to help?"

"Sure." The view might help her stop brooding, in any case. Explosive orgasms aside, she hadn't managed to spend much time getting to look at Andrew without lust and empathy fogging them. As long as she didn't touch him... "Toss me the rag?"

He did, and the muscles in his arm flexed as he waved to the far wall. "That one. We're not quite done sanding this side of the room yet."

Bare arms. He should always have bare arms. She caught the cloth and moved where he'd directed, but couldn't resist the urge to peek at him again.

He was beautiful.

If life was fair, she'd be able to savor touching him. Instead of awkward, jumbled encounters, there could be slow seduction. Kissing. God, she wanted to *kiss* him, just feel his mouth on hers and enjoy a growing urgency that didn't swallow them both whole. To have an orgasm that was more than misfiring synapses and emotional overload. She wouldn't have the knot of worry in her gut, the fear that needing him had so badly damaged the foundations of her control that she'd never master her gifts when he was there to make the world fuzzy.

The damp rag left wet streaks on the wall as she swiped it in slow, aimless circles. If life was fair, it would just be the two of them in the room. So easy to picture Andrew as he was now, sweaty and covered in plaster dust, muscles flexing, eyes dark... The way he looked at her before empathy exploded, like he wanted to touch every inch of her.

They'd never been naked. He'd never even gotten a hand into her pants, or under her shirt. She'd never felt that beard against her breasts, or her stomach, or—God help her—her *thighs*, and the mental image of Andrew coaxing her knees apart threatened to blow her brain into little pieces.

She wanted life to be fair.

His hand closed over hers as he corrected her technique. "Straight lines down the wall."

He was breathing too hard. So was she, but oxygen couldn't be making it to her head, because the world was fuzzy around the edges. All she could see was her hand, trapped under his. If she eased her other hand up the wall, would he catch that one too? Pin her to the wall and skate along the darker edge of the fantasies she tried to pretend she'd never had?

His fingers slid down to her wrist, closed around it firmly for a moment—and let go.

In a second, she'd be panting. This arousal might be in her head, but it still twisted up her body. Tightened her nipples, made her ache. Made her wet. She rocked back and found Andrew still behind her, and arousal had curled around him too.

His erection pressed against her, and she could see the dizzy, frantic series of events unfolding before her as if she had Julio's precognition. His hips rocking against her ass, maybe one hand drifting around her body, into her pants, pressing between her legs until the rough touch of his fingers sent her—

Julio. Oh Christ, if Andrew's touch shattered her control, her projection wouldn't just affect him.

Kat tore away from his body with a whimper, stumbling so hard she slammed into the opposite wall.

Julio jumped back and plucked one of the buds from his ear. "Kat, what the hell?"

Air whistled through her teeth as she stared at him, taking in confusion in upraised brows and a hint of concern in his widened eyes—

And nothing else. No arousal. No desire—thank *God*, no lust—and relief weakened Kat's knees until she slid to the floor with a soft *thump*. "You can't feel it."

"Uh, feel what?"

Adrenaline was making it worse. Her heart pounded until the world throbbed with it, and she couldn't make herself look at Julio. Not with Andrew a few feet away, intense and barely contained. She had to wet her lips twice to speak. "Andrew?"

His answer shouldn't have been an answer at all. "Julio, get out."

Out of the corner of her eye, Kat caught a glimpse of Julio scrambling toward the door. A moment later it slammed shut, and she sucked in a breath. No, panted. She was panting, tiny hitching breaths as the intensity of the need between them twisted again. "He couldn't feel it." It was important. She *knew* it was important.

Andrew closed the distance between them, towering over her in a way that sent her base instincts wild. "I feel it," he said, and Kat forgot why anything else could possibly be important as he lifted her, pinned her to the sheetrock with his hips and groaned.

For a terrifying second, Kat thought she might come from the sound alone.

The sheer insanity of her response woke reason. They couldn't do this. His skin was hot under her hands, arms bare, muscles flexing as he held her up, but they *couldn't do this*, couldn't fall into each other like helpless, rutting fools every time a stray fantasy caught either of them. It was absurd. Untenable. Like living the porno version of their lives, where every situation dissolved into impractical sex.

It was getting worse. She hadn't even touched him this time, not until he was already hard, caught in the grip of whatever made her dig her fingernails into his shoulders and whimper every time he ground against her. Lust. Blind lust, and not romantic at all when they didn't have a choice.

Desperation seized her, and she squeezed her eyes shut and ignored her body, shut it out with discipline borne of training under Callum's strict tutelage. He'd put her through hell, but nothing so hard as this. Nothing like trying to ignore the sweet, dark thrill of her back against the wall and Andrew's hips redefining the meaning of bliss with every perfectly timed rock.

Finding a half-trance was damn near impossible. Stretchy yoga pants were faint protection from the jean-covered erection grinding between her thighs, and Andrew liked grinding into her too much. Throbbing heat gave way to little bursts of sensation, pleasure thick with the anticipation of release, and Kat fought for the will to continue. She wanted this, wanted every second he touched her, every scrap of emotion that bled from him, even the feral possession, *especially* the ravenous, animal need—

—but she wanted more. More than lust. She wanted him to *choose* her.

Whispering his name, she twisted the power flooding her and let it go, invoking the filter that bled feeling into color.

With her eyes closed, she couldn't see the effects, but she could *feel* them. The emotional silence echoed, like the quiet after a violent explosion. It took a moment for her to connect to her own body again, to find the physical sensations that had seemed pale compared to the psychic maelstrom.

Or maybe not so pale. Warm tension pooled between her legs, and she moaned when the tiniest shift of her hips rubbed her against Andrew. "Oh..."

Instead of backing away or putting her down, he groaned again and caught her mouth in a blistering, hungry kiss. Teeth scraped her lower lip, and the growling noise he made in his throat drove her mouth open on an answering gasp. Then it was his tongue, hot and dangerously intent, and by the time she found the willpower to tear away, she couldn't think.

Hell, she couldn't *breathe.*

It made her words come out husky and halting. "Did it—I tried to stop it—"

"Open your eyes, Kat," he rasped. "Look at me."

So much color.

She had to squint until the first flare faded into a brilliant aura of greens and blues and silvers and golds. He glowed when he looked at her, and it wasn't the usual reds of lust and love, because what he felt for her wasn't a clean human emotion.

Andrew was the colors of the wild edged in passion and jagged pieces of pain and need sharp enough to cut, and it stole her breath when she realized it was all real. Not a product of her empathy, not a passing affection magnified a thousandfold by an endless loop.

He loved her, even with the rough edges scratching away at his soul.

His brows drew together in a frown. "You look like you can't believe I haven't stomped off yet."

"It's..." Words failed her, as she watched the colors tremble in the air between them. "You're like the aurora borealis. On acid. I could get drunk on you."

His frown faded into confusion. "The synesthesia again?"

When she touched his cheek, this time, she felt it all. Warm skin. The scratch of his beard. Giddy pleasure at such a simple feeling sent laughter bubbling up. "It's not a perfect solution, but I thought...I thought without the backlash, and the feedback loop, that you wouldn't be so out of control. That you could choose."

"Choose what, you?" He rubbed his face against her hand. "I did. I *would*. It's not about me being out of control, not like that."

"I don't think you'd usually choose against the wall, in front of Julio."

"No," he admitted, "but it's not the end of the world, either. Julio understands."

She stroked his cheek again, thrilling at the quiet intimacy in the gesture that stood in such stark contrast to the sheer sexuality of their position. "I'm only good at understanding feelings in a vacuum. When they're clear and external and not terribly personal. It's messy, when they're mine. Or about me. And after everything...it's so easy to worry that maybe you didn't want me like that. That I'd...I'd forced you to want me."

Andrew laughed and shook his head. "*That's* what you worry about? That I wouldn't want you if you weren't getting your horny feelings all over me?"

Her cheeks warmed, accompanied by the bite of embarrassment. "If you've been having horny feelings about me all this time, you've been keeping them nice and bottled up. For all I knew, I was just turning you into a deviant with me."

"That's bullshit. And completely hilarious." He glided his thumbs over her heated cheeks and smiled. "You're not a deviant. And me wanting you isn't dependent on the empathic feedback you're throwing at me. It's there all the time."

"Oh, I might be a little deviant." Turning her head, she caught his thumb between her teeth for a heartbeat before releasing him. "You just don't know because you haven't managed to get naked with me yet."

His voice dropped to a murmur. "It means a lot to you, doesn't it? Both of us being in control?"

"Maybe not both of us. But one of us. One of us *has* to be in control." She nipped at his thumb again. "Maybe not always the same person...but we're too dangerous to both just let everything go."

"Are we?" His lips skimmed her collarbone, and oh God, she felt it this time, felt it like a full-body shock, like touching a doorknob after dragging her feet across her living room carpet. Her head thumped against the wall as she tried to push closer to his mouth, wanting more. Everything.

He danced kisses up her throat and jaw, and his mouth met hers again, this time in a slow exploration that was everything she'd ever imagined in her hazy, girlish daydreams. Intense and careful, and going on and on until her lips felt too sensitive and growing urgency forced tiny whimpers from her as she squirmed closer.

He lifted his head finally, his jaw clenched, his throat working. "Control." He touched her mouth again and squeezed his eyes shut. "You're right. One of us has to have it."

Color flared with the wild intensity of a star going nova, and Kat framed his face and kissed his chin as his love for her danced through the air. "Me. I can have it right now. Put me down, Andrew, and trust me."

He groaned, but did as she asked. "I trust you."

Oh, the power. Her hands shook with it as she spread both hands against his chest and urged him backwards. Not so far, just until his shoulders hit the wall he'd been sanding.

Then she smoothed her hands down and hooked them in his belt as she dropped to her knees.

Strong hands gathered her hair, tangled in the locks. "This is what you want to do?"

"Yes." She eased his belt open, then tugged at the zipper, shivering as the teeth parted. "Next time, you can be in control."

"Never," he rasped. "I'll never be in control with you looking at me like that."

Her own control was under full-scale assault, but she clung to it by a thread as she eased down his boxers and freed his erection.

With the synesthesia, teasing him was as easy as painting by the numbers. Touch here for need, stroke there for blind lust, mix them together and hear him groan as the air danced in brilliantly colored fractals. Surely stuffy, proper Callum had never imagined such a use for it. But it was effortless and *perfect*, and when she smiled up at him and applied her tongue to all of those newly discovered sensitive spots, the way he groaned and tensed made her reevaluate her list of favorite hobbies. Surely this should find a place near the top—watching the colors flare as Andrew came to pieces under her mouth and hands.

She loved it when his fingers tightened, pulling at her hair as he guided her movements, showing her what he liked. Still a dominant wolf, under the skin, and it drove her determination to higher levels. Even on her knees, she could bring him to his.

Maybe she lacked the technical proficiency to go down on him in deep-throating style, but she followed the eddies of his emotions until she found the perfect balance of stroking hands and tongue, unable to tear her gaze from his face as he dropped his head back and whispered her name.

Then his hips began to move, tiny thrusts that took him a bit deeper into her mouth.

He couldn't stop himself. He was helpless. Putty in her hands.

She loved it.

Andrew started to talk—soft, sweet words interspersed with expletives, dirty pleas that fell just short of being commands. He tensed, moaned, and finally pulled her hair painfully. "Kat, holy *fuck*."

For the first time she wished for telepathy. She couldn't reply, couldn't whisper that she was dying to see him come. To see ecstasy steal over his face as he came undone under her touch. To speak she'd have to stop, and nothing was worth that.

Instead she applied her mouth with increased fervor, moaning her encouragement as she tried to put all the things she couldn't say into her eyes. *Come* and *now* and maybe even *I love you.*

He came with a shout and a thud as his head banged back against the wall, not once but twice. A shudder ran through him, and he clutched her hair even tighter.

Every sense was alive. Filled with him—the taste of his release on her tongue, the smell of his aftershave, his panting moans and the grip of his fingers tugging helplessly at loose strands of her hair. And the sight of him...open and overwhelmed, sated by her touch and alive with light and colors only she could see.

The perfect moment, crystal clear and all hers. Whatever came next, she'd have this—the moment she knew he belonged to her.

Andrew laid a trembling hand on her cheek. "Kat."

Her smile was probably more than a little goofy, and she didn't care. "Hi."

His answer was breathless, dazed—and equally goofy. "Yeah, that."

Later she'd acknowledge that this was a temporary respite at best. That she needed help to unravel whatever tangle of empathy had twisted her up with Andrew. Later she'd worry about the data Ben was decrypting, and her mother's past, and Derek's child and the possibility of terrifying futures.

Now she eased his clothing back into place with gentle hands and rose. His chest was solid and warm beneath her cheek, his skin hot to the touch as she curled her fingers around his arm. "I can't hold this forever. And not if I'm not in control."

"Doesn't matter." He lifted her again, coaxed her legs around his hips. "We'll take turns."

"I don't..." She hesitated. Swallowed. "I'm not ready to let it go yet. I like feeling you. I mean...just physically. Without all the empathy."

"Then we'll keep going slow."

Kat nodded without lifting her head, unwilling to relinquish the odd peace that came with listening to his heart beating under her ear. "Slow is good. Fast makes it too easy to not deal with problems, and that never ends well for anyone."

He sighed softly. "You've been hit with a lot over the last few days."

She had, more than she could begin to process. Every time

she tried to start, her brain skittered into a thousand worst-case scenarios. "I can't handle thinking about that damn letter, because this isn't even all of it. In a few days, Ben's going to have those files rebuilt and decrypted. I don't want to deal with any of it until I can deal with all of it."

Andrew tightened his arms around her. "I get it. Triage. Look at the big picture, not bits and pieces of information."

If the big picture didn't break her. "I can't get to a place where I think I'm okay and have the floor fall out again. It'll hurt more."

"I understand."

He did. She could tell from the warm golden glow that encompassed her. It made it easy to ask for what she really needed. "Can we just...not talk about it, then? There's other stuff to deal with, anyway. Like finding out if we're still being followed, and figuring out why I'm getting my empathy all over you when Julio couldn't feel it."

"Plenty of things." He kissed her again, a simple graze of his lips. "Can you get in touch with Callum and ask him about the empathy thing?"

She thought about her tutor. Straight-laced, coldly handsome Callum, who was rigid, severe and utterly impersonal. She thought about his designer suits, and how she'd never seen his hair mussed or out of place, like he'd stepped out of the pages of a men's style magazine—or an ad for overpriced cologne. She thought about how she'd never discussed *anything* remotely personal with him.

She thought about having to explain her sudden inability to avoid dry-humping her way to orgasm against a shapeshifter's thigh.

Not in this lifetime.

"I'll talk to someone," she promised, mostly because she wasn't ready to tell him who she had in mind. Callum might be the expert when it came to twisting empathy into a weapon, but when it came to sex with dominant shapeshifters...

Well. Any empath who climbed into bed with Alec Jacobson every night knew all there was to know about navigating the rocky path between psychic power and alpha instinct.

Chapter Ten

"Are you sure Alec can't hear this?"

"No, honey." Carmen finished winding her hair up on the top of her head and secured it with a clip. "He's on the phone in his study."

"Good." Fidgeting with the laptop, Kat adjusted it until the camera was just right, then sighed. "I've got empathy sex problems. Really, really fucked-up ones."

The other woman's expression didn't change. "Okay. Is it a control issue?"

That was Carmen—calm and practical, no matter how potentially embarrassing the subject matter. Kat didn't know if the talent was an empath thing or a doctor thing, but it was damn soothing. "It's not control, I don't think. I mean, not uncontrolled projection or anything. I've had slip-ups in the past. My range is wide enough that people would be affected. And they're not."

"So it's more...focused on one person?"

Too late, Kat realized Carmen might have no idea who they were talking about. "It's not Miguel," she said quickly. "Andrew. It's—I promise, I would not call and ask you for advice about sex with your brother."

The other woman laughed. "I know. Alec told me he talked to Andrew, I just didn't want to assume anything."

"It's Andrew," Kat repeated. "And it's...I don't know. I worried about imprinting, at first...but it's not just me. And it's not projecting, but he feels everything I do. And it gets out of control. Fast."

Carmen barely hesitated before asking, "Did you build your shields around him?"

"Of course not." The answer came automatically, with so little thought that Kat forced herself to pause. She'd tried to hold shields around other people, to block them from her gift, but to bring someone *inside* her personal shields would be too intimate, like letting them inside her skin.

Déjà vu. A knot formed in her gut until she remembered why. *It's like you're inside my skin.* Wasn't that what she'd told Andrew, that night in his bed? Nerves twisted as she tried to deny it, to find a reason she hadn't been so stupid and reckless. "How would you even do that? Callum taught me entirely new shielding techniques, and I've barely seen Andrew since then."

"Obviously, you didn't do it during your work with Callum. But, since then, have you been in any situations where you might have unwittingly rebuilt your shields around Andrew?"

The past week played itself out in her memory, a jumble of emotional highs and devastating lows. She'd lowered her shields a dozen times—she did that constantly. But to rebuild them completely, so fundamentally that even the foundations could have shifted to bring Andrew inside—

Oh, shit. "The burnout."

Carmen leaned forward and propped her elbows on the polished wood of the desk. "That sounds like the sort of terrifying scenario where you might have done it instinctively."

Terrifying instinct. Perfect. Almost as undesirable as having to tell Carmen the whole truth. "I might have gotten shot a little bit. Things were...complicated in the aftermath."

"You might have..." The woman trailed off, stared for a moment and then returned in full doctor mode. "Have you been checked out? Where were you hit?"

"Hold on." Kat eased her chair back from the desk she'd claimed in one of the unused offices. Her T-shirt sleeve pulled up easily, and she twisted to show Carmen the mostly faded scar. "A healer took care of it. Well, one who's a doctor and a healing priestess. She said it wasn't bad."

Carmen peered at the screen and nodded, mollified. "Looks like a graze. Whoever treated it did good work."

Settling into her seat again, Kat straightened the laptop and met Carmen's gaze. "Alec doesn't necessarily need to know. Andrew said there's a lot of shit going down up there, and I'm plenty safe with him and Julio lurking around, waiting to eat assassins."

"Are you talking to me as a medical professional or as a friend?"

A loophole, one that would keep Alec and his overprotective instincts in the dark. Kat stomped on temptation. "As a friend. If you think he needs to know, tell him. But we're handling this. *I'm* handling this. It's my mess, and I don't want to get shuffled aside while everyone else cleans it up."

"I get that." Carmen tilted her head. "Call me back if the shield thing doesn't work. I think that's the answer, but there are a few other possibilities."

"Is it..." Kat picked her words carefully. "Is that something people do? Bring other people inside their shields? Isn't it dangerous?"

"It takes trust," Carmen answered slowly. "Absolute, unending trust. It's not inherently dangerous, not usually, but you're not a typical empath, Kat. You might be a special case."

So Callum had told her. He'd beaten it into her with every lesson, stressing the responsibility that came with their power with a straight-faced seriousness that dared her to turn it into a joke.

She'd never dared. "I haven't hurt him yet. But things escalate so quickly, and not just when we want them to. And the more intense we get—"

"I know." Carmen spoke with the voice of experience, something confirmed by the hint of color that rose in her cheeks.

Oh God. The last thing Kat wanted to visualize was Alec's sex life, but it was impossible to stop. At a lower level, the feedback she shared with Andrew would be useful for all *sorts* of boundary-pushing sexual adventures. Hadn't she used the same trick to find out what Andrew needed? How easy would it be to test the lines between dominance and submission, or pleasure and pain, with feedback as a perfect, unfailing guide?

Her cheeks must be redder than Carmen's—the downside to having awkward conversations by videoconference instead of telephone. "Okay. Well...it's not working for me. Just in case, could you explain how to make sure I keep him outside my shields when I rebuild them?"

"Yeah, I can do that." The older woman cleared her throat and began to explain.

The tips of Kat's ears were red when she came out of the office, and Andrew wasn't sure he wanted to know. "Have a nice chat with Carmen?"

"Educational." She flopped onto the couch, legs sprawled haphazardly, and covered her face with her hands. "I'm an idiot. I spent all this time worrying about imprinting and weird psychic phenomenon. I missed the stupid truth because I didn't want to admit it."

He set his book aside and pulled her hands away from her face. "What truth is that?"

Instead of looking at him, she stared up at the ceiling. "It's what I always do. I cling to you. I've been doing it since I met you, and now it's just...habit."

"If you've been doing it for that long, how is it just now throwing us off?"

"Carmen thinks I rebuilt my shields around you. And it didn't make sense, until I thought..." The words trailed off. Tension tightened her eyes and kicked up her heart rate. "I know when the first time was. I should have realized, because it's the one thing in my life I can't forget."

The night of his attack. It had occurred to him before, to wonder what protected him from Kat's lethal projection when the strike team members had fallen victim to it. He'd thought at first that it had been his own injuries, the fact that he'd been mostly unconscious anyway. Only after spending time with Carmen and Julio had another possibility emerged. "That's how you kept me safe."

"I don't think I was thinking about it that clearly. I wanted you shielded. And after—" A hitched breath. "My shields were wiped out by the burnout in Mobile. And when we were being chased? I—I thought about that night. I used the pain, and protected you from it. That's probably why it got worse after that. I rebuilt my shields on the drive back, and I was clinging to you pretty hard."

"So it wasn't imprinting after all." Andrew pulled her into his arms. "And now you need to put me outside of your shields."

"Yes." She rubbed her cheek against his shoulder, and an echo of her pleasure hit him, sweet and soft but still hungry enough to stir his body.

He shifted her until she was stretched out beside him on the sofa. "How do you do that?"

"Drop my shields and then rebuild them. Carefully." She tilted her head to peer up at him. "And make sure I keep you on the other side."

She'd been so worried about the effect her empathy had on him and their time together that Andrew felt only sheer relief. "It'll be better for you, and I'm all for that."

"I know." Her sudden smile was shy. "I think I can do it now. It might take a few minutes..."

"Take all the time you need." He wasn't going anywhere, not until she told him she needed him to go.

With a nod, she closed her eyes. Her breathing evened, then slowed. A tiny furrow appeared between her eyebrows, the only external sign of effort until she caught her lower lip between her teeth.

The world went silent.

He hadn't noticed it until it ceased, the soft murmur of something that must have been Kat's aura, comforting and ever-present. He missed it immediately, though he would have died before letting her know that.

"Did it work?" Kat asked a moment later. "I'm thinking a really dirty thought. The kind of dirty that'd make yesterday look tame."

It still turned him on like burning—that she was fantasizing about him—but the echo had vanished. "Pretty sure it worked, yeah."

She reached for him, twining their fingers together. "So. No emotional craziness. No assassins shooting at me. Just...you and me. On a couch."

"The true test," he murmured. *Mundane* didn't scare him, especially not when there was nothing normal or usual about it.

Kat took a breath. Took another. Her fingers tightened around his hand. "This is like starting over. Except not, because there's so many things we haven't talked about."

He'd put himself and their relationship in the same category as the rest of the problems plaguing Kat. She'd get around to him when she dealt with other stuff—and he'd be ready. "No rush. Get through the rest of this shit first. For now, we can just...be."

She shifted her weight, curling into his side with her feet tucked under her. "What are you reading?"

He showed her the cover. "The last thing my mom published before she died. I've never read it." But helping Kat search for information about her mother had prompted him to pick it up.

"I've read it." Her fingertip traced the edge of the book. "I've read a lot of her stuff. Not just because she's your mother, either. I went through a phase when I was nineteen...read nothing but feminist theory for about six months. Alec hated life."

"I bet he did." It was easy to imagine the sorts of heated debates his mother might have gotten in to with Alec. "I used to think the whole shapeshifter thing was a chauvinistic mess. You know, before. Now I know it's not about gender at all. Derek sure the hell isn't the boss of Nick."

"I always thought Nick was an exception. That Alec treated her like an equal because she was the werewolf princess. Because her dad's the Alpha." Kat slid her fingers off the edge of the book to twine with his. "But now I've seen him around Zola, and you're right. It's not gender. It's power. He treats Miguel and Sera the same, because they're both weaker than he is."

His mother, who had dedicated her life to studying power differentials in all their forms, would have been fascinated— once she understood. "It seems complicated until you're in it, I think."

"Because there's shapeshifter power and family power and emotional power..." Amusement laced her voice. "Sexual power. It's like the most complicated dance in the world, and no one teaches you the steps until you're getting your toes stomped on."

"Or you're the one doing the stomping."

Kat settled her cheek against his shoulder. "I think we step on each other's feet a lot."

"Doesn't matter, though." He stroked her hair and smiled. Her proximity had always excited him, but now it soothed him, as well. "We're figuring it out as we go."

"We are." The tension seemed to be leaving her, drifting away as her body relaxed more fully against his. Attraction was there, and the barest hint of arousal, but she seemed content cuddled against his side, almost as if she was savoring the physical contact. Even her fingers made slow circles over his, tracing his knuckles and up to his wrist before meandering down again.

A quiet moment, the sort of thing most people would take for granted. But not Kat, who was obviously starved for the simplest of contact.

He could give her that. It couldn't last forever, not with the shadow of whatever they'd uncovered on that zip drive looming over them, but for now...

Yes, he could give her that.

Chapter Eleven

Three days of peace shattered with the rumble of a motorcycle engine.

The warehouse's downstairs kitchen was close enough to the main entrance that Andrew heard not only the engine, but the dull thump of boot soles on the pavement outside. He didn't drop his dishtowel until the side door rattled and the bell buzzed.

Kat glanced up, peering at him over the top of the laptop she'd opened on the island. "Are you expecting someone?"

"Not particularly, but sometimes people show up." He waved her back, walked to the door and opened it.

The man on the other side looked like trouble, from his scuffed boots to his sunglasses. His leather jacket was unzipped just enough to reveal a shoulder rig, and tattoos climbing down the sides of his neck and disappearing beneath a black T-shirt. He had a duffel bag over one shoulder and a grin that outdid Alec at his most arrogant.

He also had an aura of magic that felt like nothing Andrew had ever encountered before.

When he spoke, it was in the flat cadence of TV newscasters, though a hint of southern drawl lurked around the edges. "You must be Andrew Callaghan. I'm looking for Kat. My brother sent me."

Ben's brother, the one who liked to play with swords. "Patrick, I guess?"

"Patrick McNamara," he confirmed, holding out his free hand. "Nice to meet you."

"You too. Come in."

As the newcomer stepped into the warehouse, Kat appeared in the kitchen doorway. Her eyes lit up, and she took two excited steps forward before jerking to a halt. "Oh shit. How bad *is* it?"

Patrick McNamara looked like trouble—or like the kind of guy you'd send in to deal with trouble. Andrew laid a hand on Kat's shoulder. "Maybe we should all go sit in the kitchen and talk."

Kat didn't move, but her shoulder was tense under his fingers. "How bad is it?" she asked again.

"Bad, Kat." The man nodded to Andrew and lifted his bag higher. "I've got the printouts in here. Ben didn't want to take the chance they'd get intercepted."

Andrew hesitated. "Want to lay them out on the counter, Kat? We can look at them together, or you can have some time."

She drew in a steadying breath before shaking her head. "If it's big enough for Patrick to drive over here personally, it's not just about my family."

Despite the truth of the words, no one else had quite so personal a stake in the information contained in those printouts. "Did Ben give you a rundown before you left?"

"The basics." Patrick followed them across the open entryway to the kitchen tucked in the front corner of the warehouse. "I read through the highlights. There's a lot of information here, and it's a crazy kind of scary."

Kat cleared her laptop out of the way so he could start pulling out files. "Information about..."

"Psychics." The folder he pulled out looked like the one Ben had given them with fake identification. "Kids, mostly, or people who were kids ten years ago. Whoever drew up these files was looking to build an army of psychics and planned on using them to break the world wide open."

Andrew took the proffered folder, thick with pages, and flipped it open. As soon as his eyes focused on the list of names on the cover sheet, he understood why Patrick had given it to him instead of Kat.

Psychics of Interest. A list, and lengthy enough to be exhaustive. He recognized too many of them—ones he'd heard in passing, and even people he knew. Members of their community.

Not to mention the woman Kat's mother had trusted with her daughter's life. "Peace Kristoffersen had a power called psychic obscuration. That's what she was talking about, why Alyson gave her the key. The cult literally *couldn't* find her."

He flipped the pages, and his blood ran cold. There were other lists—*To Watch* and *Eliminate.* Callum, Kat's mentor, was on that one, along with a few others Andrew didn't recognize.

The last section wasn't a list but a collection of dossiers complete with pictures and a header on every page that left his hands shaking.

Of Particular Interest.

A much-younger Kat smiled up at him from one page. It detailed her strengths and weaknesses, as well as her most appropriate uses—*morale and personnel control.* "Jesus Christ," he whispered.

Kat was oblivious, her attention on another set of papers. "This is what she meant." Her voice held an edge of horror. "Turning me into a weapon."

Andrew shuffled the remaining papers. "There must be three dozen dossiers here."

She caught his hand and pushed one paper toward him. "It's not recruitment, Andrew. It's enslavement."

Patrick cleared his throat as Andrew stared down at neat specifications for a collar and an accompanying charm. "It's a prototype, and according to the notes, they made one. Slap the collar on a psychic, and anyone with a whiff of psychic power can control them. Use their powers, do whatever they want."

None of the information on the lists was groundbreaking. Even if Kat's mother had taken it all, it would be easy to reconstruct, something the cult could have done ten times over in the years since her death. "That must be it, then. She must have taken it, and they have reason to think she wouldn't have destroyed it." He frowned at the schematics. "So why didn't they build another one?"

"That's just the user manual," Patrick said quietly. "The wizard who built it died around the same time this disk was made. His house was razed. Ben's pretty sure it's the last thing Kat's mother did before they killed her."

"So this is their only shot." If it wasn't so damned dangerous, if Kat hadn't been *shot* already, Andrew would have laughed. "All their eggs in this tiny basket."

"They could be looking for another witch or wizard," Kat pointed out. "They could be trying to make another one. But I think, if they'd managed? They wouldn't be risking this much. Chasing me around has the potential to drag the Southeast council into this. And hell, Derek and Nick and Nick's dad."

"The whole Conclave would get involved in something like this," he corrected. "Though they obviously meant to intercept the drive before you had a chance to decrypt any of these files, the fact that they didn't has upped the ante. You could leverage this stuff into a *lot* of help."

"There's something that's not in the files." Patrick leaned back, draping his arms across his chest. "Ben didn't print it out. Made me memorize it. GPS coordinates, and we're pretty sure it's where the collar ended up."

Andrew pulled his phone from his pocket. "Did you run them?"

"Nope. Didn't want a record left if something happened to me."

Patrick rattled off the number for Andrew to enter as Kat opened the third folder, her eyebrows coming together. "They were outlining missions. Not vague goals either. This one uses

Ben to obtain additional sources of funding by shaving interest off of thousands of corporate accounts." She flipped a page. "These are detailed. Insanely detailed."

"And useless without the collar." The GPS search program on his phone returned the results. "It looks like a spot out in the middle of Terrebonne Parish, south of Houma. The back end of the bayou."

Kat snapped the folder shut and pushed it away from her. "So we go find it," she said quietly. "We go find it, then we fly to Wyoming and let Michelle Peyton use her badass Seer magic to erase it from existence."

It sounded simple, easy. "We have to plan on being followed, one way or another, which means we plan for a fight."

"Which means we bring Julio." Kat glanced up at him. "And Anna. I don't think we should waste time calling people back from all over the country. We should go as soon as we can round everyone up."

Which left out most everyone she hadn't already named. "And Miguel," Andrew noted. "This is his fight too, whether he knows it or not."

"What about that wizard you work for?" Patrick asked. "Jackson Holt, right? Isn't he still in town?"

"He's out west, helping his wife track down a relative." The words were absent, most of Kat's attention fixed on Andrew. "Are you sure about Miguel?" she asked, almost tentatively. "It won't be complicated?"

It would be hell, especially if shit went down and they ended up in a fight where Miguel's instincts might very well lead him to try to protect Kat. "I won't love it," Andrew admitted, "but we can't afford to leave valuable people out of the loop because they make us cranky. It won't be a problem." *Nothing I can't control, anyway.*

Kat nodded and turned to Patrick. "And I guess that's why you're here."

"I've chased down a rogue psychic or two in my day," he

agreed. "We better assume they know they'll be facing shapeshifters, though. The question is if they'll underestimate your friend Andrew, here."

"Most people do." He was a new wolf, barely a year made. A mongrel mistake. "Not as many do it twice."

Patrick lifted his bag. "Well let's not give them a second chance."

The bayou was just remote enough to be creepy without being remote enough for a supernatural showdown, which was the perfect recipe for a nerve-wracking clusterfuck.

And Kat couldn't get her bangs to stay out of her eyes.

In lieu of calling off the vital mission until she could get a grown-up haircut, Kat settled on unfashionable but practical pigtails. Fussing with her hair as they waited for the others to arrive didn't seem very heroic, but at least it put her somewhere between her two companions on the fidgety scale.

Andrew was calm and unwavering as he leaned against the bumper of his SUV, his arms crossed over his chest. Julio, on the other hand, was taking advantage of the fact that half the outside lights were out at the tiny bait shop off Little Caillou Road, and pacing broodingly in the shadows.

Finally, he scraped his boot into the dirt and sighed. "I don't like the skulking. I think that's the part that gets me."

"Being sneaky," Kat corrected, the words muffled by the ponytail holder held between her teeth. She finished gathering the rest of her hair and tied it off into a second pigtail just high enough to keep her vision unimpeded. "Shapeshifters should do it more often. Not everything has to be a full frontal assault."

"If this freaky-ass cult had mounted that sort of attack, we wouldn't be hanging around in the dark. And the *cold*, damn it." He shoved his hands in his jacket pockets. "We'd be done and out for beers already."

Kat turned to pick up her gun and glanced at Andrew. "Is that what we're doing after we save the world from psychics? Getting beer?"

"Sure." He was looking off down the dark highway, and the drone of a car engine materialized. "That's what we always do after we save the world."

They were night and day. Julio edgy and intense, Andrew utterly motionless. She remembered the jittery moments after she'd been shot, when color had faded from them world around him. "Are you all right?"

He smiled suddenly, and she knew he was trying to reassure her. "I'll be better if I don't have to get naked in the bayou tonight. Julio's right. It's cold as balls out here."

Nothing sexy about nakedness when it was a prelude to a fight. "I've never seen you as a wolf, you know."

"No." He straightened from the bumper as the noise of the engine drew closer. "No, you haven't."

He hadn't even paused to consider. Just *no*, and now she wondered if it was deliberate. If he was hiding that part of himself from her.

Tonight, if things went badly, he might not be able to hide. Kat checked her handgun carefully, deciding in the end to leave the safety engaged. "Anna's car?" she asked. "Or is that Patrick? I can't really tell cars from motorcycles."

"It's both," Julio answered as headlights came into view over a small rise. "Anna's little sportster and one mammoth bike, from the sound of it."

Sera was safely ensconced at Dixie John's for the late shift, and Anna had left from there with Miguel in tow. Three shapeshifters, one telepathic shapeshifter, an empath and a bounty hunter whose tattoos held more magic than anything the Ink Shrink had ever created. Ben had hinted once that his brother's ability to compete with shapeshifters was due to some sort of mystical exchange, a boon paid for in blood and ink, but the one time Kat had pressed for details, Ben had become evasive to the point of avoidance.

Not that it mattered *why* the tattoos worked. Patrick held his own against monsters every day. Andrew and Julio were council members. Anna had been trained in combat by the Conclave. Kat and Miguel had psychic power to burn between them, and gifts that lent themselves well to offensive attacks. The gun clutched in her hands might make her feel secure, but it was nothing compared to the power of her mind. Whatever waited for them in the frigid night, they were equal to it.

If she repeated their qualifications enough times, maybe she'd even believe it.

Swallowing, Kat slipped her hand into her pocket and pulled out her phone. She'd copied the GPS location from Andrew, because someone who wasn't going to end up on four paws needed to have it. "I did a quick sweep a few minutes ago to check for followers, but Miguel can do one too, when he gets here. He's got a wider receptive range than I have."

A silver car slowed—barely—and whipped into the gravel lot, kicking up dust. It had barely stopped before Anna shut off the engine and climbed out. "Someone tell me this guy on the bike is with us."

Kat bit her lip to hold back an entirely inappropriate laugh. "Yes."

Patrick made a less showy entrance. He parked, dragged off his helmet and smoothed down his dark hair. "You drive like a maniac, lady." It sounded like a compliment.

Anna rolled her eyes and started to turn toward him. "Yeah, I drive the way I..." The words faded away, and she snapped her mouth shut. "You're lucky I didn't shoot you."

Basic shields didn't block out surges, but Kat wouldn't have needed the tingling shock to recognize attraction that intense. Anna looked discomfited, maybe even pissy, but Patrick just grinned at her and swung his leg over his bike. "Anna Lenoir. You screwed me out of three grand last year. I chased McPherson across seven states before you put him down."

Whatever else, she recovered quickly enough to shrug. "When he showed up in Vegas, that made him mine."

"That's what my client said when he refused to pay up. Don't suppose he cut you a check?"

"No such luck, cupcake." She pounded on the roof of her car. "Out, Mendoza."

Miguel stepped clear of the passenger side door with a sigh. "Want me to listen for company, Kat?"

Kat hesitated, then glanced to Andrew and Julio. Four shapeshifters, and if there was one thing she'd learned from Alec, it was that wolves lived by their hierarchy, whether they wanted to or not. "Who's calling the tactical shots here?"

Andrew squared his shoulders. "Kat, you and Miguel are on lookout. Patrick and Anna too, only more with eyes and ears and less with psychic ability. If there's trouble, it's not the kind we can plan for very well, except that they'll probably bring a shifter or two. So we fight."

"And if we're outnumbered?" Anna asked quietly.

"Then we need to make damn sure that, no matter what else happens, these crazy fuckers don't get what they're after. So someone needs to take responsibility for it, and cut and run if necessary." He looked around. "Any volunteers?"

None of the shifters looked like they wanted to offer to run *away* from the fight. Neither did Patrick. Kat braced her feet and met Andrew's gaze squarely. "I can do it. I'm not that fast, but I don't need to be. If I can get clear of the fight, I can make sure no one can get close enough to matter."

Andrew dug his keys out of his pocket and held them out to her. "You keep whatever we find," he whispered, "and if things are bad out there, you get gone."

"You better follow me," she replied just as quietly. She reached for the keys and caught his hand as well. "I can agree. I can promise. But you shapeshifters don't have the monopoly on blind instinct."

He nodded, with only the barest movement of his head. "Now, where is this thing, anyway?"

Kat pocketed the keychain and retrieved her phone. "A quarter mile northwest of here." She indicated the tree line behind the ramshackle shop. "That way."

They made their way quietly in the darkness, past a dilapidated storage shed and two cars that hadn't run in any of their lifetimes. It grew darker when they entered the trees, and the steady, low drone of the gnats on the swamp faded.

In its place rose another kind of buzz, one that she thought she was imagining at first. The itch started at the base of her neck, then skipped down her spine until goose bumps dotted her arms. "What *is* that?" she whispered.

"Magic," Patrick replied quietly. "Big, scary magic."

"We must be close." Julio looked unusually pale in the scant moonlight.

The backlight on her phone had shut off. Kat used her thumb to activate it again and squinted at the display. "Twenty feet or so? At this point, the buzz is more accurate than the GPS."

Andrew hefted his shovel and spun in a slow circle, finally settling on a direction. Five sure steps later, he stopped. "Here. It's right here."

He began to dig.

Kat slipped her phone into her back pocket, tightened her grip on her gun and stepped close to Miguel. "Have you picked up anything?"

"Nothing," he whispered. "But I don't like it. It's not—not *quiet*, exactly. It's...silent."

"As the grave." Anna began disrobing as she offered the words, kicking off her boots as she tugged her shirt over her head.

Kat half-closed her eyes and cracked her shields, just enough to let her power ease out in a slowly growing circle. She brushed Miguel first, whose excellent shields couldn't hide his unease—or his vague appreciation of Anna's naked form.

Patrick next. Kat pushed past him quickly, uninterested in sharing his far more intense interest. Julio was his usual pool of steady strength, and Andrew was quiet concentration. She flicked past Anna and got a sense of steely determination and the tiniest flicker of satisfaction.

The circle widened. She used Callum's trick of quieting the minds she'd already touched, relegating them to silence by imagining them each packed away in a cardboard box. Her own imagery—not as fancy as Callum's chalices, chains and locks, but it worked.

Beyond her group...nothing. Stillness that spoke of the utter absence of people. She could keep pushing. Test her limits, stretch herself thinner, like warm taffy. Eventually she'd find minds. She could dip into the hearts of every person in ten miles, taste their emotions and know their fears.

Instead she held her power in a tight sphere. Five hundred feet in all directions, and if anything disturbed that quiet, she'd know.

Magic zipped through the air, raising the fine hairs on the back of Kat's neck, and a pale wolf shot off through the trees. Anna, making her own sort of perimeter sweep.

Miguel reached for his shirt, and Julio stopped him. "You might need to use your words, baby brother."

But Miguel only snorted out a laugh. "It's all right, Julio. If I need my words, they'll be there." He dropped the rest of his clothes, knelt and shifted. He was a lean man, tall and almost slender, and his wolf form reflected that.

He ran off, and Andrew struck something with his shovel. The sound rang out, hollow and metallic, and Kat eased closer to Patrick. "Is this what it always feels like? Like someone's about to jump out at you at any second?"

"Sometimes." Patrick had stripped off his leather jacket in spite of the cold, leaving his arms bare of anything but the full tattoo sleeves that ended at his wrists. Each hand held a gun. "These are the good times, though. The bad times are when it doesn't feel like that, and they jump out at you anyway."

"Yeah, speaking of jumping..." Julio arched an eyebrow. "You really want to have a couple of honking guns at the ready? This isn't exactly an unpopulated area."

Patrick grinned and lifted them both. "No one will hear these. Silent and untraceable. You don't want to know what they run on the black market, though. I could have had a beach house in Malibu."

Andrew knelt and uncovered a battered metal container. "Looks like a fire-resistant lockbox." He looked up at Kat and held her gaze. "It's locked, but I can open it, no problem."

Opening it felt risky. So was leaving without being sure they'd gotten what they'd come for. "We should check."

He wrenched open the lid a split second before a howl shredded the night, and an even louder shout reverberated through Kat's mind with an echo that felt like Miguel, smoky and smooth.

"They're here."

It was all the warning they got before emotion exploded five feet behind her. Feral anticipation, determined focus, and a satisfaction that crawled over her as she spun around. Two men stood behind her, one already in motion, lunging past her toward Andrew. The other...

Shock held her in place. She recognized the dark eyes and floppy hair, that half-cocked smile that made him look like he was laughing at a joke he would share in the next breath. Christopher Gilbert. The man who'd taken her to dinner and discussed movies adapted from video games with such enthusiasm that she'd been enjoying herself for the first time in months—until a shapeshifter jumped them on the street and he'd vanished into the night while she'd fought off her attacker with a stun gun.

In the aftermath, Jackson had broken it to her that there

was something fishy about the guy. Bad news, the wizard had called him, but Kat hadn't cared. She'd had Miguel by then, and the newness of their relationship, and little thought to spare for the sort of guy who'd run out on his date while she was being mugged.

Run out—or teleported away.

It took two seconds for the thought to form, and two seconds was already too long in a fight with shapeshifters.

"Kat, down!" Julio surged past her, swinging the shovel, but the man vanished.

Andrew had the other one on the ground, landing blow after blow, but a second later Gilbert reappeared, his boot already en route to Andrew's face. It connected, and Andrew howled as his head snapped back.

They were moving so fast, almost too fast to see. Magic snapped through the air, and at least a half dozen emotional flares burst into existence, staggered in a semicircle in the direction Anna had run. She caught her breath and shouted a warning as she raised her gun again. "More coming in from the road!"

Vicious snarls rose in the night, the snaps and growls of more than one fight. Julio had managed to divest himself of half his clothes, and Andrew recovered enough to punch Gilbert in the side of the knee. The blow connected before he could dematerialize, and his grunt of pain hung in the air after he'd vanished.

The shifter Gilbert had dropped on top of them rolled to his side, then reached for the box. Her gun was a weapon of last resort, but she had a more powerful one at her command. Eerie calm had settled over her, a tribute to Callum's training, she supposed—or Zola's. It seemed easy to touch the shifter's aura, and it didn't take much. A push. A whisper of danger, of the right flavor of fear, and instinct had the man scrambling blindly to his feet, poised to face a threat that wasn't there.

Which made him an easy target for Patrick, who proved his

guns were silent by slamming a bullet between the man's eyes.

The fights in the forest drew closer—Anna and Miguel, undoubtedly pushing the interlopers closer to them. Closing the fight to a workable distance.

Kat sensed Miguel before he tumbled out of the trees in a tangle of fur and limbs. He landed hard, rolled again and sank his teeth savagely into the other wolf's throat. His opponent thrashed and fell still as Miguel reared back with a snarl.

Another flash of emotion coalesced before her, and Gilbert reached for her only to be knocked aside by a flying form. Anna, who must have startled him, because she bore him to the ground and snapped her teeth shut on his arm before he disappeared.

Julio hit the ground on four paws as Andrew rose, cold rage spilling from him. He barely moved, just stood, his hands clenched into fists and his head cocked as if listening for something.

Kat concentrated on the people around them. Pain flickered from the dead and dying, but none of the gravely injured were their own. The interlopers were mostly fear and nerves now, with one pulsing light of rage barreling toward them from the direction of the road.

"One coming in behind you," she told Andrew, surprised at how steady her voice sounded. How cold. "And he's mad."

"Good," he growled. "So am I."

The man broke free of the trees, and Kat got the second shock of the evening. If she hadn't seen Gilbert, the features would have been naggingly familiar, the sort of echo that might keep her up at night wondering where she'd met him before. But there was no mistaking him here, now, as the anger inside him twisted up his face when he caught sight of her.

He'd attacked her before, smashed her head into a car before she'd rammed her stun gun into his side and left him unconscious on the side of the road with a self-reliance that had given her back a bit of her own pride.

Clearly he hadn't forgotten. Neither had Andrew, who scooped up the shovel and launched himself past the fray with a roar.

The man dodged his first swing and grabbed the shovel, snapping off the business end with a vicious jerk. Undaunted, Andrew swung the handle up and slammed the shifter across the side of the head.

A soft *pop* and a laugh had Kat spinning again, her gun swinging up. Gilbert grinned at her. "Try to pull the trigger before I disappear again. How many shots will you get out here before someone calls the cops?"

Out of the corner of her eye, she saw Patrick spin and lift his arm. His weapons were silent, but the movement of her eyes must have been enough warning. Gilbert disappeared again, and the bullet dug into a tree a few feet past where he'd been standing.

Another growl jerked her attention back to Andrew, who dropped his opponent with one last blow. The remains of the shovel handle disintegrated in his grip, and he tossed the shards aside and bent low. "Get up. No cage to save your ass now, so you get up and *fight me.*"

A snarl. The shifter twisted his head, gaze sliding over the small clearing. All of his allies were down. Anna, Miguel and Julio stood as wolves, tensed and ready. Patrick had his feet braced on either side of the unearthed box and both guns up.

No rescue, not unless Gilbert popped in and out again. Sudden desperation spiked through Kat hard enough to force a gasp from her lips, leaving her breathless. "Andrew, look—"

The shifter lunged upwards. Not at Andrew.

At her.

He didn't make it off the grass. Andrew hit him, over and over, until Julio—who had regained his human form and gotten half-dressed at some point—stilled his arm.

Before Kat could draw another breath, magic popped and an arm materialized around her throat.

Everyone froze.

Gilbert's hoarse command stirred her hair. Stirred her rage. "Nice and easy, guys. Hand it over, no tricks, or I'll disappear with her."

He'd disappear with her either way. She'd seen her own face in those files, had read every nauseating word over Patrick's protests. They'd slap the collar around her throat and aim her at the nearest opposition. She could start riots, burn out minds, force pain and rage and fear on anyone they needed subdued.

She could kill, which was what Gilbert never should have forgotten. Everyone else was dead, everyone who wasn't one of *hers*. And she knew what she was doing this time, thanks to Carmen's careful explanation. She brought them all into her shields effortlessly, too easily, so easily it was dangerous, and she didn't care. She gathered them to her like picking up stones from the beach, even Miguel, who could have fought but didn't.

She clutched them to her. Anna, who was so tough but so brittle, like she might shatter if you hit her in the wrong spot. Patrick, whose confidence defied arrogance—he had nothing to prove, except he *wanted* to prove everything when he looked at Anna. Julio and his sturdy strength, like a deeply rooted tree, unshakable, and Miguel who trembled with the need to fight-kill-rip-tear.

Andrew. She pulled him the closest, cradled him against her and ached at his weariness, at his fear, and yet even tired and scared, Andrew was the one who burned the brightest, with a rage that could break open and devour the man who held her.

They were all imperfect, and beautiful and, for one shining moment, Kat loved them all.

Then she let go, crashing into Gilbert's mind with all the rage inside her, fed by the helpless fury of the minds wrapped safely within her own.

He didn't make a sound. He didn't release her either, not quite, just *shook*, a fine tremor that bloomed into violent trembling as he dragged in one shaky breath after another. His pain echoed through her, terror so blinding she felt like the cruelest kind of sadist when satisfaction twisted in her gut.

Not enough to make her stop. Not until Gilbert fell, his body jerking in fits and starts, his eyes wide open and unseeing. Only then did she ease back, letting the power drift away like smoke after snuffing a candle.

Kat couldn't look at Andrew. She didn't want to look at *anyone*. Gilbert twitched helplessly on the ground, a husk of a body with a mind that would never be whole again. Dead, except for the technicalities. "Patrick, could I use your gun? Mine's too loud."

Silence, until Andrew rasped, "Give her the gun or do it yourself, McNamara."

Patrick moved toward her. Wary, slow, his eyes filled with worry and, almost worse, a quiet assessment. Alec had done that endlessly in the first days after she'd shredded through Andrew's attackers. Watched her the same way he'd watched Julio upon his arrival, studying him for strengths and weaknesses, quantifying his usefulness—and his danger.

Living through it once had been enough. Kat quietly slipped the others free of her shields and retreated into herself until she'd have time to rebuild them properly. Then she held out a hand.

"Kat..." Patrick almost sounded pained. "You don't have to—"

"I already did." She kept her hand out until Patrick reluctantly handed over one of his guns. Letting him finish what she'd started wouldn't wash the blood from her hands. Nothing would.

No, this she deserved to feel. Every gut-wrenching moment of it, a suitable punishment—and a necessary reminder.

So she took careful aim and ended Gilbert's suffering with a bullet between the eyes.

The gun didn't make a sound. Neither did Gilbert's head,

really, or if it did, she couldn't hear it over the pounding in her ears. It seemed wrong, somehow, like a human life shouldn't be that easily extinguished. It should be louder. More horrifying.

God, it was quiet. So quiet that Kat wanted to hug Anna when she spoke, if only for breaking the silence. "I know a guy, a cleaner. I can call him."

"The party might not be over," Miguel interjected. "There was someone else in the woods. A lookout, I guess. Definitely not really there."

Andrew sighed wearily. "Astral projection?"

"That'd be my guess."

"Then we need to get gone." He rose to his full height. "Kat and I will take the collar and head back. Can the rest of you stay until Anna's guy shows up to take care of the mess?"

No one protested. Patrick took his gun back with a shallow smile and tucked it into its holster, then turned to say something to Anna, as if the matter was already settled. Maybe they all had faith that she and Andrew could handle any threat.

Maybe none of them wanted to climb into a car with her.

Kat pushed the thought away and moved to retrieve the box. With the metal lid torn, it was easy to open, to lift the collar and charm and clutch them in her numb fingers. Adrenaline had faded, leaving the night chilly for a shapeshifter and damn near freezing for her. "I'm ready to go," she told Andrew, unwilling to lift her gaze higher than his chin.

He didn't speak. Instead, he picked her up and walked toward the SUV.

It was stupid, and weak, and she let him do it. She let him do it because it gave her the chance to close her eyes and rebuild her mental protections. Andrew was there, his faint relief drowned in worry, but she resisted the urge to build her shields around him. To cling to him as a distraction from her own thoughts.

She wrapped herself in layer after layer of icy steel, until her fortifications were solid. Until her mind was her own.

Not a pretty place to be. Gilbert's last seconds replayed over and over again, the terror in his animal noises, the utter vacancy of his eyes. She knew suffering. She'd felt it a hundred times, a thousand times, all the ways humans could hurt themselves and each other. With all the pain in the world, the last thing she should do was add to it.

But she'd made her choice. Not the first time, either. The last time had been to protect Andrew, and the aftermath felt burned into the back of her eyes in jolting, overlapping memories. Nick driving her away from the city. Jackson trying to talk her down. Andrew's blood had been everywhere, on her dress, in her hair.

Last time, he'd damn near died under her hands. This time he was whole. Strong and unshaken. So she found it painfully amusing that her body reacted in the same way. When Andrew set her down, she barely had time to shove the collar into his hands before she staggered two steps away and threw up everything she'd eaten that day.

At least she hadn't puked on Anna's pretty silver sports car.

Chapter Twelve

He'd almost gotten her killed.

No, that wasn't fair *or* quite right. It wasn't strictly his fault she'd almost been kidnapped, stolen away to serve whatever heinous uses this goddamned cult had dreamed up. Not his fault, but he was responsible.

It probably wasn't what Alec had in mind when he'd told him to step up to the plate.

Andrew kept his attention strictly on the road. He had to make sure they weren't followed, that they had a fighting chance of making it to Michelle before the cult caught up with them. But driving in silence afforded him the advantage of hiding—his fear, worry and, most of all, his self-recrimination. Kat wouldn't have it. She'd chalk it up to guilt and tell him to knock it off.

Maybe someday he would.

The drive back to New Orleans was desolate, a never-ending exchange of one two-lane road after another, followed by interminable stretches of interstate. Through it all, he pushed down worry in favor of focus. There'd never been anything he couldn't do if he tried hard enough, and this was one more thing on the list: *keep Kat safe and destroy the collar*. He could do it because he had to, because the alternatives were unthinkable.

He headed home, toward the building he shared with Julio, the official base of their council operations now. Home was also work, though it still seemed odd to think of it that way.

No wonder he'd let the alpha-bastard shit take over his life.

He drove slowly down the street toward the building, hesitating when he saw a familiar truck. "Are Jackson and Mac back in town?"

"No, they're still in Colo—shit." She sat up straighter and smoothed a nervous hand over her hair. "Alec called Jackson. He must have."

"The question is when." Not that it mattered, and this was a million times better anyway. "You think Jackson can get rid of this thing for us?"

"Maybe." Her smile looked tired and feeble. "After he's done yelling at me for not calling him."

"Yelling at *us*, you mean."

"He might take pity on you, mostly because Mackenzie won't." Kat shot Andrew a look that was almost sympathetic as she reached for the door handle. "Manly shapeshifters who don't ask for help make her cranky."

As it turned out, they both looked cranky. When Andrew and Kat walked in, Jackson met them near the door with his arms crossed over his chest. "You two having a nice night?"

Kat's spine stiffened as a shred of life returned to her otherwise exhausted face. "Swell. I thought you were still out west."

"We were, until we got wind of a crazy party no one bothered to invite us to."

"There wasn't time." Though the truth of the words was undeniable, Andrew couldn't keep the apology from his voice. "God knows, we could have used you out there."

Some of Jackson's anger faded into obvious concern. "What's going on? You may as well tell me."

So Kat did, laying it out without embellishment or emotion, though she seemed willing enough to gloss over the fact that she'd been shot. Throughout the explanation, Mackenzie's gaze kept flicking to Andrew, her face growing increasingly worried with every word.

When Kat finished, Jackson ground his teeth and shook his head. "I don't even have time to yell at you. We need to destroy that stuff *now.*"

"Here?" Mackenzie asked. "Or do you need supplies? Or backup?"

"Have to poke at it to be sure." He took the collar and charm from Kat and turned them over in his hands. "If it has protections, I might need Mariko's help. Together, we could short those out. The likelier scenario is that no one ever bothered with that because they didn't anticipate anyone *wanting* to destroy it." He huffed out a sigh. "We wizards are a damn self-important lot."

"I'll get anyone you need," Andrew whispered. Just so long as it got done.

Mackenzie touched her husband's shoulder. "So go poke at it. We'll be right here, and we'll track down whatever or whoever you need."

He headed off toward the converted—and warded—supply closet in the corner of the warehouse, and Andrew faced Mackenzie with his best grim look. "Hit me with it, Brooks. I can take it."

Mackenzie didn't look away from him. "Kat? You want to go help Jackson?"

She looked like she wanted to flee, but she held her ground. "Andrew?"

There were so many things he needed to say and ask, and no fucking *time.* "It's okay, sweetheart. Mackenzie likes me. She'll probably only mostly kill me."

It made her laugh, even if it was choked and died after a startled moment of sound. "Well, as long as you're only mostly dead... I'll be with Jackson."

When she was gone, Mackenzie raised both eyebrows. "If I were you, I'd have her in the supernatural version of witness protection by now, and I'm not even suffering from testosterone poisoning. Whatever this thing is—" She waved her hand, taking him in from head to foot. "I'm not buying it. What gives?"

"I can't shuffle her off like that without me," he answered as he made his way over to the refrigerator in the corner. "After I get this taken care of, sure. Until then..."

"Wolves." She shook her head. "You never just grab your people and run. You've got to save the world on your way."

"Comes with the territory." He cracked open a soda and snorted. "Literally."

"Jackson's my territory. That's the long and short of it. And Kat..." She trailed off. "Shit, Andrew, there's nothing I can say there that's a damn bit of my business. But Jackson loves her like she's his baby sister, and I've seen how wrecked she's been. Just tell me you know what you're up against."

He'd thought he had a handle on it for the first time since waking up at Alec's, shivering and overloaded on scents and sounds he didn't understand. He and Kat were finally communicating, getting close to figuring out what the hell they were going to do to move beyond it, and now...

Now they could be starting all over again, square one, because Kat had had to do it again—use the empathy she thought of as nothing more than a burden as a lethal weapon.

So he told Mackenzie the truth. "I don't know. I thought so, but I don't *know.*"

Sympathy filled her eyes. "Honestly? She's surrounded by overprotective badasses. I think maybe she's trying to prove she's an adult by turning herself into one, even if it breaks her."

If it were as simple as that, it'd be easy to deal with. "It's not about proving it to other people, Mac. It's about her."

"And what about you?" Mackenzie hopped up onto the counter and crossed her legs, the pose deceptively casual when her energy pulsed with what she was—a cat deciding if she wanted to pounce. "You were an architect when I met you. Now you make Rambo look like a weenie."

"For your information, I was a badass architect. Not that much has changed." A lie, but just a tiny one. "Guns and fighting, that's all. I probably needed to learn it anyway."

"Uh-huh. And I saw what you did with it." She gestured, taking in the building around them. "You're doing good, you know. When I found out what I was, Jackson had to explain the shapeshifter world to me. And it scared me worse than knowing there was a crazy Seer out to get me, because it was pretty damn hopeless. You're changing that. Maybe not for cougars and lions and coyotes...but it's a start."

She was saying the sorts of things that always made him uncomfortable, and Andrew fought not to fidget. "I'm doing what Alec asked me to do. It's not exactly heroic."

"Tell that to the people who have new clinics in their cities. Alec can only get his work done because no one dares screw with him while you're watching his back."

"Maybe, but all that makes me is good backup." Which was just fine with him.

"Tell me again why Kat's not in a bomb shelter somewhere?"

"Because I'm not letting her out of my sight. Try to keep up, Mac."

She flipped him her middle finger with a cheerful grin. "Why aren't *both* of you in a bomb shelter somewhere, smartass?"

No matter what, it kept circling around to that question, and you either got the answer or you didn't. Until the night he'd almost died, he hadn't. Now, he couldn't imagine blowing off the responsibility, even if it meant sacrificing his own wants. He wasn't the first, and he hoped he wouldn't be the last.

The crowd at Mahalia's was typical for a Wednesday night. Led Zeppelin spilled out of the jukebox, almost drowning out the drone of chatter and the clack of pool balls. Andrew scanned the room and spotted Julio and Anna by one of the pool tables. "Over there," he said, low in Kat's ear.

She pivoted, then relaxed when she saw Sera bending over the pool table to line up a shot while Miguel watched. "Everyone's here," she said, so relieved that she might as well have said, *Everyone's safe.*

He laid his hand on the small of her back. "Let's go give them the heads-up."

Sera completely missed her shot as they approached, sending the cue ball sailing past everything else on the table to slide neatly into a corner pocket. She straightened with a sigh that turned into Kat's name. "I thought you guys were never going to get here."

Kat jerked her head toward the bar, where Mackenzie had stopped to talk with the manager. "Jackson was doing his thing."

"Took a while, but we got it done." Jackson accepted the beers Anna offered and passed one to Mackenzie.

Kat shook her head when offered a beer and glanced at Julio. "Is Patrick in the back? We should probably talk."

"He's in the office," Anna said, already heading toward the hall.

It was eerily quiet in the converted stock room behind the office. Magical soundproofing kept all the noise of the bar out, and would ensure the details of their conversation remained private.

Julio, for one, didn't wait to start that conversation. "The thing's dead, right? The collar?"

"As a doornail." Kat leaned against the door, looking like she'd rather be out at the pool table with Miguel and Sera. Fractures had begun to appear in her icy calm almost as soon as Jackson laid the inert metal on his workbench, declaring it well and truly destroyed.

On the other side of the room, Patrick snapped his phone shut. "I put the word out on this cult as soon as Ben gave me the name, and he's starting to get some intel back. Might as well find their nest and burn them out once and for all, right?"

"That's it, then." Anna hopped up to sit on the table along the wall. "We stay on our guard, just in case, and finish them off."

"That's it," Jackson agreed.

Andrew stepped to the middle of the room. "I'll call Alec in the morning. The cult members brought wolves with them, which means the Conclave might want their pound of flesh."

"They can have it." Kat closed her eyes. "The worst part is over, though. They can't build their little psychic army any time soon."

"Calls for a celebration, right?" Jackson drained half his beer and wrapped his arm around Mackenzie. "Keep your eyes peeled. If anything happens, raise the alarm."

Julio filed out after them, and Anna followed suit. Patrick paused to squeeze Kat's shoulder. "Chin up, Katherine. You did good."

"Thanks, Patrick." To someone who didn't know her, the smile might have looked real. Patrick seemed to buy it, and he nodded to Andrew before slipping out of the room.

As soon as the door closed behind him, Kat tried to pull Andrew's mouth down to hers. He stayed rigid and wrapped his hands around her wrists. "Not so fast, sweetheart. We need to talk."

"You could have died out there. I could have died out there." Her fingernails scraped against his neck. "I didn't kiss you last time, and I regretted it for a year."

"Kiss me all you want. *After* I make sure you're not still spinning."

"I'm always spinning, Andrew. I don't know how to stop." She tugged against his grip, trying to slide her hands toward the back of his neck. "You could make me stop. I wouldn't be able to spin if you had control."

Responsibility was one thing, but she was talking about the kind of control he'd never wanted. "That's never been my thing. I didn't know it was yours."

She laughed shakily as her eyes fluttered shut. "You're my thing. Wanting you is the only thing in my life that hasn't changed."

The cracks in her composure grew with every breath, and Andrew eased her away. "Kat, it's been a shitty night. Just...sleep on it, and we'll talk tomorrow."

"No." She took a step back, just one, then braced her feet. "I can't do this anymore. I can't heal a little and then rip off more of the scab. I can't live with all this shit hanging over my head."

The words sliced at him. "I'm sorry about what happened tonight. I'm sorry you had to do it again."

"Not tonight," she grated out. "Fourteen months ago. You're a wolf because I lost control. Because I was scared, and I panicked, and I made those bastards attacking us panic."

"No." The denial escaped without thought, but with more than a little panic. "You did what you had to do."

"Later. Later, I did what I had to do." Her fingers curled toward her palms. "At first, I was weak and scared and out of control. I screwed up. And if you won't be *mad* at me for it, we're never going to be anything but two people who lie about the worst day of their life."

He couldn't hear what she was saying. She had to stop and, for a heart-stopping second, he wanted to scream at her. So he shut it down and answered calmly. "What happened wasn't your fault."

"Stop being a damn coward, Andrew. Be mad at me. Hate me." Her blue eyes were ice as she glared at him. "And if you can't do either of those, just 'fess up and admit that you think I'm a stupid kid who shouldn't be held responsible for anything she does."

His careful, hard-won control didn't snap. It split—right

down the middle, like his heart. Like his *life*. "You want me to be mad? To hate you? Fine, I hate you."

Her face split too. Relief, and pain, and when she spoke, her voice was tight with what could have been rage or tears. "I ruined your life. And then I ruined mine. Some days I don't know which of us I hate more."

"How could you not *know*?" The question had eaten him up inside, and it spilled out now. "Being around Alec and Derek, knowing how close to the edge they get sometimes... How could you not know that flipping your shit on a bunch of wolves was going to make them crazy?"

"I wasn't thinking. He said—" Her jaw clenched. "It doesn't matter. I didn't make a choice. I lost control, and I'm sorry."

His anger faded as suddenly as it had formed, exhausted by her pain, leaving him tired and ashamed. "Are we finished taking care of what you need, Kat? What makes you feel better? Because I feel like ass."

"Why?" Her voice broke. It broke, and she broke with it, shattering before his eyes. "Because I'm not like you and Anna and all the other badasses? Because I can't take it if you treat me like an adult?"

The truth was far simpler—and a hell of a lot more damning. "Because all hating you will do is cost me everything else. Whatever I didn't lose that night." *You.*

She choked on something lost between a laugh and a sob. "We lost each other anyway. And I can't—" She lifted her hands and scrubbed at her eyes. "If this is what I needed, what do *you* need?"

It was impossible, literally. "I need for it not to have happened."

Another helpless laugh. "We're both fucked, I guess."

"Yeah." Anger bubbled up again, this time directed entirely at himself. His own selfishness was yet another thing he hadn't been able to protect Kat from, and he really did hate her a little for making him admit it. "So what now?"

"Now..." She shrugged. "I guess we figure out if we can forgive each other, or we give up. We can't build anything good on hating each other and being afraid to admit it."

They had to be the only people anywhere, ever, who needed to despise each other, and it almost made him want to laugh. "I hate you, Kat," he said again. "But I don't want to, and not nearly as much as I hate myself."

She wet her lips. "Do you hate yourself over me?"

He clenched his hands into helpless fists. "How could I not?"

"It's recursive. That's what I keep thinking. We just... We hurt each other and we hate ourselves, and we hurt ourselves and we hate each other. One of us has to..."

"To what?"

She swallowed, then reached for him, stretching up to frame his face. "It broke my heart when you pushed me away. But I forgive you."

He caught her wrists again, but he didn't pull her away. "Kat..."

"I forgive myself for killing those men, because it was all I could do. And some day, I'm going to forgive myself for not being able to be cold about it."

"Stop." He took a deep breath to ease the tightness in his chest. "I'm going to say it again, and you need to know that I mean it. You did what you had to do. It's easy for me to blame you, but if you hadn't unleashed on that strike team, I'd be dead anyway, and you'd be—" He couldn't say it.

So she did. "He told me he was going to make me watch you die. And if that didn't convince me to give them access to Alec's files, they'd torture me."

No matter what he wished for himself, he could never think she should have allowed that to happen. "You did the *right thing.*"

"But not on purpose." She leaned her forehead against his

chin and sighed. "Tonight I did it on purpose. That's better for everyone else. Worse for me."

He drew her into his arms. "You stopped him from getting the collar."

"I know." Her voice sounded small. "I did what I had to do, so shouldn't it feel like it was worth it? Justified?"

"Some of us aren't cut out for killing, sweetheart. No matter what."

"Still makes me feel weak."

"Because you're not bloodthirsty?"

"Because I want to do what the rest of you are doing. I want to make our world better, and not be the girl who's sitting on the sidelines, or back at the office fixing the computers."

"You haven't been paying attention." He tucked her face against his neck and sat on the edge of the table. "Julio and I have been finishing work on the other lofts over at our building. Carmen and Alec have been organizing clinics. What is it exactly that you want to do?"

"I don't know." She slipped her arms around his waist and sighed. "I finished my PhD...but I can't go back, Andrew. I can't go live in the human world and get a job and be normal. I don't fit there."

"Kicking ass isn't the only way to fit in my world, either."

"I know." Easing back, she finally met his eyes. She looked old and tired and oddly amused. "No one ever really feels like they fit anywhere, anyway. I know that. You'd think it'd make it easier to feel so lost."

"You're not lost, Kat," he whispered. "It's just...a rough spot. If you weren't going to pull through it, you'd know by now. But you are."

A nod. Perched on the table, he wasn't that much taller than her, and she took advantage of it by leaning in to kiss his cheek, lips soft and tentative. "This is it. This is us facing the worst we've been. And I *am* spinning, but that won't stop until I start fighting for what I want instead of obsessing over what I can't change."

He didn't argue. "One step at a time." It was all either of them could ask.

Chapter Thirteen

Dixie John didn't serve breakfast to the public, but he had a habit of opening his doors when enough supernaturals wanted an early meal—especially if Sera smiled hopefully and promised to help out in the kitchen.

Her friend slipped into the back as Kat settled at one of the hastily pushed together tables in the center of the room. No one looked like they'd slept much, except for Patrick, who followed Sera and came back with a pot of coffee. "There's more coming."

Kat accepted the first mug. She needed it, since alcohol combined with a mere four hours of sleep had her blinking groggily at the world. Andrew, Julio and Miguel, on the other hand, mostly looked hungry.

At least Anna didn't seem to be faring much better. Kat pushed the second cup of coffee toward her. "Did you get any sleep at all?"

"Some." She sniffed the brew and took a tentative sip. "Too much whiskey last night."

It would take a lot of whiskey to leave a wolf *that* hung over. Kat's celebration had been tinged with the knowledge that more enemies could be out there. Two beers had seemed like plenty, even spaced across the hours before Andrew drove her home. She didn't think he'd rested any more soundly than she had, but at least they'd been together. Awkward and uncertain, but together, in all their celibate glory.

It was a start.

But an uneasy tension lay heavily in the room, belying the congenial atmosphere, and this time it wasn't just her and Andrew. The others smiled and joked, but beneath the surface a thousand tiny gestures painted a complex and curious picture.

Callum had been the one to insist she pay attention. Empathy had made her lazy when it came to people. Leaky shields and pushy emotions meant she *always* knew what people were feeling. Callum had told her to watch, too, to understand body language. She could almost hear his voice, crisply enunciated and perpetually serious. *Not everyone has a Rosetta Stone for the human soul, Katherine. It's a strength. Use it.*

So she did, watching the people around her as small talk washed over her. Anna had claimed a seat as far away from Patrick as she could get, and Kat would have bet her next paycheck it was deliberate, though she wasn't sure why until she noticed the way Patrick kept trying to catch Anna's eye. On the rare occasions he succeeded, the look Anna shot back was more *fuck you* than *good morning.*

Sera, by contrast, wasn't a mystery at all. She brought out toast and sausage and managed to take everyone's requests without actually looking at Julio once. Her studious disregard had passed casual a few months ago, but Julio remained oblivious to the way Sera avoided him.

He was less oblivious to her ass, which he seemed plenty willing to appreciate, and that was one emotion Kat was heartily glad she wasn't being forced to share.

Next to Julio, Miguel just looked tense. Since his telepathy was every bit as strong as her empathy, she didn't blame him. Kat caught his gaze and lifted her eyebrows, a quiet question they'd asked one another a thousand times. *Too much noise?*

His lips pressed together in a line, an expression that almost managed to look like a smile even though it wasn't. Then he nodded and dropped his gaze to the table.

"Are you headed out of town soon, Patrick?" Andrew asked.

"After I eat, probably." Patrick leaned his elbows on the table, and Kat found herself staring at the way his tattoos moved when his forearms flexed. "Alec called me after he talked to you. The Conclave's moving a little slow in agreeing to officially hire me, but Alec asked me to get started anyway."

Andrew gestured across the table with his mostly empty juice glass. "You should take Anna with you. She was planning on running down a few leads."

"Oh, I don't know about that," Anna interjected. "He works alone. Don't you, Patrick?"

His jaw clenched. "Not always. Two heads can think smarter than one, right?"

"That depends on the heads."

Julio looked up, one eyebrow arched. "Did I miss something?"

"No," Anna said quickly. Then she shrugged. "It's fine. The job's important. We can pool our resources, get it done."

No one disagreed, and the conversation shifted, turned to discussion of plans and tactics. Julio and Andrew had responsibilities in New Orleans—responsibilities she'd already kept them from. Psychics weren't a wolf concern, not when the bulk of the threat had been neutralized. Patrick and Anna chased down crazy supernaturals professionally.

In the hour before dawn, Kat had stared at the ceiling and wondered if resolution was important enough to press the issue. To insist that Patrick let her go with him. But Andrew would follow. Even in sleep, his arm had curled around her, hand splayed possessively across her hip. They'd barely moved past kissing in the days since she'd removed him from her shields, but the physical seemed inconsequential in the quiet moments. When none of the pain mattered, because he looked at her like she was the person who made him glad he was alive.

Andrew would follow her. He'd rip out those places that had been remade with an alpha's need to protect his people, and focus all of that protection on her. He'd neglect duty, neglect himself and everyone in the world, and it might kill the man he'd become.

He would follow her, she knew it in her bones, and that made it worth staying.

Under the table, she reached for his hand and twined her fingers with his, the soft intimacy a thousand times more arousing than the wildest empathy-induced orgasm.

Let Anna and Patrick chase her past. She was chasing her future.

The paper shredder made a very satisfying sound.

Seated on Andrew's couch, Kat watched it turn one page at a time into tiny strips of paper with black spots that seemed entirely innocuous. There were easier ways to destroy files, of course, but she'd made Andrew stop by Jackson's office so she could abscond with the shredder.

It was cathartic, reducing a cult's scheme for world domination into bits of paper spaghetti.

Andrew eyed the growing pile of shredded paper apprehensively. "Are you sure we don't need a copy? Some sort of list...?"

"Ben made me a script." She picked up the page that listed the psychics who needed to be eliminated and stared at Callum's name for a moment. Then she fitted it into the shredder and watched it vanish. "I can use it on the corrupted files I pulled off the zip disk if I ever need to recreate the lists."

"So it's better than encrypted." Andrew nodded. "That's smart."

"Ben's smart," she agreed. Opening the next file revealed a smiling picture of her own face, twelve or thirteen at the most. Ben's color laser printer had recreated the vivid colors of what must have been a surprisingly high-resolution scan a decade ago. Her eyes were so blue. So young. "This is what my mother saw," she whispered, tracing the boundary of the photo. "This is when she lost it."

Andrew stroked a hand over her hair. "She probably had reservations already, but that... Yeah, that would do it."

"This is why she told me about imprinting when I was too young to even understand it." She moved her finger until it passed over the neat list of her uses. Controlling people. The one thing she'd never wanted to do, because she knew in her gut how horrible it could be to have someone else's emotions guiding your choices. "My powers were out of control when I was a teenager. Puberty sucked. It wouldn't have been so hard to break me. Remake me."

"Hey." He turned her face to his with a gentle hand on her chin. "She made sure that didn't happen."

"I know." His eyes were as green as hers were blue. The colors of an oversaturated summer day, endless skies and perfect grass. The file slipped to the floor, and she raised her hand to touch his cheek, to feel his beard under her fingertips. "She protected me, even when she was crazy. Even when she was lost."

"That's right. We destroyed their experiment, and we're going to find the rest of them too. Shut it all down, forever."

They were supposed to be going slowly. Taking a step back from grinding their way to orgasm, or empathy-fueled blowjobs. But his beard scratched her fingers, and every touch seemed so important, now that she was feeling them with her body instead of her mind.

Rubbing her cheek against his palm, she let out a shaky sigh. "I feel like I shouldn't be shy. We've practically had sex already."

He kissed her cheek and spoke, his breath blowing over her skin. "Not like this, we haven't."

If her heart pounded any harder, people would hear it on the street below. "Are we about to have sex?"

"Don't know." His voice deepened. "Do you want to?"

A helpless laugh escaped her. "I've wanted to since about the time I discovered my sex drive. I was a late bloomer."

"Mm-hmm, and there'd be no harm in waiting a little longer, either. It all depends on you, Kat. What you need."

Kat closed her eyes. Breathed in the scent of him. "I want you to be in control this time. Just for a bit, because I've never—" She took another breath and imagined dragging in courage with the oxygen. "All the stuff I said to you in the hotel, about my emotions being hardwired...it's not wrong. It was the wrong reason for what was going on, but it's not wrong. I don't know if I can keep everything together the first time I have sex with someone I love."

His breath hitched, and he dropped one hand to her shoulder. Pulled her closer. "I don't think anyone can." His mouth descended on hers, coaxing and desperate all at once.

It was Andrew, and her, and her empathy was locked down tight enough to survive the psychic version of a nuclear bomb and she still lost the ability to think when his lips parted over hers. Her brain lurched drunkenly between sensations, thrilling at his kiss and reveling in his touch, and then she managed to get herself into his lap, and *that* was the best yet.

He settled her carefully against his erection and broke the kiss to blow out a shaky breath. "Bedroom. If I'm in control, I'm doing it right."

Freedom from responsibility might have its perks. She kissed his jaw, then higher, moving toward his ear. "If you're in control, you have to get us there. I'm busy."

He rose but swayed. "How busy? Because if you're going to do that..."

Kat laughed and hid her face against his neck. "You could set me down and make me walk, you know. I'm not tiny. Not even with Zola chasing me around her dojo ten hours a week."

His hands tightened on her thighs, held her closer. "You're perfect."

There could be no doubts that he meant it, not when the

words caught in his throat and came out so rough they sounded like his beard felt, rasping and scratchy enough to send heat spiraling through her. "I believe you."

He headed toward the bedroom, a low laugh rumbling out of his chest. "You sound surprised."

"Do you really want to talk about cultural pressures and female body image right now?"

"No." He laid her on the bed and straightened, reaching for his shirt. "No, I really don't."

Fabric hit the floor, and Kat decided that Andrew needed to be naked. Constantly, or at least until she burned through every fantasy she could come up with.

Most of them involved her being naked too, so she dug her fingers into the hem of her T-shirt and yanked it up. The bed dipped, and his hands joined hers in guiding the garment over her head.

Shirtless. Shirtless was progress. She ignored his pants and her bra and wrapped her hands around his ridiculously solid biceps so she could tug him back to the mattress with her. "I don't know where to touch first. I want everything."

"We can take our time, hit on everything at least once."

Touching him thrilled her. She spread her fingers wide against his chest, and it felt so good. Just touch, so simple, so laughably mundane. He could bend steel and she could kill with her mind, and she was drunk on the simplest brush of skin against skin.

"No empathy, right?" Andrew asked, his breath stirring the hair at her temple. "You're getting giddy."

"Because it's you." Easing her hand to the side, she savored the feel of him under her fingertips until her thumb found his nipple.

He sucked in a breath and slid his fingers into her hair to cup her head. "It's me."

Kat lifted herself up onto her elbow and pressed a kiss to

his shoulder. "Have you thought about this? What you'd do if you had me in your bed?"

He considered it with too much gravity to be believed. "About every fifth heartbeat or so, I think."

A few inches up, and her mouth hovered over his ear. "If you tell me one of your fantasies, I'll tell you one of mine."

"Do I get points deducted if mine includes costumes?"

"Depends on what kind. No metal bikinis."

"Damn it." He smiled—a joyous expression edged with heat. "Princess Leia's hot."

"Perv." And because joking with him, *laughing* with him, was the hottest thing of all, she closed her teeth on his earlobe and moaned.

Andrew rolled her, pinned her hands and body to the bed. "We have to go slow."

Gentle as he was, the fingers around her wrists were strong and unyielding. She liked the weight of his body, the thrill of being on the receiving end of his focused intensity. "I thought we *were* going slow. For us. We're redefining glacial, here."

"Not quite." He eased his hands down her arms, all the way down her sides. "Trust me. Once we get going, it'll be anything but glacial."

"I was talking speed, not temperature." Her nipples ached enough to make her bra uncomfortable, the wrong kind of friction when she wanted his hands, or his mouth. "You are really hot."

He answered with a hoarse noise of encouragement as he slipped one hand beneath her and unhooked her bra with a quick motion. A practiced move, and relief swelled at the fact that it wasn't her first time, that his confidence and intensity could be sexy instead of blindly intimidating.

Andrew slid the lacy fabric free and tossed it behind him, but when he bent low again, he touched his lips to her collarbone, her shoulder. The middle of her chest.

Too slow. Kat clutched at his short hair and groaned. "I'm not a virgin. We can go slower the second time? Or the fifth?"

His mouth skimmed her breast as he raised his head to meet her eyes. "You're not a virgin," he agreed as his cheeks reddened. "But this isn't—I'm not—"

"A tiny man?" she guessed, trying to keep from smiling. He was stammering. "Andrew, I've seen you with an erection. I didn't faint. I'm pretty sure it will all work out, anatomically speaking."

He didn't share her amusement. "I just don't want to hurt you," he whispered.

That subtly, the power shifted again. Maybe it would always be like that between them, a seesaw of give and take, Andrew's desperate need to minimize the danger to her body against her equally powerful need to protect his mind and heart. They could hurt each other, destroy each other, so easily—so *accidentally*—

They could. But they wouldn't. For the first time, she was sure. Kat lifted her hands and cupped his face. Gave him the power, because right now she had plenty to spare. "Then we'll go as slow as you want to. Until I'm whimpering and begging and ready to kill you for how bad I need you inside me."

His eyes darkened, but he smiled again. "The death threats are sexy." Then he kissed her, slow and deep.

And endless. Not that he couldn't kiss, oh *hell*, could he kiss, but the sheer sensuality of his tongue teasing against hers had her twisting restlessly long before he decided to move on.

To her neck, next, which had her arching her head back in a silent plea that he granted with a soft nip. He must have liked the way she whimpered, because he did it again and again, until her breaths rasped in and out and she wondered if it was possible to go insane from too much physical pleasure.

Then he moved to her ear. Licks. Nips. He kissed her until she whispered his name, then switched to the other side and started all over, working his way down her throat with a concentration that made her consider snatching the power back and taking him.

But he needed this. Needed every moan he coaxed out of her, needed the pleasure that made her skin flushed and sensitive. Needed her to be ready for him, as if she wasn't already aching and wet, embarrassingly aroused and ready to beg in earnest.

She did, when his beard scratched across her breasts, his mouth hot and open on her chest. "Andrew...oh, my *God*, please—" She caught his hair, tried to tug his mouth to her nipple, babbling helpless pleas that she'd have to deny later.

"Please what?" He tugged at the button on her pants.

"Your mouth..." She didn't finish. Not when it might distract him from finally taking off her pants.

"My mouth," he agreed. Then he closed his lips around one nipple and sucked hard as he opened her pants.

It felt so good she spent a terrified moment wondering if her shields had shattered. But no—it was her own pleasure, physical and mounting under the skillful play of his tongue. Or maybe deeper than physical, as if his calculated, deliberate seduction stroked across months of fantasy and years of longing.

She needed him. Wanted him. Loved him.

Andrew's movements took on an edge of desperation as he yanked her pants and underwear off her hips at the same time. He groaned without lifting his mouth or breaking contact, and his hand slipped between her thighs.

This was critical overload. Too good, too much, and not enough by half. She tried to move her legs apart and groaned when she found them tangled in her pants. "Off," she whispered, twisting to try to reach her clothing without losing the heat of his mouth or the sweet relief of his fingers.

But she lost both as he straightened, up on his knees, and tossed the rest of her clothes aside. "Night stand," he whispered.

It took her five seconds to understand and twice that to roll to her hands and knees and drag open the drawer. Inside she found an unopened box of condoms tucked next to a couple of paperbacks. Mysteries with vague covers and huge shiny fonts, and she couldn't believe she was paying attention to books when she could hear Andrew unzipping his pants.

She grabbed the box of condoms and turned to find him naked beside the bed, staring down at her with lust and desire and a tenderness that turned her inside out. "Lie down, Kat."

For the first time, she saw the cracks in the control, saw that the restraint that seemed so much a part of him was hard-won and too easily shaken by everything she did.

So she eased back against the mattress, the box clutched in one hand. He took it from her with careful movements, pulled one free and put it on.

The bed dipped under his weight as he stretched out beside her, still moving slowly, deliberately. He touched her face, smoothing his thumb over her lower lip.

"How?" she whispered, unable to look away from his face. "How do you want me?"

"Just like this." Andrew dropped quick, soft kisses on her face as he moved over her and settled between her thighs. The head of his cock rested against her, ready but not pressing deeper.

It could be anticipation...or fear. Kat rubbed one foot over his calf as she nipped at his chin. "I know I'm human. I know you don't want to hurt me. But I could stop you, Andrew, no matter what. You can let go, because I've *felt* what's inside you, and I trust you."

"I know." He kissed her, his hips flexing. "That's the best part." The flexing turned into a gentle rock, forward and back, each motion bringing him just a little deeper inside her.

If her empathy had been weaker, she could have shared it with him. Opened her heart and wallowed in the pleasure he took from her, from how it must feel to press forward one torturous inch at a time. She could have given him the giddy joy that accompanied her body stretching to accommodate his cock.

Dropping her shields would leave them vulnerable to the uncontrolled feedback, but she had words. And she used them, clutching at his shoulders as his next rock pushed deep enough to steal her breath. "I've wanted this for so long. You, inside me."

He gritted his teeth, and his arms shook, muscles standing out in sharp relief. "Did you mean it? Let go?"

A fraction of his strength would leave her broken, and she didn't care. Couldn't imagine a world where any need he had could be met with her pain. "Show me. All the things we've been missing."

Andrew bent his head and caught her mouth with a hoarse groan as he thrust deeper—not too deep, but enough to dance the line between too good and too much. Moaning, she tightened her legs around his hips, a silent plea for a moment to adjust, then licked his lip.

He froze, then returned the tiny caress. "A minute?"

"A few seconds," she corrected, rocking up. Taking him, taking the pleasure and the hint of discomfort, the sensation somehow more perfect because it was as imperfect as they were. The rough edges and pain made it real, made it worth it, because it wasn't easy and they wanted each other enough to fight.

So she bit his lip and growled. "Deeper. I want all of you."

He echoed her growl as he eased into her, slowly but not stopping until his hips rested against hers. "Better?"

"Perfect. Told you it would be..." It was the best she could manage when every sense was overwhelmed with him. She smoothed her hands over his tense shoulders, restless now. She tried to ignore the heat of his skin and the way his cock felt, buried so deep. Ignored it just long enough to issue *her* warning. "If—if I come, I could slip a little. Even with my shields in place...if I'm feeling that much, some of it might leak through."

"*If* you come?" he asked, his voice tight.

Kat groaned and dug her head back against the bed. "Why do you think the porn-star orgasms freaked me out so much? It's never been—been easy before. But it's never—" She met his eyes, his wild, damn-near feral eyes, and wondered if her heart was in her own. "It's never been you."

"It's me." He stared down at her as he began to move. "It'll always be me now."

The way it should be, the way it needed to be, and she *was* glad she wasn't a virgin, that she knew how to find his pace and meet his steady thrusts, that she could enjoy the friction and the skillful way he found the right angle, like he'd turned all of that intense concentration on claiming her through pleasing her.

And he did. It got harder to focus with every moment, the slow build of give and take, of deep thrusts and the way he lifted one of her legs higher on his back and growled low in his throat.

Words began to bubble up, a lifetime habit of babbling taking a turn for the obscene as his next advance kindled a wild anticipation, a climax suspended out of reach. "Harder, you can fuck me harder. Make me come, make me beg to *stop* coming..."

Andrew covered her mouth with his and thrust harder, the muscles in his back rippling as he moved. So good, so good she couldn't stop the frantic animal noises, or the way her fingernails left scratches down his arms when the first heat of orgasm bloomed.

She came in stages, in slow motion, or maybe it just lasted forever. Her body seized, drawing tight and tense. She had time to turn her head and gasp in one frantic breath before everything exploded outwards, pleasure and pain and *her*, all the tension and longing releasing in one moment of utter, reckless abandon.

His arms collapsed, and his elbows dug into the bed as his careful rhythm broke along with his control. "Kat. *Kat.*"

Instinct prompted her, or the vague memory from last time, the echo of his satisfaction. She lifted her chin and turned her head, offering him the vulnerable spot where her pulse beat with the too-quick tempo of her body's shuddering release.

He bit her as he hit his peak, a rough caress that would surely leave a bruise, but the pain was nothing compared to the sound he made, completion and pleasure so profound that she couldn't stop herself from reaching out to him.

Just a little, a tiny crack in her outer layer of shields, but Andrew flooded her with a possessive joy that triggered something primal in response. It tumbled free in breathless words, maybe not the right ones for a dominant shapeshifter, but the right ones for them. "I love that you're mine. I love being yours."

He rolled to his back, taking her with him, and wrapped both arms around her. He didn't say anything at first, only panted for breath as his trembling subsided. "Did I hurt you?"

Exasperated, Kat stretched up and bit his chin. Hard.

"Can't help it," he murmured with a smile. "Thought you would've figured that out by now."

"Uh-huh." She settled her cheek back against his chest, where she could enjoy the way his heart thudded loud and fast. "And you need to figure out that if you hurt me, you'll be the first to know. I've got some pretty scary defenses, even when I'm not feeling lethal."

"Shh." His thumb stroked over her neck, over the sensitive spot where he'd bitten her. "I meant this."

Kat shivered and arched into the gentle touch. "It's a symbol. Even if I didn't kind of like it, I'd get off on knowing how much *you* like it."

"It's not about that," he protested quietly. "It's about needing it."

"The symbol?"

"The *mark*."

"So that everyone else would know? Or so I would?"

"I don't know—both?"

She lifted her head so she could meet his eyes. "I *do* know. I think I've always known. Maybe that's why I never pushed, even when everyone laughed and said my big dumb crush wasn't a secret. I wasn't ready for this. It was too...forever."

His expression had turned grave. "It doesn't have to be, not if it's too much for you. I swear, Kat, sometimes I think I'd live with half your heart if that was all I could get."

If he kept saying things like that, her heart might thud its way out of her chest. "You don't have to. It's not in very good shape anymore, but it's all yours."

"I want it." Not a shred of doubt. "I love you."

She'd known. She'd felt it, seen it in the wild colors that surrounded him. But hearing it... Such certainty. Such quiet passion. It tightened her throat until her words came out in a whisper. "I love you too."

He closed his eyes for a moment before shifting her to the bed, settling her gently. "I'll be right back."

Kat eased under the covers, her limbs shaky, as Andrew headed for the bathroom. Her neck throbbed where he'd bit her, and she'd no doubt have the sort of bruise that people pretended not to see but couldn't stop staring at.

The shapeshifters would recognize the symbol. Julio would probably ignore it. Sera would smile knowingly, and Miguel... Miguel hadn't felt the need to mark her. It had been part of why they'd worked so well together, that affection that never crossed the line into possession. Sex had fizzled, but their friendship hadn't.

Except for the fact that she'd been avoiding him since Andrew had come back into her life.

Kat rolled over on her back and closed her eyes. She could think about navigating ex-lovers and shapeshifter instinct in the morning. Tonight was about her, and the man who crawled back into the bed and gathered her close. With Andrew's arms around her, the world could be just the two of them. Crazy cults and complicated friendships drifted away, leaving her at peace.

They could do this. Together, they could do anything.

Chapter Fourteen

Andrew dodged Kat's swing and tumbled her to the mat. "I don't think you *want* to hit me, sweetheart."

She snarled her frustration before baring her teeth at him. "Oh, I do. I really, really do."

"I don't believe you." Not with the punches she'd been landing, and not when he knew she could hit harder. "I can take it, you know."

"Doesn't make me like it." Sighing, she rolled to her feet and shook her hands. "It was easier to hit Alec. He inspired rage."

"No argument here." Andrew arched an eyebrow at her. "While I'm really, really glad you like me, liking me too much to hit me might make this sparring thing difficult."

Behind him, the top stair creaked. Kat's gaze jumped past him as Zola spoke. "That is why we will teach you to fight as a team."

It made sense—but, then again, Zola usually did. Andrew rose and faced her. "Like you and Walker?"

"Yes and no. Together, you will fight with body and mind." Zola pointed to Kat. "She is holding back. Not fighting as I taught her. Katherine?"

In the mirrors, Andrew saw Kat's cheeks turn pink. "I didn't want to hurt him," she muttered.

If he didn't know how real her concern was, it would have

been mortifying. "Hurt me how?"

Zola leaned back toward the stairs and shouted something in French. Then she gave Kat a stern look.

Kat winced. "Callum taught me a few things... I don't know, kind of like punching someone with my brain. An empathic jolt that throws them off. But I work with Zola because I have to stay calm enough to do it, and get fast enough to do it before a shapeshifter breaks me in half. Which I'm still working on."

"So, you don't want to punch me with your brain." He blinked. "A surprisingly weird thing to say out loud, actually."

Her lips pursed, like she was trying to hold back a laugh. "Hey, your brain doesn't want to hit me either. If you pull those punches any harder, they'll be going backwards."

Not admitting it would mean lying to himself as well as her. "I guess we're even, then." He'd killed a man with his bare fists, and she'd done the same with her psychic ability, so no wonder they were loath to use those weapons against one another.

"Enough." Zola gestured to Andrew. "Your instincts will not let you strike at her with strength she cannot meet. So you will watch her with Walker. See what she can do. And then..." The lion smiled, wide and predatory. "You spar against us."

Walker appeared behind Zola. "What's up?"

She nodded to Kat. "Andrew must see of what she is capable, so that he may fight at her back."

"You're supposed to come kick me around," Kat said, bouncing on the balls of her feet. "I can't punch Andrew. He's too pretty."

The lion laughed. "I should be offended, especially since you look happy enough to smash my ugly face in."

Kat caught Andrew's gaze and smiled at him like they were the only ones in the room, wide and open and lopsided. "I'm happy."

"Uh-huh." Walker shook his head with a laugh. "Bring it, Gabriel."

She did fight harder, that much was obvious immediately as she ducked a blow and whirled away. Walker was moving more slowly than usual, but the fact remained that Kat was human. She would never be as fast as a shifter, no matter how much she trained.

It was easy to see Zola's influence in her movements, and that she'd been trained in a very different style. Defensive, her focus on evasion, until Walker lunged toward her.

Her left hand fisted as her eyes narrowed, and Walker stiffened. His foot came down too soon, at an awkward angle, and Kat struck fast, slamming into the back of his knee hard enough to send him to the floor before she hopped away.

Next to Andrew, Zola lowered her voice. "She is good, finding the right moment where a small push can devastate. But she does not press her advantage. Her instinct is always retreat."

And it always would be. If necessary, she'd protect herself and others, but her first choice would be to extricate herself from the situation. "She's still human, Zola. Without someone at her back, retreat is her best option."

"Now, at her back, she has you." Zola was tall enough that she didn't have to tilt her head back very far to meet his eyes. "She knows how to push. You know how to finish what her push has started."

"Teamwork." The more he thought about it, the better it sounded. "How's it working out for you and Walker?"

"Soon enough, you will see." Her gaze shifted back to the fight, and her mouth softened. "For him, I have even learned more English. What will you learn for Katherine?"

A simple answer, despite how long it had taken him to come up with it. "Everything."

"Good." Her fingers brushed his arm. "I am proud of you. Of the work you have done, to learn. I have taught many, many students...but you are the best."

"The most determined," he corrected, though her words

elicited a smile. "You just happen to be the best teacher."

"Mmm, flattery will help you little." She lifted her voice. "Enough. Walker?"

He turned, a question in his eyes. "What do you think? A demonstration, or should we jump right in?"

Before Zola could answer, a distinctive musical tune drifted up from Andrew's bag. "Figure it out while I grab this call," he said, already crossing the floor.

It was Patrick's number. Andrew flicked the screen to answer, his heart pounding. "Did you find something?"

"Yeah." Patrick's voice sounded numb. "Bodies. A whole lot of them. It's not quite Jonestown, but it is one ugly, ugly mess."

"What?" Keeping his tone modulated was an impossibility, and Kat and the others turned to frown at him. "Say that again."

"It looks like a mass-fucking-suicide up here. At least one of the bodies is the astral projector Anna saw in the woods."

So they'd found the cult—maybe. Andrew reached for his keys. "Where are you?"

"Outside an abandoned church a few miles off of I-10. Just north of Pass Christian." Patrick cleared his throat. "They found out Anna and I were coming, I'm guessing. This scene is fresh, and way too big for any of my contacts to cover up."

"I'll call Jackson." If anyone knew how to route that sort of investigation, it would be him. "Sit tight, but you and Anna keep your eyes peeled for trouble. We're on our way."

Kat was breathing too fast when he hung up. Zola and Walker stared at him—but then, they would have heard Patrick's side of the conversation. Kat watched him too, her eyes unblinking. "Something happened?"

"They found the cult." He dropped beside his bag on the bench and grabbed his shoes. "Get your clothes. We're going to Mississippi."

"I need to go in." Kat's voice was resolute, unyielding.

Jackson and Mackenzie stood outside, and Andrew raised a hand in greeting as he engaged the parking brake. "I don't know if that's a good idea. The way Patrick described it..." He grimaced. "It's not going to be pleasant."

"I know." Kat rubbed her hands against her jeans and stared ahead. "I don't like dead bodies. They're so empty they echo, and it feels wrong. But I need to see it. I need this to be over in my head."

"I can tell you," he insisted. "When I get out, I mean. Kat, really—think about it, okay?"

"I am. I did." She finally shifted in the seat to meet his eyes. "Death doesn't give me nightmares. Not like killing or feeling someone die."

The kind of death Patrick had described was enough to give *anyone* nightmares, but he knew how she felt. Some things couldn't be told, only experienced. "All right."

Jackson opened Kat's door as Andrew rounded the vehicle. "We've got to make it quick," he told them. "A buddy of mine has the right authorities on the way, and anyone who doesn't want to make a statement needs to be gone by the time they get here."

"I don't think we'll be hanging out." Andrew closed his hand around Kat's. "Ready?"

She nodded and tightened her fingers until her grip bordered on painful. "Is Anna inside?"

"With Patrick," Mackenzie confirmed. "They're getting pictures and whatever else they need."

This close to the small block building, the scent of burning flesh was strong enough for a human to detect. Andrew had to fight not to recoil from the doorway, but there was no turning back. Answers lay inside, information they needed.

It certainly looked like a tiny country church, with rows of long benches and a small pulpit—the kind of place that preached fire and brimstone. Andrew shuddered and blinked against the acrid smoke that hung heavy in the air and stung his nose.

Anna rose from where she knelt by the stage, a haunted look in her eyes. "Patrick's in the back. That's where the—where the bodies are."

Kat took a breath. Took another, and this one was shallow and unsteady. "I'm never going to be this person, am I?"

Andrew pulled her close and buried his nose in her hair, inhaling her clean, sweet scent. "It's a bunch of burned bodies, sweetheart. No one is this person, not really."

"It doesn't matter if I shield, or if they're not already dead." Her shudder made her entire body tremble. "I've felt agony. I've known what it's like to die from it. I thought it wouldn't be as bad...but I can't stop imagining what they went through. I can't stop feeling it."

Kat had more reason than most to turn away from this place. Not only because of the pain and death, but because *their* fates could have been hers. The thought left Andrew's hands shaking as he kissed her head and released her. "I'll be out in a minute."

"I'm going to go stand with Mac and Jackson." She managed a tiny smile. "No shame in that, right? Mac's a badass."

"I'll come with you," Anna said quickly. "It's a little much for me too, and I don't mind admitting it."

Kat brushed her fingers over Andrew's before retreating, Anna at her side.

In the back he found Patrick snapping a picture of one of the corpses. The bounty hunter glanced up, his eyes numb. "You may not want to be back here. A shapeshifter sense of smell is not an advantage."

"I can handle it," Andrew lied. "Which one is the guy from the other night? The astral psychic?"

Patrick straightened and crossed the room, stepping over outstretched limbs and skirting spots where paper and wood still smoldered. "This one. We found their IDs on the desk in the back office."

"Maybe they didn't want to chance not having their families be able to identify them."

Patrick shrugged. "We left them. Anna got pictures so we'd have the names and info."

Andrew knelt by the corpse, the only one untouched by the flames. Foamy spittle flecked with blood had dried around his mouth, and his face was frozen in a rictus of pain. "They didn't burn themselves alive, I guess."

"Not quite." Patrick gestured toward the far corner. "Looks like poisoning. There's a tub over there, along with a few bottles—phenobarbital, cyanide and Valium. Jackson said—" His mouth tightened. "He was pretty sure whoever mixed it up had suicide in mind."

The astral projector must have gone last, after torching the others. It'd take a crazy person, all right, to still want to chug poison after watching his friends die ugly, excruciating deaths. Crazy—or dedicated. "Are there any other notes, documents? Anything in the office?"

"A lot of it burned. They had files, but they brought them in here." Patrick nodded to a mess of ashes. "Anna dug some stuff out of it. Not sure what else is salvageable, though."

The last, desperate acts of people with no options. "The astral psychic must have told them what happened. There aren't many bodies here, all things considered." A quick, nauseating count. "Ten. Maybe not enough to mount another attack, especially if they sent their best fighters the first time around."

"Maybe not, if they're all psychics." Patrick turned off his camera and pocketed it before giving Andrew a serious look. "Especially if they had Carmen Mendoza's name on a list and thought her husband might have seen it."

"Carmen? Shit." The carnage Alec would have visited on the remaining cult members eclipsed the scene before them—and they would have known it. "That's as good a reason to off yourself as any. It'd hurt less."

"That's the truth. And it's not even taking into account what they've done to Kat. Making a move on her was a last-ditch effort, guaranteed to bring down a world of pain if they fucked it up." Patrick nodded to the bodies around them. "Maybe they were ready for that."

"Maybe." Andrew closed his eyes and suppressed a shudder. "Do you guys have everything you need? I don't know—samples and pictures and stuff?"

"Yeah. It'll take us a few days, running down the info and tying up loose ends. Anna's going to check the IDs against what we found. But every lead we chased to get here seemed to indicate there were a dozen of them at most." Patrick dropped a hand to Andrew's shoulder. "I think it's over, Callaghan."

His tension didn't abate. It would take time for him to believe it, to relax and let down his guard. "I'm not used to trouble being over," he admitted.

"Because trouble's never over," Patrick replied, in a tone that said he understood. Completely. "But there's trouble, and there's catastrophe. And we're on the other side of that now."

"Yeah." He couldn't draw a deep breath, not until he'd gotten about a hundred miles away from the place. "Let's get the hell out of here before the cops show up."

Patrick actually laughed. "If I had a dollar for every time I heard that…"

Sometimes, you either had to laugh or lose your fucking mind. "Me too."

Outside, Jackson leaned against the sloppily painted wall, hurriedly pressing buttons on his phone's keypad. Mackenzie and Kat were huddled around Anna and her phone.

Kat broke away as Andrew approached. "Some of the names on the ID match the lists. The list of kids to recruit."

A mirror of her greatest fear, realized. "That doesn't mean they were here voluntarily."

She stopped a foot away, her hands fisted. "Voluntarily or not...it would have been me. If my mother hadn't—" An unsteady breath, but she didn't look spun now. She looked like she'd finally found somewhere firm to stand. "Whatever kind of crazy she was, it wasn't this. She had lines, and that means I can find them too."

The words gave him pause. "Was that even still a question?"

"It has to be, at least a little. As long as I'm asking it, I'm okay."

She never *wouldn't* ask it, and Andrew had to get used to that. He reached for her, pulled her close and whispered against her hair. "You're okay."

"I know." This time, she sounded like she meant it. "Are we almost done here?"

Behind them, a squat building held death, the remnants of an obsession that aimed to destroy the lives of far too many people. But at the moment all he cared about was the woman in his arms—her life and her happiness. "Let's go home."

Chapter Fifteen

Two weeks. It had been two weeks since she'd spent any time in her own damn apartment.

Kat shifted, trying to find a comfortable position. The leather couch was the same one Derek had given her when she'd first gotten her apartment, though somewhat scratched and worn from lack of care. She'd spent hours on it every week, her feet propped up on the coffee table and her laptop balanced on her legs. Three weeks ago she'd spent an entire Saturday afternoon in this exact spot while Sera worked her way through two DVDs of one of the eighteen billion *CSI* shows.

Two weeks, and it didn't seem like home anymore.

Miguel arched an eyebrow at her. "You're fidgety."

Kat made a face at him and shifted again, tucking her feet under her. "It's been a weird couple weeks. I don't know if I remember how to relax."

"You'll figure it out." He turned his attention back to the video game he was playing, though a particularly vigorous movement snapped the thumbstick on the controller. "Shit."

It had happened enough after Miguel's transformation to a full-blooded wolf that Kat had started keeping extra controllers in the closet. Of course, it hadn't been happening lately, and that stirred worry. "You doing okay? You were looking rattled the other day at breakfast."

"I'm fine." The words came too quickly.

With Miguel, she never felt guilty about snooping. Other

than Callum, Miguel was the only person she knew with shields strong enough to keep her out if he wanted to.

And he did. Her gentle psychic touch slid across shining steel, slipping right past him. Worry twisted into concern, and she reached out to touch his arm. "If you decide you're not...tell me? Please?"

"Kat—" His words cut off in an exasperated sigh. "I'd tell you, I swear. But there's nothing wrong with me that time and a good, long run won't fix, okay?"

"All right." She settled back against the couch and watched him. "I guess...I don't know how this goes. There are so many rules I don't get. The ones that no one explains, like what it means to your instincts if I'm with Andrew."

"Honestly? Not much." He tossed the busted controller aside and used the remote to turn off the television. "We were never going to be a thing, not like you and Andrew. There's no sense in getting upset about it. I mean, it's not like I didn't know."

He always had, because she'd never lied. There was no reason to—both of them understood the futility of lies when dealing with powerful psychics. It was why she told the truth now. "I was avoiding you. If Andrew had tried to tell me I couldn't hang out with you...it would have gotten ugly. I couldn't handle any more ugly last week."

Miguel snorted. "If Andrew had a problem with me, I'd know better than you. He couldn't hide that, any more than I could lie to him if I wanted you for my own. Some things, you just can't do."

A dish clattered in the kitchen, and Sera stuck her head out. "He's right," she said, proving that she'd been enjoying the shapeshifter pastime of eavesdropping on conversations they shouldn't have been able to hear to begin with. "If Andrew was having instinctive issues with you and Miguel, he wouldn't have been able to leave you here. The place smells like Miguel, you know."

A thousand little cues, and sometimes Kat wondered if interpreting the subtle intricacies would ever feel natural. "Uh-huh. To my human nose, the place smells like pizza. Is it almost done cooking?"

Sera ducked back into the kitchen, her voice drifting back down the hallway. "Five minutes."

"Five minutes," Kat echoed, nodding to Miguel. "If a run would help, why don't you go take one after we eat?"

"Yeah, maybe," he replied vaguely.

Andrew's words came back to her, the ones he'd whispered before he kissed her goodbye. "*It's just some guy throwing his weight around. He thinks Julio and I are weak, so we're going to talk to him, face-to-face. I'll come to your place when we're done.*" They'd seemed innocent, at the time.

They had *better* have been innocent. "Is there a reason you can't leave?"

Miguel tensed. "Are you going to get pissed off if I say yes?"

She was going to kill Andrew, or at least beat him within an inch of begging for death. "I'm already pissed. I'm going to be fucking furious if you lie to me."

He shrugged a split second before someone knocked on the door. "You're not going to get to be alone much anymore. You need to talk to Andrew about it."

Stunned, Kat stared at him as Sera started for the front door. "If something else came up with the cult, they should have told me. That shit was supposed to be over—"

"It's not the cult," he argued.

"What's not the cult?" Anna asked as she walked in, a battered knapsack slung over one shoulder.

"Kat was just demanding to know why she's being babysat."

The woman chuckled as she dropped to the sofa beside him. "Welcome to being involved in wolf politics. I can't think of anyone on any of the regional councils who doesn't employ at least casual security for their families."

Kat opened her mouth to protest, then closed it again. Andrew and Julio were members of the council, but they didn't have families to protect, not besides Miguel and— "Carmen. Are you telling me your sister puts up with a bodyguard and hasn't strangled Alec for it yet?"

Miguel reached for the soda he'd left sitting on the coffee table. "Carmen's had one since they went to New York. It's not optional for Conclave members. Even Alec finally stopped fighting it."

The world tilted. "Alec. *Alec* has a bodyguard?"

Anna plucked the soda can from Miguel's hand. "Like he said—it's not optional. There are too many people who'd like to avoid challenges with Conclave members and are willing to fight dirty to do it."

Kat pinned Sera with a look. "Did you know?"

"Me?" Sera tossed her kitchen towel over her shoulder, a casual gesture that didn't distract from the tightness in her eyes. "I'm a coyote, Kat. A backwoods hick coyote. I don't have a clue how shapeshifter royalty lives."

Maybe Andrew hadn't known, either. She'd give him a chance to say that, before she screamed at him. "So every time some wolf gets pissy with Julio or Andrew, I'm going to end up with a babysitter? Just because I'm dating a council member?"

"For a while." Anna seemed unapologetic. "This is the life, Kat, love it or hate it. The same thing would've gone down if your cousin had taken that council spot he earned instead of running off with Nick."

In some ways, it still had. From the day Derek had married the Alpha's daughter, Kat had weighed all of her decisions against the sure knowledge that she could be used as leverage. Hadn't that been part of the reason she'd pushed herself in endless rounds with Zola? But in New Orleans, she'd been removed from that. Outside of the immediate sphere of John Peyton and his enemies.

It wouldn't be the same with Andrew. His enemies would come to him, and she'd be at his side. It wouldn't matter that she could turn their brains to Jell-O and erase their existences—she *looked* like a tempting target. They'd come after her, again and again, and she'd have to defend herself. How many times could she use her mind to crush out someone's life before the darkness started to numb her to the horror of it?

They were all staring at her, even Sera, until the timer went off in the kitchen and she swore and took off to rescue the pizza.

Kat looked at Anna. "It's more complicated than I realized."

"It always is." She made a face and then dug the video game controller out from behind her back. "Anyway, I'm the next shift, so...get lost, Mendoza."

He rose, but his troubled gaze remained on Kat. "I can stay, if you want."

His turn to be protective, her turn to smile and pretend she was fine. "Go on. I'm sick of boys, anyway."

"Yeah, yeah. Girl time." He gathered his stuff and left silently.

"He must be going nuts not to stick around for pizza," Anna observed.

"He has good days and bad days." Kat leaned back and closed her eyes. "Jesus, Anna. Who the hell does someone like Alec hire as a bodyguard? He's already the scariest person I know."

She laughed. "It's not his job to be scarier than Alec, just to make sure no one can sneak up and get the drop on them. To take over Alec's role of raving, paranoid lunatic, if you will."

"Sounds like fun." At least she'd recovered her sense of sarcasm. "I'm not sure I want one of those following me around. I didn't like having Alec following me around, either, and I was a lot more tolerant at twenty."

Anna pulled a tattered paperback out of her bag. "Now that? Is none of my business."

It *wasn't* Anna's business, and the fact that Kat was tempted to press the issue was proof of how far she'd come from jealousy and self-consciousness. Whatever Anna knew—or didn't know—about Andrew and his plans to put Kat under 24/7 surveillance, she clearly had no intention of breaking alpha ranks.

The dominant shapeshifters rarely did...and Sera's Sharpie reminder on the bathroom mirror was starting to make a lot more sense. *No fucking alpha bastards*, indeed. Kat had climbed into bed with one, and this was what came of it.

Deciding to save her ire for its intended target, Kat cast about for a change of topic. "Is Patrick still in town?"

"Don't think so. He had to go meet a contact about a job." The book lay unopened in Anna's hands. "You know, working with him wasn't as bad as I thought it'd be."

It didn't seem like a very noteworthy comment until Sera appeared with a pizza stone in one hand and a six-pack of Heineken in the other. "Jesus, what did he do to change your tune? Cure cancer and rescue a litter of kittens?"

"I appreciate a certain level of ability and efficiency." Anna tilted her head and flashed them a wicked grin. "Plus, did you see those tattoos? Too bad he's off limits."

"Says who?" Sera settled the food on the well-abused coffee table and took a beer. "If you're not going there, I sure the hell am."

"Uh-huh." Kat didn't need beer, but she did lean forward and claim one of the corner pieces from the pizza. "Don't let the road-warrior act fool you, guys. Patrick's squishy hearted. The tattoos aren't a bad-boy thing. They're magic."

"Magic," Anna agreed. "Only way for someone like him to stay alive, doing what he does."

"He'll never say where he got them or what they do..." Kat trailed off and grinned. "I've heard he can hold his own against shapeshifters, though. I mean, he must."

Anna grabbed the remote control, turned on the TV and

began scanning through the channel guide. "So, what're we watching tonight?"

It was about as subtle as the way Sera could spend two hours in a room with Julio without looking at him once. Avoidance and denial, and it made Kat want to laugh. She'd spent so much time feeling unattractive and awkward and violently jealous of Anna and Sera, and they were just as lost and insecure as anyone else.

Whether you were a blonde *femme fatale*, a bombshell redhead or a geeky brunette, men were still a pain in the ass. Some truths were apparently universal.

It didn't take an empath to see Kat was pissed.

Andrew parked the car, pulled up the emergency brake and turned to her. "What did I do?"

She shook her head. "Inside. I'll talk inside."

It had to be the fact that she'd been under guard. All the way into the warehouse and up to his loft, Andrew considered the possibilities, and it was the only one that made sense. He dropped his keys on the kitchen counter and turned, bracing his hands on the granite as he faced her. "I was going to talk to you about it."

"But you didn't." She eased the wide strap of her laptop bag over her head and set it down next to the door. "Which is a whole different and way more serious issue than the fact that I have to have guards to begin with."

"By the time I thought about it, there wasn't time." He retrieved two bottles of water from the refrigerator and held one out to her. "It's no different than what we were doing when the cult was still active. I figured we could talk about it later."

Kat stared at the bottle of water for a few seconds before taking it, though she immediately set it down. "There was time to tell Miguel and Anna."

"There was time to ask them to watch out for you. I didn't have to explain *why*."

"And you thought I'd get pissed off or not trust you? If you just told me without explaining?"

"Give me some credit, Kat. I thought it would wait, is all." And he hadn't wanted her to worry, but admitting as much might just upset her more.

Instead of replying, she jerked at the zipper on her jacket, tugging it down in abrupt, rough movements that showed she was still angry, still clutching at her temper. She slid out of the garment and tossed it over the back of the couch. "I found out that I might have to have a bodyguard for the rest of my life from someone else. And I felt like a stupid kid again, like every time someone shuffled me off into a closet because bad stuff was going down but no one wanted me to know about it."

"I'm sorry." It was the very last thing he'd ever meant to do. "I don't think you're a kid."

Kat closed her eyes and sank to the cushions with a groan. "I know. But it's—it's a sore spot, and it's always going to be. I need you to be the one person who is painfully, brutally honest with me when things are dangerous."

"Okay, I screwed up." Andrew perched on the arm of the couch. "The guy Julio and I were dealing with today has a chip on his shoulder about the council, and it doesn't matter that I don't have legacy. He'll push my buttons like anyone else's, and I don't really think he cares how he does it."

"And people are already figuring out I'm one of your buttons?"

One thing didn't change, no matter who or where you were—gossip. "People like to talk."

She tilted her head back and stared up at him. "I don't love the idea of a bodyguard, but I can get my head around it, as long as we get a few things clear upfront."

"Such as?"

"I get to decide who. And how." She shifted to her knees, so her head was closer to his. "And we get Jackson or Mahalia or *someone* to ward your loft and my apartment well enough that I can have time alone when I need it. If this is a shapeshifter threat, then magical protection is enough. I'm not going to live the rest of my life like we did the last couple weeks."

"Done." He touched her hair, relishing the way the soft strands slipped through his fingers. "I really wasn't being a jerk this time. There's been so much going on, that's all."

She leaned into his hand and offered a tiny smile. "I was furious. I wanted to come back here and strangle you with some cat-5 cable. And then I *did* give you credit. I thought of every time you choked back your instincts so you wouldn't smother me, and I realized I should trust you." The smile faded. "And then I wondered if you didn't trust me. If you thought I'd be so reckless that I'd fight this just to—"

"You were worried the other night," he cut in. Maybe if she understood *why*... "Freaking out about the cult stuff, and thinking you might go off the deep end. Maybe—maybe I didn't want you to think that your life's going to be one never-ending string of boss fights that are going to push you closer and closer to the edge."

Her lips twitched. Pursed. She clenched them together as her face scrunched up, like she was fighting to hold in laughter. She fought it until her face was red. "Boss...fights?" Her mirth spilled free, the sound filling his ears as she dropped her forehead to his leg and laughed until she shook.

He sighed. "You know, aside from my unfortunate use of video-game terminology, that's really not funny."

"I know, I know..." She gasped in another breath and stared up at him. "I just...I love you, Andrew. I love you enough to have bodyguards or babysitters or whatever the hell else it takes, because you're not going to let me get anywhere near the edge."

He dragged her closer. "Not if I can help it."

"I've got dark places inside me, but that's not all bad." Her hand landed on his chest, fingers spread wide. "I figure I can spend the next few decades letting you see all of them. If you can handle them."

If anything, her dark places matched his. "As long as you need me the way I need you. Everything else is...everything else."

The tip of her tongue teased over her lower lip in a quick, nervous gesture. "I don't even have words for what I need. I could let you feel it?"

He had no reservations. "If you want."

She left one hand on his chest and lifted the other to his cheek. The first tickle ghosted over him as her eyes drifted shut, just a hint of affection.

Then love bloomed, and a passion that bordered on feral, instinctive desire. Control—his loss of it, that was what she needed. For his need for her to overrule everything else.

They tumbled to the couch, her mouth under his, open and hot. He couldn't think, couldn't stop himself from turning her over, across the arm of the couch with her knees digging into the cushions.

He couldn't stop himself—but she could. If it was too much, too far, she could stop him.

She didn't. Instead she moaned, and the wild emotions vanished as her head slammed back against his shoulder. "Just like this," she said, the words breathless. "God, *just like this.*"

He accidentally tore her shirt, but the fear he expected didn't come. Her shields were intact, and he wasn't beyond control, dangerous, just...

"I need you," he mumbled against the smooth, newly bared skin of her back.

"Good." She squirmed, yanking the tattered fabric over her head, every movement grinding the curve of her ass against his hips. "Don't let me hold back. Don't let me hide from you."

They'd always locked themselves away like that, and it had

very nearly killed them. "No hiding." He licked her back and pushed at her pants.

They were loose—stretchy, like yoga pants—and slid down easily enough. Kat whimpered, one hand groping for the back of the couch, and dropped her head forward. "I had this fantasy about a hundred times."

"Only a hundred?"

"Sometimes we were in a bed. Or over the table." She shivered. "Sometimes you made me come. Just with your fingers or your mouth, because you wanted me to beg before you'd take me. But sometimes it was just this, and then you were inside me..."

So many possibilities, and it would take years to explore every one of them. "I can do that."

"Make me come?" Almost a question, but then she laughed, low and throaty. "I know you can. Make me come, Andrew. Please, *please*, I don't care if it's fast or hard, I just want to feel you—"

His hands shook as he rolled on a condom and gripped her hips. She wiggled impatiently, and he distracted her by dropping tiny bites across her shoulder blades and the back of her neck as he worked into her slick heat.

She was panting by the time he made it halfway in and moaning before he thrust home. Her fingernails scratched the upholstery of the couch as her body clenched around him, already primed for release. Her shaky plea confirmed it, made him grit his teeth and press his forehead to her bare skin. "So close, please...touch me, please touch me."

Andrew slipped one hand around her until his fingers found her clit. "Kat."

"Oh—" Just a sound, a gasp, and she flew apart, her release as fast and easy as the wildest of her empathy-fueled orgasms. But there was no feedback this time, no projection, just Kat coming hard around him.

He thrust once and then again, clenching his teeth against

the need to follow her. But her orgasm went on and on, dragging him along, and driving her higher proved an impossibility. Pleasure tightened along with the rhythmic clasp of her body, and he shouted her name as he gave in to it, to the intense throb that started at the base of his spine and cascaded through him.

Kat slumped forward over the arm of the couch, her head down and her hair brushing the floor. Underneath him, her body was lax. "Holy shit."

He couldn't speak, so he traced his lips over the dark lines of the tribal tattoo that wound its way from her hairline down between her shoulder blades. "Mmm."

Goose bumps dotted her arms. "It doesn't bother you, does it? The tattoo?"

"Bother me?"

"The mark." She tilted her head, baring the side of her throat where he'd bitten her the first time. "I marked myself."

He soothed the spot with his tongue. "I'm not sure it works that way, Kat."

"Oh, good." The words slurred together. "Not that I'd mind. If you wanted to bite the back of my neck."

"Uh-huh." Andrew laughed. "Don't worry. I won't gnaw your tattoo off."

A giggle escaped her. "I think the blood is rushing to my head."

He pulled away carefully and eased her upright. "Better?"

"No." She slumped back against his chest and turned until her lips brushed his throat. "Giddy."

Her skin was hot against his, her heart pounding. "Not just from the head rush, I hope."

She bit him with a playful growl. "Not even a little."

Just to be sure, he pulled back and met her gaze. "You're not still mad, are you?"

A tiny furrow appeared between her eyebrows. "No," she

said after a moment's pause. "I'm not mad. This time. If you do it again…"

"I won't. Next time—" A single deep breath eased some of the tightness in his chest. "Next time, I promise I'll talk to you."

"And I get to pick my own damn bodyguards."

Maybe she didn't like hanging out with Miguel anymore—or maybe Anna was getting under her skin. "Was there a problem tonight?"

"No. But there's a difference between spending time with friends and my friends having to spend time with me because I can't be left alone." She tilted her head. "Do you understand? If this is real, and necessary…it can't just be people we know. I don't want to be a personal obligation. I want to be a professional job."

"Okay." It would entail searches and interviews, but surely Jackson knew people who did that sort of thing. "For what it's worth, it sort of *is* Anna's job. Not with you, obviously, but in general. Maybe we could hire her for the time being, if it's not too weird."

"Anna's okay. And I can hang out with you and Julio." She wrinkled her nose. "And Miguel, if he's a suitable deterrent to the cranky shapeshifters of the world. The Mendoza name, I guess?"

"That's part of it." She probably wouldn't believe the rumors circulating about him, the whispers that the ritual magic that had awakened his wolf had left him half-feral and dangerous as hell.

"It's fine, until we can find someone permanent. I just don't want my friends stuck babysitting me forever." Her eyes grew serious. "I'm going to put up with it. Because if someone's around…maybe that's deterrent enough, and no one will get hurt."

There it was, the very real worry that she would have to use her abilities to hurt, to wound. "Better to head off trouble before it starts," he agreed.

Kat eased away and started straightening her clothing. "Next time I poke you into fulfilling my dark fantasies, I'm going to strip first. You ripped my snarky T-shirt."

"Just go ahead and tie me to a chair." Intuition and instinct drove the words. He could easily break any bonds, but that would be part of the draw for Kat. She would like that, having his strength barely leashed and him *not quite* at her mercy.

Her sudden thoughtful expression proved him right. Abandoning the shirt, she swung a leg over his thighs, straddling his lap as she braced both hands on his shoulders. She smiled, as wicked as her eyes were curious. "Tie you to a chair, huh?"

"If I let you." The words were a bluff. He'd let her because he didn't have it in him to deny her anything she wanted, and he'd love it—because it was her.

Chapter Sixteen

Julio's loft wasn't so different from Andrew's, with the glaring exception that Julio had an excuse for the place to be completely undecorated. Unlike Andrew, Julio had only moved to the warehouse recently, after Alec had funded the renovations and Andrew had finished the plans for them.

Kat dabbed the paintbrush into the corner and squinted her nose at the beige color. "You could have gone with something more interesting, you know. If I owned my apartment, I'd paint it purple and blue or something."

Julio made a face. "I don't think I'm really the purple type."

Laughing, Kat rocked up on her toes to smooth the brush over the last bare spot. "Red? Red's manly, isn't it?"

He stepped back and considered the wall with a tilt of his head. "Green might not be so bad. Something dark."

Meddling was bad, but sometimes Kat couldn't resist. "You could ask Sera. She's good at decorating. Before she moved in, all I had on my walls were posters I hung up with thumbtacks."

"Probably not the greatest idea ever." He grinned and laid his paint roller aside. "Your roommate avoids me like the proverbial plague. I figure she's got her reasons."

"Well, yeah." Kat waved the paintbrush at him. "You're all hot and growly, and she's on the wagon. Sera wants to be independent, and you're the top-shelf liquor of dominant shapeshifters."

"Uh-huh. That, or she doesn't want her father to murder

me in my sleep."

A valid concern. Sera's father had been a trauma surgeon and a mercenary before settling down to run New Orleans' supernatural clinic. But of all the years Kat had known Franklin, her clearest memory was his hands coaxing hers away from Andrew's torn body as she sobbed and Andrew bled and bled—

She pushed away memory with rigid self-control and turned back to the wall. Andrew was whole. Andrew was *hers*, finally, and some day she'd stop having the nightmares where he bled to death and she never got to say goodbye. "Franklin is a scary man," she managed. Too little, too late, but the best she could do.

Julio remained silent for a moment before snatching away her paintbrush. "Enough work. Time for fun. What do you want to do? And don't say play cards, because you cheat, and don't think I haven't noticed."

"I don't cheat," Kat retorted, grateful for the chance to laugh. "You just suck. How can a precog be *that* bad at poker?"

He huffed. "As if I'd be so self-serving with my visions. I'm here for the good of mankind, you know."

It was a joke, but it was Julio, and she knew that somewhere underneath the smiles and the teasing, he was just like Andrew. A hero, the kind who'd laugh about it and claim it wasn't true, but who'd quietly do the things that needed doing. Whatever it took to keep the people around him safe.

Julio probably wouldn't be any more comfortable with the praise of the truth than Andrew was, so Kat let him have the joke. "Yeah, yeah. You're God's gift to something, all right. How long have we got until Andrew's done with shapeshifter politics for the day, anyway?"

"Hours. He promised he'd pick up some of the stuff I've been handling."

"Huh." She'd avoided Andrew—and, by extension, Julio—so adeptly for the last year that she barely knew the scope of what the two of them did every day. "If I buy you a beer or three, will you tell me exactly what a council member does?" *And how I can start helping?*

He didn't consider it for long. "Hell, yeah. I'll drive."

It didn't take long to clean up the brushes and paint supplies, but Kat made good use of the time, pestering him with questions about the day-to-day running of the wolves' territory. She was still going as they stepped out onto the sidewalk, wiggling her way toward finding some place she could fit. "What about the changed wolves? I know Alec used to look after them, but is there a formal support system now?"

"Not quite." His keys jingled as he dug them out of his jeans pocket. "There have been plenty of inquiries, though. People putting out feelers about Andrew, seeing if he'd be up to the task."

She'd suffered through Derek's transformation with him, unwilling to abandon the cousin who'd been unwilling to abandon *her*. Andrew hadn't been able to accept her help, but Miguel had, and she'd watched him struggle with the same problems. She'd struggled with him, with an understanding only empathy could provide.

Excitement sparked inside her for the first time, the sort of excitement she'd never felt with her endless job searches. "I could help with that," she offered hesitantly. "I mean, help Andrew. I know I'm not a wolf, but I can feel the things they feel. I can know who needs help, and when."

"I guess you could, huh?" He locked the outside door behind them. "Talk to him about it."

"I need to talk to you, too. And Alec." She waited until Julio turned, so she could meet his eyes. "I want to be a part of it. Not Andrew's girlfriend or Alec's secretary. I want to help people who went through what Derek and Andrew and Miguel did."

"Good luck with—" A pained grunt swallowed the words as he stumbled and pressed his fingers to his forehead with a grimace. "*Damn it.*"

"Julio?" Instinct drove her a step closer to him. Training prompted her to go for her phone, urged on by the sudden flash of Julio's fear. Get the phone, call for help. Better to feel stupid if nothing was wrong than to—

"*Run.*" He blindly shoved the keys at her. "Get the car and go."

His fear vanished, swallowed whole, and the abrupt silence was so unnerving she fumbled with the keys. Something tingled over her skin, like getting in the way of one of Jackson's spells, and Kat shuddered as her phone slipped from her fingers.

Silence. Stillness. The calm before the storm, and she made it three steps before magic snapped through the air, painful enough to drive her to her knees. Physical discomfort faded under a wave of suffocating claustrophobia, and Kat screamed as she threw herself against the harsh cage that had snapped shut around her mind.

With Alec stuck in New York most of the time, Jackson had to work twice as hard to keep up with the clients at their small investigative firm. Alec's name was still on the window, but it was a one-man show these days.

Andrew fidgeted in the office chair and looked at the piece of paper Jackson held out. "What's that?"

"It's a cashier's check." He waved it harder, then sighed and laid it on the desk. "Alec had me get a couple for Patrick and Anna, and they deserve it for the work they did in tracking down that cult. I already sent McNamara his, but I thought you could just give this one to Anna."

"Okay." Andrew picked it up and blinked at the amount printed on it. "The Conclave pays well for that stuff, huh?"

"Didn't come from the Conclave." He took off his glasses and rubbed his eyes. "They wouldn't pony it up because Anna's still *persona non grata* up there. They consider her a defector, at best, and we all know how they feel about rogue threats. Alec paid up."

"It's hard to think of her that way." It didn't matter that she hadn't *done* anything. The Conclave had trained her to be an assassin, and she'd quit on them. She wasn't a person to them, not anymore—she was a time bomb with legs. A sobering reality, and a reminder that things in their world weren't always what they seemed.

"The Conclave's ineffective," Mackenzie pointed out from her perch on Alec's abandoned desk. "Do you know how long it takes for them to work through their so-called justice system? It's been a year and a half since the mess went down with the cougar Seer, and they're still holding the wolf who worked for him. Alec told me some of the people in their holding cells have been there a damn decade."

"A big reason Alec and Carmen had to get up there," Jackson drawled. "Even if it left me holding the bag here."

Andrew tapped the edge of the name placard on the desk. "Can you hire someone to help you?"

"I've got some feelers out," he admitted. "With the kind of cases we get, it's not really as simple as hiring a newbie with a fresh PI license. I need someone like McNamara."

He was practically brooding. Andrew hid a smile. "So ask him to join up."

"Can't. He's not one for operating inside the normal boundaries of the law, you know."

"Right, that might be an issue."

"You'll find someone, baby." Mac's fond smile faded. "In the meantime...can I give Mr. Council here a piece of my mind, yet?"

"Only if you promise to keep it civil, darlin'."

"I'm always civil." But when she turned her gaze on Andrew, she looked damn near feral. "You know how Jackson and I have been chasing down rumors of orphaned cougars? Turns out it's not as easy as it should be, because this country is lousy with orphaned shapeshifters."

That he could believe. "What sorts of situations are you finding?"

"A lot of wolves. Some who have one or both parents who were turned, then ended up on the wrong side of the local pack structure. Some who are on the streets, or group homes." She glanced at Jackson. "We found one in an orphanage last week."

Andrew sat straighter. "Shit. How old?"

"Eight." Mackenzie's voice took on an odd note—almost like the protective purr of a mama cat over her cub. "Once Jackson's got everything tied up here...I think we're going back for him."

If he grew up alone, there was no telling what would happen to the boy. "I think it sounds great. Where's the orphanage?"

"Colorado." She leaned forward again. "But it's not enough. Even if we save one of them...we need something here, in town. While you and Alec are throwing around all this money, throw some at all the damn kids who get left behind because our screwed-up world keeps killing their parents."

"I'll check with Alec, see what we can do. When it comes to orphaned kids, though, finding the money might be the least complicated part of it all. Those kids can't just disappear from society, so it's all got to be legal."

"People have been throwing money at problems like this for years," Mackenzie replied. "And there's Carmen's cousin, Veronica. She's got a legal degree from a top school and understands. I bet I can talk her into helping me. But the wolves are the only ones who can protect and fund it."

"Kenzie's already got it figured out," Jackson said affectionately.

His wife smiled. "Because you helped." Turning back to Andrew, she raised both eyebrows. "I was lucky. I got adopted by people who loved me and took care of me. Even if we can't give them all families, we can give them chances. So help me make it happen."

"All right. I'll try." Andrew's phone vibrated and then rang, and he tilted his head toward the back room as he dug it out of his pocket. "May I?"

Jackson waved him back, his attention on his computer. "Knock yourself out."

It was Patrick calling, and Andrew's gut clenched as he answered. "Hello?"

"We fucked up, Callaghan." Patrick's voice was rough. Choked. "We missed something."

The knot in his stomach seized. For one breathless, agonizing second, he was sure he was going to puke all over the boring office carpet, but his voice—when it came—sounded steady enough. "What happened?"

"Ben is missing, and I found his girlfriend in their apartment. Her neck's broken."

Lia. "Fuck." Andrew's hands started to shake. "Does it look like a burglary gone bad? Anything like that?"

"What it looks is well-planned." A motor revved in the background. Patrick's voice evened, turned cold and detached. "I'm about to get on a plane back to New Orleans. Can you call Anna and have her start trying to track down properties attached to any of the IDs we found? Or anyone related to them? Once I'm in the air, I'll send her what I've got."

"Right after I've called Kat," he promised. "We'll regroup when you get here. We'll—" His throat closed. "We'll find Ben. I swear that we'll find him."

Andrew had already speed-dialed Kat's cell phone by the time he reached the doorway back into the office, and the pale faces that greeted him removed the last of his hope that Ben and Lia had run afoul of some new and unknown threat.

Jackson held up a faxed page. "My contact in Biloxi says the ME's office started the autopsies on the bodies from Pass Christian. Two of them had already been autopsied once, so they rushed tissue samples through the toxicology lab and found significant amounts of embalming fluid in seven of them."

"That's why they burned them." The numb words seemed to come from someone else. Some*where* else, miles away. "Most of them were already dead."

"And they staged it to look like a group suicide." Jackson swore.

Andrew started as the ringing in his ear gave way to Kat's outgoing voicemail message. "Try calling Julio. He's with Kat, he's—" Stupidly, he ended the call and redialed her number. "He's with Kat."

Mackenzie already had her phone out. "On it. I'm sure they're—"

Her voice cut off. Julio's outgoing message spilled out of her earpiece, quiet and even more damning because the phone hadn't rung at all.

Andrew moved without thinking, straight for the door. "Get Anna on the phone. She and Patrick have to run down the leads they have left, see if they can find out where the cult might go to ground."

Jackson swore again. "Fuck. Someone should stay here where we have database access just in case they come up with something."

"I'm going to check the lofts and a few more places." His heart was splitting apart, but he sounded so *calm* that he couldn't help but marvel absently. "If I don't find Kat and Julio, I'll come back, and we can figure out where to go from there."

"Shit, all right." Jackson snatched up his phone receiver. "Be careful, damn it."

"Yeah." He took a deep, bracing breath as he stepped out into the chilly, early evening air. Kat was smart—even if she and Julio had gotten snatched, she'd know what the cult was really after. And she'd tell them whatever was necessary to keep them hanging on, waiting, hoping for a chance to trade her for their precious collar. They had Kat, but she—

They had Kat.

His key chain shattered in his hand, and the metal teeth

lining his keys dug into his palm along with the shards of plastic as he sagged against the rough brick building.

He had to pull it together and *hold* it together, because the one thing more important than anything else was finding them soon—and alive.

Chapter Seventeen

Her head hurt.

No, scratch that. Her whole body hurt.

Kat groaned, then wished she hadn't. The noise set off a throbbing in her skull, an impressive feat when her brain felt about as solid as cotton balls. The only thing that registered was pain—her wrists, her arms, her ankles, everything *ached*—and the fact that she couldn't seem to pry her eyes open.

Drugged. She'd had surgery once, to have her appendix removed. She'd been just fourteen, but she'd never forgotten how it felt to claw her way back into consciousness through that terrifying haze. The anesthesia, making her so numb and confused that her senses had woken up at different times. Her ears first, and then her sense of touch, and she'd listened to her mother whisper to her father that they had to get her discharged before the charm wore out...

The charm. A silly bracelet with two wooden beads, and her parents had paid five thousand dollars for it. Kat remembered the brush of her mother's fingers tying it around Kat's wrist as she struggled to wake up, remembered the feeling—like a soft blanket wrapped around her empathy, cutting her off from the world. A desperate gamble, to bring an empath into a hospital when hormonal spikes put her powers beyond her control, but she'd been so sick, and her parents had been so scared.

She felt that way now. Sick, sore. Scratching her way into coherency as *something* coiled around her mind. Not a comforting blanket this time but cold steel, someone else's psychic strength stifling her own.

Memories were too chaotic to grasp, but her brain was starting to move now. Falling into familiar patterns. Math.

Pain plus drugs plus psychic blocks equals...

Fuck. This time the groan was worth the pain. She deserved it, if she'd let herself get kidnapped.

"It's about time you woke up," a rough but familiar voice whispered. "We've got to get out of here, damn it."

Ben's voice, and raspy, like he'd been chain-smoking again. She'd heard it a thousand times over her headset, exchanging teasing insults as they hacked and slashed their way through online video games. Her eyes felt glued shut, but she managed to wet her lips enough to speak. "Ben?"

"Yeah. Hey." Something jarred her chair, making the legs skitter across the floor with the grating sound of metal on concrete. "Open your eyes, Kat."

That set off the pounding again, like an entire drum line practicing on the inside of her skull. "Ouch. Fuck, Ben." She got her eyes opened, and squinted at the floor between her feet. She had paint on her left boot, boring beige paint that stood out against the scuffed black leather.

Beige paint. "Julio. I was with Julio."

"The guy they keep dosing with horse tranquilizers?" He jerked his head toward the corner. "They've got his chair chained to the wall, just in case."

Without thinking, Kat tried to lift her hand to rub at her eyes and winced when metal dug into her wrist. Handcuffs, cold and unyielding.

She wasn't going anywhere.

In the end she settled for blinking until her vision cleared. Julio *was* slumped in the corner, but no one had taken a chance on handcuffs holding him. Chains held his arms to his body as well as his legs to the chair, enough of them that it would have seemed absurd if it hadn't been so damn terrifying.

Kat looked back to Ben, who was scruffy and exhausted. "Where the hell are we?"

He shook his head. "All I know is I've been here for *days*. They're holding Lia too, but they won't tell me where. They just keep asking questions."

Days. That was important for a reason, but her mind still wouldn't make connections. "What are they asking?"

"The collar." He grimaced. "They must have traced my activity somehow when I was pulling records."

"Oh God, Ben—" For the first time, she understood shapeshifter guilt. It formed a knot in her gut and made it hard to speak. "I'm sorry."

"Don't. I figured out the risk early and I kept taking it. I knew what I was doing." He blew out a harsh breath. "But now we need to get the hell out of here so I can find my girlfriend and rain down some vengeance on these motherfuckers."

"Fine. Guilt later, rage now." Kat closed her eyes and slid her senses along the cool metal barrier holding her empathy in. "Are you blocked too? Or have I got some sort of bad magic mojo just on me?"

"There's someone. He's been keeping me locked in since I got here."

"Damn it." No empathy. She'd gotten so damn cocky about how nothing could touch her. She'd indulged in fits of moral crisis over how dangerous she was, had angsted that her power was so brutal she had to accept a bodyguard to save her attackers from her own lethal skill.

She should have been learning to squirm out of handcuffs.

It hurt, but she tried anyway, twisting her wrists as she looked at the corner again. "Julio? God damn it, Julio Mendoza, wake the fuck up."

Nothing. Not a single groan, not even a whimper.

Ben swore under his breath. "Two of the cult whackos have

been arguing about his drug dosages. Whether they've given him enough to kill him."

So no shapeshifter, either. Just her and her brain—not even the most useful parts of it. Kat drew in a calming breath, dragging the air deep and holding it as Callum had taught her.

"*I don't need to learn how to breathe,*" she'd told him.

"*Most people do*" had been the typically Callum-esque answer.

Breathing didn't help her situation, but it did help her fear. A minute later she craned her head to look at Ben. "Okay, we're smart. We're a couple of geniuses. Let's rescue the shapeshifter and get the hell out of here. Are you handcuffed or tied?"

"Cuffed." Ben scooted his chair closer to hers. "Near as I've been able to tell, we're not in a city. Sometimes when it's quiet I can hear crickets outside, but no cars unless someone's coming or going. That's all I've got."

She wiggled, but the chair was solid. Maybe Julio could have bent the metal to free his arms, but Kat was just as likely to dislocate something. "Blocking our powers takes expensive charms or sustained effort. Have you got a charm tied to you somewhere?"

"Not a damn thing."

So somewhere, not too far away, a spell caster or a psychic was watching their power drip away as they fought to keep Kat and Ben contained. "Then I'm going to make life hell on whoever's shielding us. I've got psychic fuel to burn."

Ben's eyes gleamed with a surprisingly feral light. "Together, we can make one hell of a headache."

Across the room, Julio stirred with a low grunt. His chains rattled, and he mumbled something unintelligible.

Relief surged. Whatever they'd done to Julio, he was strong enough to survive it. All they needed to do was get free. "Wake up, Julio. Wake up. There's beer. And naked women."

Another mutter was all she got as his head fell back and

lolled to one side.

Kat closed her eyes and gathered her will. Slowly, like a hard drive spooling up, until she was wound tight and damn near vibrating with the need to let go. To *push.* "Ready?"

Ben's handcuffs clinked as he clenched his fists. "Ready."

"Me first," she whispered. "Give me ten seconds, then throw everything you've got at them."

"Got it."

Maybe she'd learned something from watching the wolves circle, but her strategy was pure Zola. A testing jab against the shields, then a strong push with half of her strength. No projection—not when breaking through could injure Ben and Julio—but every scrap of sensory empathy she had.

For eight seconds she pushed against the barrier. It stretched with her, like a rubber band pulling taut, but didn't snap. On the ninth beat, she eased back, as if giving up, and for the briefest moment she swore she sensed satisfaction lacing the walls of her mental prison.

Zola's favorite trick—encouraging an opponent to underestimate her.

On ten, Kat gathered her strength and slammed it outward.

For one moment, one *heartbeat*, the iron cracked.

The man who slammed through the door held a gun in his outstretched hand. He pointed it in Kat's direction for a moment, then lowered it. "That's a bad idea, Miss Gabriel. Len is here to protect you and your friends, and you're making that difficult."

If it had just been her...but it wasn't. Ben and Julio were just as helpless as she was. Gritting her teeth, Kat let the mental attack fade away. "Tying us to chairs and drugging us was part of the protection too?"

"Yes." He held up the gun, its barrel pointing at the ceiling as he brandished it. "Otherwise, we may have no choice but to kill anyone who may not have the information we need."

The collar, Ben had said. Clearly whoever had kidnapped him didn't realize Jackson had already destroyed it.

If she told them, they might not believe her. If they *did* believe her...

Time, that was what they needed now. Time for Jackson to cast a spell or for Anna to use her contacts. Kat licked her chapped lips and winced. "May I have a glass of water?"

"No."

Without empathy, Kat had to fall back on the lessons Callum had forced her to learn. Body language. She took in the blank expression, the cold eyes, the easy grip on the gun. This wasn't a tense man, or a frightened one. This was a man so far gone into madness that he wasn't even angry.

Dangerous. He was dangerous, and he clearly wanted her to start talking. Fast.

Kat swallowed. "What do you want to know?"

His jaw clenched. "Where is the *collar*?"

Truth or lie. She had a split second to decide. "I don't know."

The man shook his head. "Try again, Miss Gabriel."

We don't have it. An answer guaranteed to make them all useless—and therefore expendable. So she met his gaze and put everything into the lie. "I told you, I don't—"

His dispassionate expression didn't change as he lowered his arm and shot Ben.

The sound was deafening. Like thunder in a closet, rattling through her almost hard enough to distract her from the sick feeling of something wet and warm splattering across her face.

The shot.

He'd shot Ben.

He'd *shot Ben.*

Shock held her rooted in place as the man turned without a sound and left, leaving Kat alone in a room with an unconscious shapeshifter and the lifeless body of her friend.

Chapter Eighteen

Most of the faint hope Andrew still harbored died when he found Kat's cell phone wedged in a storm drain outside the warehouse. Julio's car was still parked on the street, and there was no sign of either of them.

He kept it under control as he drove to Kat's apartment. Mackenzie and Jackson would be checking any and all of the public places they could have gone, like Mahalia's or Dixie John's, so he could do this. With any luck, they'd be watching an old sci-fi movie with the lights down and the telephone ringer off, and they wouldn't even realize Kat had dropped her phone.

The last shred of possibility, and it flared into desperation as he stood outside the apartment and heard movement inside. He pounded on the door. "Kat?"

He had to knock again before the door popped open. Sera stood there in sweatpants and an inside-out tank top, both clearly hastily donned. "Kat's still at Julio's..." She trailed off as she studied his face, then swore softly. "What happened?"

He gripped the edge of the doorframe. "They're not here?"

"No." Sera pivoted and got to the dining room table in two steps. She picked up her phone and flipped through the screen. "She texted me...this afternoon. Said she was going to help Julio paint a room, and they might go out later. That was the last I heard."

If anyone had unearthed them somewhere, getting drunk

and playing pool, Andrew would've gotten a call. "They're missing."

"Shit." Sera shoved her phone into her pocket and snatched up a hair elastic from the kitchen table. "Where's the last place anyone saw them?"

"I found Kat's phone over at the warehouse." His heart thumped painfully. "I was about to go back to Jackson's office. He's—he's already looking."

"I'm coming with you." She shoved her foot into a shoe while twisting her wet hair into a knot at the back of her head. "Grab my keys off the counter, will you? Do we need something of Kat's? For Jackson, if he needs to try to use magic?"

"I've got her phone."

Sera hopped on one foot and pulled her other shoe on. "What about Julio's phone? Maybe her friend from Birmingham can track the phone to Julio, if he's still got it. Trigger the GPS or something?"

"Ben's missing too." He shoved her keys at her and turned for the door. "We've got to move."

She did, grabbing a leather jacket off the back of a chair without bothering to find a warmer shirt. "Is Anna on her way?"

"Should be." And Patrick too, someone with reason enough to hunt down the bastards who'd done this. "I'm driving."

He counted the streets and turns between the apartment building and Jackson's office, trying to find a way to keep himself centered and calm. Using the little things to distract himself from disaster.

Anna's car was parked in front of the office, but it was Miguel who met them at the door. "Nothing?"

"No," Andrew said shortly. "Jackson?"

Miguel shook his head. "Patrick sent Anna some info, and Jackson's been helping her run some of it down."

The inside of the office didn't *look* like chaos had descended. Jackson and Mackenzie were both on the phone, and Anna was scribbling something on a white board in the corner.

Sera touched Andrew's arm, just the slightest brush of fingers, but her energy swept over him like a warm breeze in a cold room. "She's with Julio, and Julio's not going to let anything happen to her. We just need to get to them."

Somewhere to the left of Alec's deserted desk, Andrew had lain on the carpet, bleeding. Dying. He had half-memories of Kat leaning over him, her tears splashing hot on his skin as she screamed herself hoarse.

"I told her this was over," he found himself confessing. "I promised her better than this."

"I know." Sera pulled at his arm, planting one hand in the center of his chest to urge him to sit on one of the empty desks. "You sit, and you take a deep breath. Then you take another. Then you find out where the cult is, and you kill every person who had a hand in kidnapping Kat. And no one will touch her again."

"That's a damn bloodthirsty suggestion for someone who's trying to calm me down."

"We all have our roles. You don't run with a lot of submissive wolves, do you?"

Jackson slammed down his phone and rose. "Not good news, I guess."

Andrew held up Kat's phone. "I found it outside our building. Can you...?"

The other man's eyes clouded. "I tried a tracking spell already. I was able to lock on to Kat, but the location kept jumping all over the map. Someone's scrambling it."

Andrew squeezed his eyes shut. The cell phone's plastic casing cracked in his hand, and he forced himself to relax his grip as he opened his eyes. "So what's next?"

"Skip tracing," Anna said from her position by the white board.

"What the hell is that?"

"We trace the paper trails. Known associations." She drew a line between two names and capped her marker. "Hazelton has a sister with a Louisiana driver's license, and one of the other cult members inherited her dead mom's rental properties on the Gulf. If we track it all down..."

"We could find where they've gone to ground." Jackson rose and walked over to examine the board. "If they're snatching people, they need a place to take them."

Mackenzie held up her phone. "Tell us what to do. Who to call."

He didn't have a clue. This was Jackson's specialty, Anna's, anyone's but his. He was an architect before he was a wolf, before he'd been tasked with taking care of everyone in his charge.

He couldn't do this.

That's complete bullshit. His mother's voice, musical and determined. She'd never accepted the words from him, and she certainly wouldn't if she were around now, with so much on the line.

Andrew stood. "Can we find out when Patrick last spoke to Ben?"

Anna didn't have to check. "Four days, he said."

So they'd had plenty of time to find a place and hole up. "We keep looking," he said finally. "We track down everything we can, every lead, and we check them all out." In the absence of magic, it was all they could do.

"How do we do that when each place could be hours away in any direction?" Miguel asked quietly.

There was only one thing he could think of. "Wynne Albrecht. We'll use the cult's own tricks against them."

Chapter Nineteen

Her face was sticky.

Kat dug her teeth into her lower lip to hold back a whimper. She wouldn't break. Wouldn't cry, and it didn't matter that tears had been leaking out from beneath her closed eyelids for hours or days or *weeks*, however long she'd been handcuffed to this chair while Ben—

No. She tried one of Callum's calming breaths and regretted it, because everything smelled like salt and metal. Tears and blood, and it hadn't been days because Julio was still slumped in the corner. He stirred from time to time, muttered sounds that weren't quite words, but Kat couldn't bring herself to speak to him. If he woke up, if he looked at Ben's body, looked at her, then it wouldn't be a dream.

It had to be a dream. A nightmare. Something new to replace the terror of replaying Andrew's near death over and over again. Catharsis. Her psyche spewing out the stress of the past weeks, like it did after controlled burnout. That was all it was.

Ben was not dead. His blood was not on her face, on her body, in her hair. Just like before, just like with Andrew, only this time it wasn't only blood but *pieces* of him, and Franklin wouldn't come and save the day. Ben wouldn't climb to his feet as a wolf because bullets didn't remake lives, they ended them. Gone forever. Game over.

No. Just a dream. Soon, she'd wake up. Wake up.

Wake up, please wake up.

Julio made another noise—a groggy sound that was almost a word this time—and a scream crawled its way into her throat, scratched and clawed until it burst free in one pained cry that raked across her nerves.

This was it. This was what it felt like to break.

"Kat." Julio coughed and whispered her name again.

Her irrational need for him to stay asleep vanished, swallowed whole by the desperate need to not be alone in her nightmare. "You need to wake up, Julio. It's important. It's really important, okay?"

He raised his head, but his eyes were glazed and unfocused. "Where are we?"

"In a garage, I think." Her lips were dry, but she couldn't wet them. Not when her face was covered in— *Stop it, Kat. Stop it.* "I think someone from the cult must have us. You and me and—and Ben." Her voice broke on the name. "They shot him."

The words kindled no recognition, but his head snapped up. This time, his gaze focused on the chair beside her.

On Ben.

Julio made a low noise and jerked against the chains as he started to breathe faster. "They want the thing, right? The collar."

"Yes." If they had a telepath, they would have plucked the thoughts from her head already. Or maybe they just hadn't had one strong enough to break through the natural psychic defenses she and Ben had. It didn't mean they didn't have a clairvoyant...or a good old-fashioned bug. "They could be listening to us."

His expression didn't change. "Did you tell them you don't know where it is?"

She couldn't tell if he was lying, confused from the drugs or honestly didn't know...and there was no way to ask. "Yes. They didn't believe me."

His gaze flickered to Ben. "How long was I out?"

"I don't know." Shame twisted with horror, made her queasy. "I freaked out, Julio. I'm *still* freaked out."

"It's okay." He looked around the room for a moment and cocked his head as if listening. The chains shook again as his shoulders flexed. He strained against his bonds, grunting from the effort, then relaxed with a curse. "They must have used magic. These things are solid."

"I'm handcuffed." It was inane. Everything she said was inane, everything she thought was inane, but it was the only way to stay calm. To keep from following Julio's gaze to where Ben sat a foot away.

No, not Ben. Ben's body.

"*Kat,* look at me." His tone brooked no argument. "I can't break these chains. You have to tell me what's going on."

"Okay. Okay." God, she would have given anything for a wisp of her empathy, for the power to reach out to him, to ground herself in his unshakable strength. "They've got someone here who's blocking me. I can lower my shields, but it doesn't matter. They've got me penned in."

"We'll figure that out. But you've got to stay with me, okay?"

"I know." She had to get back to Andrew. If something happened to her, he'd never come back from it. She dragged in a steadying breath out of habit, and wished she hadn't. So much blood, and she had to tighten her neck and shoulders to keep from turning to look at Ben. "Can you hear anything outside of these walls?"

"Footsteps." His expression tightened. "Whatever you have to do, Kat. Remember that. Whatever—"

The door opened.

A woman this time, not the man from before. She carried a small leather case, which she set down not far from Julio's chair. "Good evening."

Julio remained silent, even when the woman took an extra chair from the corner and brought it close to his, sat down and opened her case to reveal the wicked glint of metal.

Staged. It was all perfectly staged, straight out of a movie script, and Kat knew it was meant for her. Not that they wouldn't torture Julio—with Ben's blood dried on her skin, she believed they'd do anything—but the precise movements, the slow reveal, the sheer theatrics of it all... They were trying to fuck with her head.

It was working.

Kat squeezed her hands together, even though she could barely feel her fingers. "I told you, I don't know where the collar is."

"Really?" The woman pulled out a thin knife, almost like a scalpel. "From what we've heard, you planned to take it to Wyoming. Did you?"

They knew too much, and yet not enough. Kat's mouth went dry. The blade looked sharp, cold. The woman kept turning it this way and that, letting it catch the light. More theatrics, giving Kat ample time to speak as dread closed around her.

She'd seen the movies. She knew all of her lines. Quips and taunts. *Sorry, I was too busy banging your mom*, or something even cockier. *Is that the biggest knife you've got? No wonder you're overcompensating.* No, that one didn't even make sense, because it was a woman, not a man, and how in hell was she supposed to laugh in the face of danger when danger wasn't coming anywhere near her?

No, they'd killed Ben, and they'd slice Julio to pieces next. Because she was the empath, the squishy-hearted one, and she'd break under someone else's pain.

The scalpel dipped toward Julio, and Kat let out an embarrassing squeak. "Wait. Wait, don't."

Julio growled. "Kat, no—"

The blade sinking into his skin silenced him.

Chapter Twenty

No more than a quarter hour after Andrew's desperate, determined phone call, a willowy blonde stood in front of him. It didn't matter that Wynne's body was currently in Paris—she didn't need it to help them investigate the addresses Anna had managed to locate. She studied the satellite map Mackenzie pulled up, closed her eyes and vanished.

Andrew paced the floor anxiously. Astral projection allowed her almost instantaneous travel, but she had to exercise care in popping in and out of her target coordinates, or she risked exposure. They were dealing with psychics, and if they thought Kat and Julio had help coming, they might not hesitate to kill them both.

In less than ten minutes, she reappeared. "Nothing there but a vacant lot. I checked the adjacent ones too, just to be sure, but nothing."

The bell above the door jingled as Patrick shoved through it, a massive duffel bag over his shoulder and a smaller one in his hand. He stopped short and blinked at Wynne, then looked to Andrew. "You found an astral projector?"

Jackson scratched his head and eyed the white board. "It's the only way to check all these places out without splitting up in half a dozen different directions. A hell of a lot quicker too."

Wynne barely raised her head to smile absently. "I'm off again." With that, she disappeared.

Patrick swung the large bag off his shoulder and dropped it on the desk in front of Andrew. "Weapons," he said shortly. "I flew private and brought everything."

Andrew dropped to one knee and unzipped the duffel. Just about every kind of gun he could think of lay inside, along with several intricate-looking blades. "Magically silenced like your others?"

"Silenced, untraceable, warded ten ways to the underworld and at least halfway back." Patrick turned to Jackson. "I know your spell wouldn't lock on Kat, but I brought some of Ben's things."

Jackson nodded. "Give me the thing he handles the most and I'll try."

Patrick retrieved a laptop computer barely bigger than his hand and held it out. "This."

"Got it." He retreated to his desk and the map laid across it.

Anna beckoned Patrick over to the board. "I've narrowed down these possibilities. Does anything strike a chord, maybe something one of your contacts mentioned?"

"Not Tennessee," Patrick said at once, pointing to an address south of Memphis. "Not Georgia either. But I got hits on movement in Mississippi and Louisiana... I tried to get a guy on those bank accounts, to follow the money, but I'm used to having Ben."

"Either they're still traveling or they couldn't have gone far," Miguel observed.

It all depended on what they wanted—information, or something far more violent and personal. "Closer means less time," Andrew told him. "They'd have to consider that we might—" His breath cut off as magic whooshed through the room and lifted the fine hairs on the back of his neck.

He turned to find Jackson's entire desk awash in golden, glaring light. Even after it died down, the wizard stared at the map in confusion, his brows drawn together.

It was Sera who spoke, her voice soft and worried. "Jackson? Was the computer warded? Kat has a ward on one of her laptops..."

"No, it's..." He trailed off and shook his head. "Are any of those addresses up near Covington or Goodbee?"

Anna whirled and snatched up one of the files. "Yes! A foreclosed farm in St. Tammany Parish. The motherfucker's in the middle of nowhere."

Andrew's knees wobbled, and he grabbed the edge of a desk. "That's it?"

Jackson began to hurriedly fold the map. "That's it."

Mackenzie shoved her phone into her back pocket and turned to Sera, who'd already reached for her jacket. "You're staying here, honey. Someone needs to wait for Wynne, and you know what'll happen in a fight."

The coyote tensed, anger flashing across her face, chased quickly by frustration. "It's Kat."

"It's Kat," Mackenzie agreed. "Which is why we can't have you underfoot, giving our instincts hell."

Sera jerked her coat off the desk and looked at Andrew. "I'll stay in the car. I just...I can *help*. We can leave a note for Wynne."

He couldn't imagine being left behind with his friends in trouble, and the pleading look on her face was one emotional straw too many. "You stay in the car and stay *down*, for Christ's sake."

She nodded with the blind obedience of a submissive shifter, so effortless he knew it was instinct. As Sera slid into her coat, Mackenzie gave him a searching look, then turned to the white board and scribbled a note with the address.

It couldn't be more than fifty or sixty miles, less if they crossed the lake over the Causeway, but the thought of getting stuck in traffic on the bridge with no way out of it...

No fucking way. He hit the door, shouldering it open. The glass wobbled in its metal casing, maybe even cracked, but all Andrew could think of was getting out of the city.

Getting to Kat.

Chapter Twenty-One

Julio didn't scream.

He gritted his teeth. He clenched his fists. Kat felt every slice like it was cutting into her own skin, and she was crying long before the first tears of pain leaked from the corner of his eyes.

But he didn't scream.

Kat did. Ten minutes, twenty—she didn't know, and she couldn't keep track, but it didn't take long for her begging to give way to fury. Julio healed fast, his skin closing up to present a fresh, unblemished surface, if you could ignore the blood. She screamed as her fear turned to rage, as pressure built until the constriction of the psychic barriers locked around her turned claustrophobic.

She couldn't get enough air, and maybe that was what broke her. Suffocating while Julio suffered in silence, and when she finally snapped, the truth tumbled from her lips in a tangled rush. "We destroyed it already, it's gone, it's *gone.*"

The woman froze, leaned back carefully out of reach of Julio's teeth and eyed Kat. "I don't believe you."

Of course not. Too little, too late, and she didn't know if it was brilliance on her part that she'd managed to confuse the issue so thoroughly, or if the truth would be what got them killed. "Why would we keep it?"

"Why *wouldn't* you?" the woman demanded in turn, rising from her chair. She snatched up the bag and stalked out, slamming the door behind her.

A rough noise vibrated out of Julio, and it took Kat a moment to recognize it as a rusty chuckle. "You like to piss people off," he rasped.

If she started laughing, she might never stop. Blind hysteria wasn't an option. "I don't try, it just happens." There, a joke. They were back on script.

Then Julio coughed, and blood trickled from the corner of his mouth. "Use it," he said finally. "You do what you have to do, I mean it." Then his head rolled forward until his chin rested on his chest, and he went still.

Her heart stopped.

"Julio?"

No response, and panic swelled until she realized his chest was moving. He was breathing. Slow and shallow, but he was *breathing*, damn it, and Kat counted the breaths. Counted ten, and then started to worry that they were too slow. She tried timing them, but keeping track of the seconds in her head and the breaths on her finger felt as natural as patting her head and rubbing her stomach, and as useful.

So she counted, as her body ached and terror settled around her. Every ten breaths she said his name and got silence in reply.

All of the guilt seemed stupid now. She'd spent so much time cursing her gift and punishing herself. She'd wallowed and moped and done everything but etch emo poetry into her arm, because she was *so* dangerous and *so* dark. Now she was handcuffed to a fucking chair, locked into her mind, and she'd give anything for a spark of that deadly power.

She'd never felt so helpless in her life.

Julio's chest rose and fell three hundred and seventy-four times before the door opened again to reveal the woman, returning with her damned bag. She laid it at Julio's feet and slapped him once to rouse him. When it didn't work, she frowned, sat and retrieved a larger knife, one with a serrated edge.

But instead of applying it to Julio's flesh immediately, she cast a glance at Kat. "None of the others believe you, either."

Then the sharp teeth of blade bit into Julio's shoulder, he jerked awake with a muffled grunt—and Kat felt it.

Not garden-variety human empathy and not her imagination. Her power, his pain, so clear she jerked and stared at her arm as a choked groan escaped her. Her skin was unmarked, but she felt the next cut just as deeply, so bright and hot that she threw herself instinctively outward, battering against the prison that had become a trap. Emotions could come in, but she couldn't get out.

Not even when the torture began in earnest.

Maybe it was a blessing that she'd already screamed herself hoarse. Her own whimpers would have been a distraction from marveling over how Julio could feel this much agony and not make a sound. Maybe he was the god that Sera painted him in her weaker moments, when she got drunk on too much vodka and explained to Kat in agonizing detail that Julio was the sort of man a girl drowned in because he wouldn't let anything happen to her ever again.

Sera was never going to forgive Kat if Julio ended up with a bullet between his eyes.

Kat shivered. Shivered hard enough to rattle the handcuffs against the chair, because it was so damn cold she couldn't feel pain anymore. Just the beautiful numbness that brought back memories of the last time she'd been helpless while a man bled for trying to protect her.

Their captors had made a mistake. A terrible, wonderful mistake. They'd given her Julio's pain and mixed it with her own rage, and the bastard trying to keep her locked into her own mind didn't know how very, very soon he'd be dying.

Kat didn't know how long it went on, only that Julio never broke. Not on the surface, anyway, but his pain filled the vast reservoir of her gift until she wondered whether anyone who could suffer so deeply, so silently, wasn't a little broken to begin with.

She was past broken, careening into deadly. And maybe the woman torturing them knew it. This time, when she put away her knives and turned to face Kat, that triumphant little smile slipped away. Kat didn't need empathy to see uncertainty in the woman's eyes or fear in her too-quick steps as she retreated to the door.

As it slammed shut, Kat spent one idle, bemused moment wondering just how insane she looked.

Julio met Kat's gaze, his face pale and ashen. "Hold on to it," he urged softly. "Just for a little while. Keep it."

Her lips cracked when she smiled, and she didn't care. "I'm bringing you inside my shields. Don't fight me."

He didn't return her smile. "I don't think I could." Then he added cryptically, "I need time."

She was already dismantling what was left of her battered shields so she could rebuild them around Julio. "Time for what?"

A spasm of coughs wracked him. "To heal up. Then we fight, no matter what."

"All right." Brick by careful brick, she built her own wall around them. "I'm not getting out of these handcuffs, but I might be able to get you out of those chains."

"Did you get all telekinetic on me, sweetheart?"

No, she'd gotten ruthless. "Try pharmaceutical. Ever overdosed on adrenaline?"

Chapter Twenty-Two

There were no cars, no lights, nothing to indicate Kat and Julio and Ben were being kept anywhere on the property. No signs, until Andrew and Patrick circled a stand of dead pecans and caught sight of a small freestanding garage.

"They painted the windows." He gestured, guiding Patrick's gaze. "Obscuring the light."

"Wards too, all the way around that building." Patrick rubbed at the back of his neck as if it itched. "Jackson'll take care of those. Can you get a scent?"

All Andrew smelled was wet earth, dead grass and motor oil. "They're in there." And only the knowledge that it could get them killed kept him from rushing in. "We need to check with Miguel, see if he got anything."

They carefully retraced their steps back over the rise down the road. Miguel had already returned, resumed his human form and pulled on his jeans. "They're here, *somewhere*. I tried to get through to Kat, but I don't know if she heard me."

"A lot of magic in the air," Patrick said, scratching at his neck again. "Did you smell any other wolves, Miguel?"

"I don't know. A few times, I thought maybe...but it was hard to tell."

Anna slid her phone shut and hopped down off the back of the car. "We have a problem. One of my friends out west heard of some big freelance job in these parts. Magic and muscle. Apparently, it drew hardcore interest, got some hires."

Mackenzie rocked to her toes, then unzipped her jacket. "So we fight. Jackson, baby? How big a racket do you think crossing the perimeter will make?"

"With these kinds of precautions? I'd say mighty loud." He flexed his hands and stretched his shoulders. "I can handle the spells, and whoever they've got in there casting them. What we need to watch out for is a Hail Mary pass once they know we've got them."

Andrew yanked his shirt over his head. "That's me. If anyone tries it, I'll stop them. No question." And there wasn't. A strange calm descended over him as he unbuckled his belt. If anyone needed to step in front of a bullet, it would be him. He'd take that risk, be the protector.

One way or another, Kat would live.

Anna nodded slowly. "I'll be on your heels."

"Patrick?" Mackenzie's voice was muffled as she jerked her shirt over her head. Her bra was blue lace and ruffles, but her words were brutally efficient. "Go with them. I'm fast enough to be flexible, so I'll keep an open path for retreat."

And watch Jackson's back. Andrew understood the feeling. He normally avoided fighting as a wolf, but tonight he relished the notion. He'd stand before them, and they'd *know* how low he would bring them.

And then he would end them.

His jeans landed in the dirt, and he followed them down. Magic, so much magic he wondered if they'd feel it in the ramshackle garage, and then the wolf was free. He stalked through the grass, once overgrown and now brittle and brown. They left tracks, he and Anna and Patrick, but that was okay too.

The time for stealth was almost at an end.

Jackson began to chant, low, rolling words that tumbled over each other until they ran together in a rhythmic stream. Soft light began to gather around him, a subtle glow that seemed like a trick of the eyes until it intensified, almost throbbed—

From somewhere inside the building, Julio howled, a sound that fell somewhere between human and animal, one hundred percent *rage*.

The magic around Jackson exploded, might have even swept Andrew off his paws if he hadn't already been running, counting on Patrick to blow open the door and let him in to wreak his vengeance.

A roar came from above as a massive black shape hurtled off the roof. Patrick spun out of the way too fast for a human, but his silent shot went wide. The panther landed gracefully, using the momentum from his leap to charge straight at Andrew.

Anna cut him off. She was smaller than the cat, but she caught him broadside with a running leap, and they both went tumbling down, spitting and snarling, in a flurry of claws and teeth.

More shouts from inside, voices raised in warning and fear. Andrew hit the door with his shoulder and it yielded, shattering under the force of his advance.

Inside was chaos. Men and women scrambled for weapons in front of a door that shuddered as Julio screamed his rage. An older man sat in the corner, both hands pressed to his temples and his face screwed up in an expression of agony. Next to him, a woman clutched at his shoulder, screaming something that cut off abruptly as she stared at the door.

At Andrew.

Before he could move, she threw up her hand. Fire shot up in a semicircle that cut her and the man off from the rest of the room, and a second woman spun and leveled her gun at Andrew, her finger trembling on the trigger. "You self-protecting *bitch*, why don't you set the fucking wolf on fire?"

She fired a split second before Andrew moved, and pain ignited in his shoulder. It didn't stop him from lunging. She screamed and squeezed off one more wild shot, and he snapped his jaws shut on her forearm.

Julio's enraged roar drowned out her pained shriek. The inner door trembled under the force of another strike, and the man standing before it lifted both hands as if warding off an invisible force. "Kill him, Saunders. I can barely hold the door."

The remaining figure—a hulking man who smelled of wolf— swung a meaty fist at Andrew. The blow connected, driving Andrew to the floor, and the woman screamed as his teeth tore through her flesh.

He released her and rolled away to his feet, dancing clear of the next punch. His shoulder burned, but he could stand on his leg. Just a graze, maybe, and no real damage.

Zola's voice echoed in his head, warning him not to let his anger guide him. Rushing in blindly was a recipe for disaster, so he braced himself and growled, baring his teeth and lifting his tail. A show of dominance. A warning.

For one second, one telling, fatal second, his attacker hesitated.

That's right, you son of a bitch. Andrew let his growl melt into a menacing snarl as he surged forward. The man was strong, maybe strong enough to hurt him if he really got a good grip, so he'd have to drag him down. Instinct drove him just as much as anger, and he sank his teeth deep into the man's thigh.

The wolf hit the floor, but he didn't go down easy. A steel-toed work boot slammed into Andrew's back leg, and Saunders snatched at the scruff of Andrew's neck and yanked out a fist full of fur.

Inconsequential, really, that pain. For all he knew, this was the man who'd grabbed Kat off the street, covered her mouth to quell her screams and dragged her off to her fate.

No more anger. Even his rage was transformed, more animal than human, and he wrenched his head back without opening his jaws. Blood gushed as muscle and skin ripped under the force of his bite.

Saunders screamed—just once, short and agonized, and rolled away awkwardly, the desperate retreat of an animal who knew he was already dead but couldn't quash the urge to flee.

The man by the door threw out his hands, and an invisible wave tossed Andrew into the air and against the wall. He barely managed to stagger to his feet as the remaining door smashed open, knocking the telekinetic aside. The man stumbled over one of his fallen comrades and tripped into the fire that blazed in the corner.

He flailed, screaming as the flames licked at his clothes and hair, but his suffering lasted only moments. Julio gripped the man's head between both hands, twisted hard enough to crack his neck and dropped him into the blaze.

Julio looked like hell, but he was *alive*. His shirt hung in sliced tatters over scabbed, bleeding flesh, and broken chains dangled from his wrists. Another inhuman noise escaped him, a match to the feral light in his eyes, and he dropped to the floor behind Saunders. One quick, vicious movement wrapped one of the chains around the man's neck, and Julio drew it tight with a sharp snap.

Nothing stood between Andrew and the door, and he rushed through it. The first thing that hit him was the scent of blood, of *death*, and he stumbled blindly.

"Andrew?" Kat's voice, hoarse and cracking.

Kat. Andrew shook as he tried desperately to reach for that spark of humanity inside him, to regain his human form and tell her everything would be all right. But the stink of death remained, and he realized with growing horror that it was Ben in the chair beside Kat, unmoving and—

He dragged his attention away, focused every bit of his attention on the curve of Kat's cheek. She needed him to help her now, and it was the only thing that allowed him to shift.

He struggled through the change and half-crawled to her chair. "I'm here."

Blood and bits of Ben had dried on her face and neck, cut

through with furrows that showed the path of her tears. There was something off in her gaze, not quite shock, or even fear, but a detachment that was almost numb.

It seemed to take forever for her to focus on him. When she did, her gaze fixed on his shoulder. Black swallowed her eyes, until her iris was nothing but a tiny blue ring around endless pupils.

In the other room, a man shrieked in agonized terror.

He'd forgotten all about the bullet wound, and he lifted her face with his hands, tearing her gaze from it now. "Stop, Kat. You have to come back now."

"They killed Ben." She leaned forward, twisted, and metal clanged against metal. "Get me out of these handcuffs. Let me fight."

Struggling against the cuffs had cut into her wrists already. Andrew snapped the chain and lifted her from the chair. "I'm getting you out of here."

"No!" She twisted in his arms like a wild creature. "I'm not running. Put me down and help me fight, Andrew. I need to fight. I need—" A hitched breath. "So much pain. They tortured Julio, and it's in me now."

No time to argue. He pressed his lips to her temple, clutched her tighter and ran for the door.

Just outside, the flames had grown higher. The pyrokinetic could still lower the flames and come after them, and Andrew trembled, torn between his need to get Kat someplace safe and his knowledge that everyone involved here had to die or she'd *never* be safe.

Before he could make a decision, a spot of magic flared on the wall, a flash followed by a bullet that shouldn't have passed cleanly through the side of the garage. One of Patrick's weapons, and as it found its mark, the woman cowering on the other side of the flames crumpled to the floor.

The ring of fire on the concrete floor subsided, but the flames had already climbed the wall. When they reached the rafters, they began to spread quickly.

Too quickly.

Patrick lunged through the door, a sleek rifle in his hands. "Where's Ben? We need to get back to the cars. The fight's converged there."

Shit. "He's..." Andrew couldn't say it, *couldn't*, not like this.

"Patrick." Kat's voice broke on his name, and that must have been enough. Without a word, Patrick circled around them and disappeared into the back room.

Kat shuddered, pain spilling over her features. "I can stand. You need to get him."

Anna came in, barefoot and still tugging her shirt into place. "Everyone outside is down. Jackson says—" She froze, her gaze on the open doorway into the back room. She crossed to it, heedless of the fire overhead and its mounting intensity.

Andrew took Kat outside and set her down, but he stayed by her side. "Anna will get Patrick out of there. I'm not leaving you."

She tried to step away, but her knees buckled, and she ended up clutching at his shoulders. "I'll be fine when my feet wake up. Just *go*."

"I *can't*."

She actually snarled, but her eyes held pain and fear, not rage. "Why not?"

"You're all that matters." He smoothed his hands over her cheeks and tried to make her understand. "I'll save every damn person in the world if I can, Kat, but if I ever have to choose between them and you... It's not even a choice. It'll always be you."

And there it was. The answer to the question she hadn't dared to ask all those endless days ago. The reason he'd learned first aid and weapons and fighting. *Everything.* Andrew didn't want to be a hero.

He wanted to be her hero.

Her body trembled. Tears filled her eyes, but she blinked them away, and when she met his gaze this time, clear blue stared up at him. "Do I get to save you sometime?"

"Every day. More than once, if you want."

"Oh, good." She shivered again, and her eyes fluttered shut. "When Patrick and Anna get out, you have to get me to Julio. I have to try to undo what I did before it hurts him."

"It's okay." Andrew pulled her closer, tucked her face against his neck. "Everything's going to be okay."

"I killed the man who was shielding me," she whispered. "I blew his mind to pieces, and then I went back and crushed the pieces into dust. And I don't feel bad. Not at all."

"Because *they* did this," he whispered. "No choice, remember?"

Kat nodded. "Do you think—"

She stiffened as Patrick's voice rose in a single incoherent roar of grief and anger, audible over the crackle of the fire. A moment later he screamed again, this time in pain.

Kat's fingernails pierced Andrew's skin. "We have to do something."

The others had already come running, but by the time they reached the garage, Anna had made it to the door. She dragged Patrick bodily behind her, nearly lifting him off his feet even though he was easily twice her size. "One of the rafters went," she ground out.

A wide strip of the shirt covering his upper back had been burned away, revealing red, blistered skin beneath. "We need to get him to the clinic," Andrew told her.

"And you," Jackson cut in. "There's a hole in your shoulder."

Andrew had forgotten again. "I can barely feel it." Then again, that might not be a good thing. "We can handle arrangements for—for all this on the way."

Arrangements. A nice, bland way of talking about covering

their tracks, but reality was reality, and sometimes it was necessary. They could never walk away from a fight clean and free, with no worry about exposure or what came next.

Kat's hand slid into his, and he closed his fingers around hers. "Let's go."

Chapter Twenty-Three

It took Sera, Mackenzie and half a bar of soap to get Kat clean.

She ended up in the shower at the clinic, stripped to her bra and panties as the two women helped her scrub dried blood from her skin. Jackson had sprung the locks on the handcuffs before they made it back to New Orleans, but the damage was already done.

Kat winced her way through a haphazard bandaging before Sera dragged her under the spray. Then she stretched her aching hands out in front of her and watched through a dream as the pinkish water circled the drain until it finally ran clear.

Sera braided her damp hair while Mackenzie found her a pair of scrubs to wear. By the time she had her wrists clean and redressed, Andrew appeared, his own bandage just peeking out of the neckline of his T-shirt.

He took her hand and lifted it, studying her wrist. "Okay?"

"I'll be fine." Everything felt distant—surreal—except for the brush of his fingers. Shivering, she leaned into him. "I think I have a new understanding of pain now."

"Julio's going to be fine," he whispered. "Most of the wounds are already healing."

The wounds were the least of it, and they both knew it. Julio's berserk frenzy had exhausted his body, but it had taken Sera's touch to lead him back to sanity. The magic of a true submissive shapeshifter, the power to balance rage with gentle acceptance. Sera might be trapped into obedience, but the true dominants—the good ones—were just as bound by their need to protect her.

Not so different from the balance between herself and Andrew, Kat supposed, though so much cleaner. She and Andrew would always be tangled up in an edge of danger and the knowledge that they could hurt each other. It had taken her this long to realize it didn't matter. They were creatures of instinct, both of them, and their first impulse would be to keep each other safe.

Turning her head, Kat pressed a soft kiss over his heart. "What about Patrick?"

Andrew hesitated. "The burns on his back are probably going to scar. Right now, understandably, he's more upset about Ben. Anna took him to the apartment over Mahalia's to get him set up there."

Sera had been the one to break the news about Lia, conveyed in a soft whisper as she worked bloody snarls out of Kat's hair. Maybe it was a blessing, that Ben had never found out. That he'd died so fast, so suddenly, and with no idea that the woman he loved was already gone.

Andrew stroked the tears from her cheeks. "The cleaner settled everything. He managed to stop the fire too, so Patrick can bury Ben after the ME releases him."

"Okay." The numbness was fracturing. No, melting—like ice around her heart laid bare to the sun. Andrew's warmth surrounded her, and the lingering echoes of pain drifted up. She'd made it her own, and she'd used it, and now she had to let it go, let tears wash away everything but the knowledge that she'd never have to cry alone again.

He rocked her and murmured gently as she cried, soft assurances that no matter what happened, horrifying and joyous and everything in between, he would be there. Holding her.

It was enough. Not a cure, not even more than the start of

one, but it was comfort enough as she sobbed through the pain, through *Julio's* pain, the agony he'd borne that had gone beyond the flesh. He hadn't cried, not really, so she cried for both of them, until her head ached and she felt empty and hollow.

Swallowing hurt, but she managed, then rested her cheek against his chest. "I get it now. The instincts. Being alpha. It's not just because you love me, is it?"

"No," he whispered. "That's not all of it. I love you, and that's the only reason I can rein it in sometimes. Because I know the crazy alpha shit makes you miserable."

It would always be his challenge. Hers would be to love him enough to forgive him when the instincts spilled over. "I don't know what hurt Julio more. Being tortured, or knowing they were using him to hurt me and not being able to stop it."

"That." He seemed certain. "Being helpless to stop someone else's pain."

He'd been helpless to stop hers for too long. All of them had been, and maybe that was the real truth behind Alec's anger, the truth even Anna hadn't picked at. He'd watched Kat cry, and it would have been so much easier if he could have dragged Andrew to her by the scruff of the neck and forced them to make up. But Andrew had been a danger to her, so Alec couldn't stop her pain.

She didn't have to be in pain anymore. So she let it go and struggled for a smile. "Thank you for coming to get me. I mean, we were in the middle of rescuing ourselves, but I'm just as glad I didn't have to wrestle with Julio after I gave him the empathic version of a shot of adrenaline."

He didn't laugh. "Of course I came for you. Don't ever think I won't. *Ever.*"

"I didn't," she promised, lifting a hand to his face. He looked grave, as exhausted as she felt. "I'll always protect you. You'll always protect me. That's how it works."

"That's how it works," he echoed hoarsely, his eyes intense.

"Kat, I'm sorry. About everything."

"Shh." She smoothed her thumb over his lower lip. "I don't hate you anymore. Not even a little."

"Even if you should? For Ben, if nothing else?"

His name hurt to hear. Maybe it would for a long time. But this was a burden Andrew didn't get to carry. "I'm the one who dragged him into it, and I'm the one who tried to bluff the people holding us. But it's not my fault he's dead. It's *theirs*. I know you can't stop feeling the guilt, but if you're going to be with me, you have to give it up sometimes. I want a lover, not a martyr."

He heaved a shaky sigh. "It's not easy to give up, this martyr thing, but I can do it for you."

"Only when it makes you miserable." Touching his lips again, she smiled. "I know what I'm getting into. You're an alpha wolf. Sometimes I'll have to bite you to get your attention."

Andrew closed his eyes and bent his head to her touch. "And I need you to do that."

She knew, though she couldn't say how. It wasn't empathy, or instinct, either. Maybe it was like chiseling away at the new Andrew to find that the base was there, the outlines of the man she'd known. Loving him now was like learning a new programming language, like switching from C++ to Java and realizing all the important stuff was pretty much the same, underneath the syntax and semicolons.

It would be awkward for a while. But one day she'd turn around and realize she couldn't remember not knowing exactly who he was. So she kissed him, and told him the only thing she needed him to know. "I don't want you not to be what you are. You're a wolf. I love all of you."

His arms tightened around her, and his breath stirred her drying hair. "Can I take you home now?"

Home was with him. Wherever he wanted her to be. "Yes."

Empaths and funerals were a miserable combination, which made Carmen's presence a blessing.

Ben's service had been short—at Patrick's request—but Alec and Carmen's arrival had given the exhausted mourners a place to gather and grieve. It took a few phone calls and a Dixie John's catering miracle, but eventually Kat found herself enthroned on one of Alec and Carmen's newly upholstered couches.

Long sleeves covered the thick bandages around her wrists. A plate full of food balanced on her lap, filled with finger foods that she obediently nibbled every time Andrew looked her way.

Carmen took it away finally. "You can tell him I said not eating was okay right now."

"He's worried." Which was an understatement. She wouldn't be surprised if he'd spent the last two nights watching her sleep. "I'm sure my appetite will come back eventually."

Carmen's dark eyes held shadows of concern. "I want to get Callum to come back here for a while. You and Julio both could use...someone to talk to."

Protesting that she wasn't the one who'd been tortured would do no good. Not with Carmen—who knew, like only another empath could know, how little it mattered. "Callum was due another visit anyway. At the end of February."

"I think I'll call him and see if he can make the trip early."

"For Julio, if you want." Kat found Andrew in the crowd, and smiled when she caught him sneaking a look at her. She didn't need Callum. Not because she wasn't broken, but because she *had* someone to talk to. Someone who could make her feel safe until she climbed back to her feet. "I'm not going to be here, anyway," she added. "The Alpha's private jet is waiting to bring us to Wyoming before my cousin actually self-destructs. I'll be lucky if he lets me out of his sight before Nick has her baby."

"He's worried about her," Carmen said. "Maybe having you

there, safe and sound, will set his mind at ease."

"I know." Reaching out, Kat curled her hand around Carmen's. "Is Julio okay?"

"You know better than anyone what he went through." She took a deep breath. "No, he's not okay. But he will be."

"He's strong," she whispered. "I know that now too."

Carmen looked over to where Julio stood in quiet conversation with Alec. "He's strong, but sometimes I think maybe that's harder. It makes him likelier to blame himself."

"I know. I'm afraid Patrick will do the same."

"He lost his brother," she allowed. "I don't think it's possible not to feel responsible for that. But we find ways to deal with tragedy, and people to help."

"At least we have a strong community. It's better than being alone."

"Absolutely." Carmen squeezed her hand. "Give everyone on the ranch a hug and a kiss from me, okay?"

Kat opened her mouth to answer, but Carmen's gaze had jumped to Alec, who was weaving his way through the scattered crowd. He seemed uncomfortable in his crisp black suit, but Kat had to admit he looked good.

Judging by the way Carmen's eyes softened, she agreed. "Does anyone need anything?" she asked, touching his sleeve.

Alec nodded toward Andrew. "He needs to round Kat up and get out of here before Derek calls me again. I think we've reached the end of his patience."

They'd probably reached it two days ago, when Derek had gotten Kat's greatly sanitized version of the past few weeks. The explosion she'd expected had come all right, and she hadn't even told him the worst bits.

Maybe she should have, in retrospect. Admitted everything before she was within arm's reach and he could actually shake her to see if she'd rattle.

Oh well. Too late now. Kat released Carmen's hand and

rose. "Do me a favor, Alec?"

"What's that, kiddo?"

"Keep an eye on Patrick? Just for the next few days..." Long enough for him to remember he *had* a community, even if it wasn't one he'd spent much time in.

Alec glanced to Carmen, who smiled gently. "Patrick isn't alone," she said finally. "He knows."

It was all Kat could ask for, and it would have to do. For now. After murmuring her goodbyes, she picked a path through the gathering and found her way to Andrew's side. "Alec says it's time to face the music."

"So I hear." He dropped one hand to the small of her back. "Will you still love me after your cousin smashes my face?"

She loved him most when he made her smile. "Will *you* still love *me* after my cousin smashes in your face?"

"Yes," he said, suddenly serious. "Always."

Kat lifted her fingers to his cheek, stroked his beard and wondered if she'd ever get tired of the thrill of touching him. Even with sadness and grief pressing in on her from every side, he made tomorrow worth living for. "Me too."

Chapter Twenty-Four

Wyoming was mercilessly fucking cold, so cold that Andrew still hadn't warmed up by the time Derek stopped hugging Kat, and that took almost half an hour. Finally, he reluctantly relinquished her to Mahalia's care and beckoned for Andrew to follow him.

They walked down the hall to a library. What Alec had said about Derek's constant worry was evident, because his friend looked like he'd barely been sleeping. "Has Nick been all right?" Andrew asked.

"She's resting." Derek dragged a hand through his too-long hair, which responded by standing straight up. "Christ, Andrew. I don't—" He stopped and turned. "I don't even want to know what happened. I don't think I can handle it."

"It's in the past anyway," he answered. "She's safe now."

Derek dropped into a rocking chair and braced his elbows on his knees. "And you and Kat..."

"Yeah. Me and Kat." The only words that would suffice—*me and Kat*. "I'm going to marry her, you know. Well, after I ask, and provided she says yes."

"Are you asking my permission?"

"No." Maybe he should have been, judging from Derek's forbidding look, but he didn't have to. "She's not a kid anymore, man, and we—we don't want to be apart. It's time to move on."

Derek studied him in silence for long enough to be uncomfortable before looking away. "It would be nice to have my best friend back."

It wasn't until that moment that Andrew realized how much he'd needed to hear that. Nick had made an effort to pull them back together, but the specter of Kat's broken heart had lingered between them, impossible to overcome. "I'd like that."

"Good." Finally, Derek smiled. "I should beat your ass around the room for not calling me, but my high ground's a little shaky. Next time my cousin decides to play chicken with a cult? Maybe pick up the phone, Andrew, even if my wife *is* pregnant."

"Talk to my alpha. He seemed to think you had enough on your plate."

"Alec thought you could handle it, I guess. And you did."

"No, I fucked it up." And his mistakes had cost Ben and Lia their lives. "I won't next time, though."

Derek nodded to the couch across from him in a silent command. "I know. How it feels, I mean. To not save everyone."

They all did, in one way or another. "Yeah." Andrew sat and stared at Derek for a long moment, trying to reconcile the man before him with the one he'd known. "Shit, you're going to have a kid."

"And you're going to marry my cousin. If she lets you." Derek's grin was lopsided. "Long way from a couple of humans who were going to build the most badass construction firm in the Southeast. Now I live on a ranch and you're ruling New Orleans."

Andrew snorted. "Assisting, maybe."

"Uh-huh. Kat already told me that she's going to help you save the world."

After Zola and Walker taught them how to kick ass together, it was at the top of his list. "What can I say? She wants to be a big damn hero. This? I can give her this."

Derek choked on a laugh. "Yeah, well, don't forget to take holidays off. You're family, and the Gabriels spend holidays together."

He would have spent the last Christmas alone in his loft if Carmen and Julio hadn't insisted he join them. "We'll be here, you can count on it."

"Damn right you will." Leaning back, Derek raised both eyebrows. "So tell me what's going on in New Orleans. The unedited versions. For a hacker girl, Kat's weirdly in love with censoring the good stuff."

The wistful note in his voice told Andrew that Derek missed it, maybe more than he realized. So he stretched his arms out across the back of the couch and grinned. "How much time do you have?"

"Until Kat gets worried that I really am killing you."

The second time Nick threw up, Kat started to understand why Derek looked like he hadn't slept in three weeks. "Are you sure you're okay?"

"I'm fine." She rinsed her toothbrush, tossed it back in the holder and leaned against the bathroom doorway. "Only now I'm hungry again. Damn it all."

That had to be a special kind of hell. "Is this what it's like all the time? The barfing and the being hungry?"

"So far, and it's *weird*. I've never actually been nauseated and still wanted to scarf down a whole bucket of chicken." Nick dropped to the bed and fell back. "Now I want fried chicken. I wonder if Mahalia would make me some."

"Probably. Especially if you tell her I'm going to eat some too. Everyone seems obsessed with feeding me." Kat shifted to lean more comfortably against the headboard. "At least I can give you a little peace from Derek now."

"Ha." Nick rolled to her side. "You don't get it, lady. This kid has kicked his parental instincts into high gear. I'm lucky I'm not on bed rest already."

Derek had been frantic enough in the first year after he'd

become Kat's guardian...and he hadn't been a shapeshifter. "Yeah, maybe you are. He means well."

"Of course he does. He wants the best for everyone, no matter what." Nick's dark eyes shone with love. "Unfortunately, what he thinks is best for me right now is to be carried everywhere, not lift a finger, and preferably wear clothes made of safety foam."

"And you used to think I was joking about the bubble wrap. You better make sure he doesn't line the kid's walls with it."

Nick propped her head up on her arm and watched Kat. "Are you okay? I mean, Ben was your friend, and with what happened to you and Julio..."

If anyone could understand, it would be Nick. Nick, who'd fallen in love with Derek in the midst of her sister's greatest tragedy. Kat picked at the edge of the bandage around her left wrist and tried to figure out where to start.

In the end, nothing worked but the truth. "I feel like I should feel worse."

A hint of a smile tilted the corner of Nick's mouth. "Because you're happy."

"Because I've been through hell before. Andrew almost bled to death in front of me, and I walked away alone." Kat shrugged helplessly. "It hurts. Ben, and what happened... It hurts a lot. But this time, I have Andrew. And he makes it hurt a little less."

"That's not a betrayal," Nick whispered fiercely. "Anyone who cares about you would be glad, so glad that you have that."

"I know." And she did, because she could remember watching Derek watch Nick, and being so *relieved* that he was loved, even as her own heart broke. She hadn't begrudged him those moments of happiness. She'd clung to them as proof that the world had a shred of hope. "Thanks, Nick."

"Don't thank me. It's just the truth. The world can be such an ugly place, but it can also be so beautiful it takes your breath away. The trick is to try and find more of the beauty than the ugliness."

Kat couldn't stop her lips from curving up. "Andrew takes my breath away."

Nick rolled over on the bed, laughing. "Then go look at him, and send my husband in here while you're at it."

Kat stood and smoothed the blankets. "Andrew probably needs rescuing anyway." Which was an exaggeration.

She hoped.

Eighteen months of holidays at the ranch had given her a rough idea of the layout. Instead of interrupting an angry confrontation, she found Derek and Andrew in the library. Talking.

No, not just talking. They were laughing together in a way she hadn't seen in years. Not since before Derek had been turned, when they'd both been humans barely brushing the fringes of a supernatural world.

Brushing them because of her. Because she'd never been entirely human, and Derek had lived on those fringes because he wanted to give her what she needed to grow into her own as a psychic.

Knocking lightly on the doorframe, she leaned in. "Derek? Your wife wants you to go pamper her."

Derek damn near tripped in his haste to get to his feet. "Is she okay?"

Poor Nick. "She's fine. I think her request is secret code for 'leave Andrew and Kat alone'."

"Smartass." Derek pointed at Andrew. "Do we need to find you a bedroom to sleep in?"

To Andrew's credit, he managed not to laugh. "We've already been offered the guest house."

"Which we're sleeping in together," Kat pointed out helpfully, just to make Derek wince. He didn't disappoint, but as soon as his face screwed up into his big-brother-about-to-make-a-fuss expression, she laughed. "Get lost, Derek."

"Nice to see you too, Kat." But he leaned down and kissed

the top of her head before making himself scarce.

Kat closed the door behind him, then moved to stand in front of Andrew. "Hi."

He caught her hand and nudged her leg, knocking her down into his lap. "Hi."

The world fell away, taking the pain of the last few days with it. Here, in this moment, it was her and him, and Nick was right. Life was about clinging to the beautiful parts. "So. Derek didn't punch you in the face, it seems."

"Mmm." Andrew wrapped a lock of her hair around his finger. "He was more interested in whether I plan on breaking your heart again."

"And what did you tell him?"

"I told him that part of our lives is over, and we're trying something new—being happy."

They'd broken free of their endless loop. Finally. "Good answer. Especially since I'm pretty sure I already moved in with you, without either of us discussing it."

He laughed and settled his hands on her thighs. "I did hear that Anna's going to live with Sera."

"I said it was okay." Which had been a presumptuous move, she supposed, in retrospect. Enough of one for nerves to set her heart to racing. "I probably should have asked you first. I mean, asked you if you want me living with you for the rest of forever."

"You mean like I should have asked before I informed your cousin that I intend to marry you as soon as you'll let me?"

Now her heart was skipping beats, doing a funny new dance in her chest as she discovered a spontaneous interest in the institution of matrimony. "You could probably talk me around. Only if you come up with an awesome idea for a wedding, though. Mac and Jackson stole Vegas. If we do that now, we'll just look like copycats."

"Uh-huh." He kissed the corner of her mouth. "We'll think

of something. I mean, we're creative people, right? And we've got time to figure it out."

How could she have ever thought she was cold? He warmed her, even with the softest touch, and she knew now how easily he could bring that gentle heat to a boil. "We're brilliant." She murmured the words against his cheek, then kissed his temple. "We'll get married eventually, but it doesn't even matter. We're Kat and Andrew. We just *are*."

"You know, that's exactly what I said." And then he kissed her.

Soft lips, hard body, slow burn and a pleasure that transcended flesh. She melted into him, then took Nick's advice and lowered her shields. Not so much, just enough to let his love flood her, to lift her up to a place beyond bad memories and pain.

It was beauty, and she seized it with both hands and savored it, drank it down until she was giddy. Drunk. Until her fingers tightened on his shoulders and his dug into her hips, and even though they were panting and half-crazy, there was no shame in the loss of control.

No shame, and no fear. Just Kat, and Andrew, and together they were everything.

About the Author

How do you make a Moira Rogers? Take a former forensic science and nursing student obsessed with paranormal romance and add a computer programmer with a passion for gritty urban fantasy. To learn more about this romance-writing, crime-fighting duo, visit their webpage at www.moirarogers.com, or drop them an email at moira@moirarogers.com. (Disclaimer: crime-fighting abilities may appear only in the aforementioned fevered imaginations.)

He's no one's hero. She's no one's pawn.
And now they're caught in the crossfire...

Deadlock
© 2011 Moira Rogers
Southern Arcana, Book 3

Abandoned by her wolf shifter father and raised by her human psychic mother, Carmen Mendoza can't deny she's different. She craves things most women shy away from—and she has a trail of shapeshifting ex-boyfriends to prove it.

Working at a clinic for supernatural creatures, she's escaped the notice of her father's legacy-obsessed family. Until they need a pawn in their bid for power. Snared by a vicious spell designed to wake her inner wolf, Carmen's only hope is to trust the one man strong enough to soothe her darkest instincts.

Alec Jacobson was once the heir apparent to the wolves' ruling elite, until he walked away to marry the woman he loved. She paid with her life. Now he lives as a rebel, a black-sheep alpha who protects the supernatural residents of New Orleans from the wolves' barbaric class system. Too bad he can't protect himself from his need for Carmen.

Yet staking his claim on his enemy's niece will turn his city into a battleground. Unless he can find a way to stop breaking the rules—and start making them.

Warning: This book contains a renegade alpha wolf, a smart empathic doctor, very dirty sex with psychic safe-words, the occasional dominance game in and out of the bedroom, and a group of supernatural citizens ready to take on the corrupt leaders of their world.

Available now in ebook and print from Samhain Publishing.

Get in. Do the job. Get out. If only it were that easy.

Ghost Soldiers
© *2011 Keith Melton*
The Nightfall Syndicate, Book 2

Vampire hit man Karl Vance has a new target: a rogue, charismatic sorcerer building an army of paranormal creatures in Eastern Europe. The stakes have never been higher, nor the odds so long, but he's in too deep to turn back. If Karl fails to kill, the powerful Order of the Thorn will hunt down Maria Ricardi, the vampire he loves, and destroy everything he's fighting for.

When Karl is cut off in enemy badlands, he's reduced to survival mode, doing the kinds of things he'd sworn would never be part of his vampire existence. Things that will forever color his relationship with Maria...if he survives to see her again.

In Boston, Maria is haunted by disturbing dreams of Karl as she struggles to keep control of her mafia syndicate against a growing tide of threats—traitors, FBI agents, hostile crime families, and the fear that power will turn her into a creature like her hated Master, Delgado. Then she discovers Karl is walking straight into a deadly trap...and there may be nothing she can do to stop it in time.

Warning: Explicit language and intense, violent content. Assassinations, betrayals, paranormal warfare, explosions, gangland slayings, chaos, calamity, rampant pandemonium, and an occasional fiery explosion.

Available now in ebook and print from Samhain Publishing.

SAMHAIN
PUBLISHING

www.samhainpublishing.com

Green for the planet.
Great for your wallet.

SAMHAIN

PUBLISHING

It's all about the story...

Romance

HORROR

Retro

ROMANCE

www.samhainpublishing.com

CPSIA information can be obtained at www.ICGtesting.com
Printed in the USA
BVOW071433190712

295691BV00001B/10/P